SUCH PRETTY FLOWERS

SUCH PRETTY FLOWERS

A Novel

K. L. CERRA

BANTAM
NEW YORK

A Bantam Trade Paperback Original

Copyright © 2023 by K. L. Cerra

All rights reserved.

Published in the United States by Bantam Books, an imprint of Random House, a division of Penguin Random House LLC, New York.

BANTAM BOOKS is a registered trademark and the B colophon is a trademark of Penguin Random House LLC.

Library of Congress Cataloging-in-Publication Data
Names: Cerra, K. L., author.
Title: Such pretty flowers: a novel / K. L. Cerra.
Description: New York: Bantam, 2023
Identifiers: LCCN 2022014856 (print) | LCCN 2022014857 (ebook) |
ISBN 9780593500255 (trade paperback) | ISBN 9780593500262 (ebook)
Subjects: LCGFT: Thrillers (Fiction) | Psychological fiction. | Novels.
Classification: LCC PS3603.E7475 S83 2023 (print) |
LCC PS3603.E7475 (ebook) | DDC 813/.6--dc23/eng/20220517
LC record available at https://lccn.loc.gov/2022014856
LC ebook record available at https://lccn.loc.gov/2022014857

Printed in the United States of America on acid-free paper

randomhousebooks.com

3 4 5 6 7 8 9

Book design by Susan Turner

To Sara

Sorry it took me so long to get my dedication right

SUCH PRETTY FLOWERS

PROLOGUE

Dane
So Maura wants to play this weird-ass game
with me and I figured I'd let you know in case
anything happened

I fumbled my phone onto the lip of the sink. Down it skittered, against the rust-ringed drain. *Gross.* The bathroom door swished open then, letting in the sludge of a bass line.

"There you are." Rachel's neck was mottled; she was almost as wasted as me. She looped an arm through mine, the ice in her vodka soda clinking. "We were starting to think you'd gotten abducted."

I grabbed my phone and let my roommate pull me out of the bathroom. The blaze of fluorescent light in the mirror tilted out of view, sickeningly. Then the thump of the music reclaimed my body. In the belly of the bar, Rachel unwound herself from me to latch on to her fiancé, Henry, of the ruffled trust-fund hair and slight underbite. A violet tube of neon shone through the rows of alcohol bottles arranged behind the bartender. It sloped away when I tried to focus.

"So . . ." a male voice said.

Who was this speaking to me? *Oh, right.* The guy in houndstooth Rachel had been herding me against for the past half hour. He looked like a stock photo of *young professional.* I couldn't think of a reason to object to him, but I very much wanted to. He leaned forward, cupping my elbow with his palm.

"Sorry." I squinted at my brother's text still resting on the lock screen.

> I figured I'd let you know in case anything
> happened

I was tapping out a string of question marks when Henry's arm jostled me with a shot glass. He must have been feeling generous, because even Young Professional got one.

I clinked my glass against Rachel's so forcefully a bit of vodka sloshed over the side. Rachel shrieked and gripped my shoulder, shaking with silent laughter.

"Skumps!" I cried.

It was our little inside joke, an allusion to the stupid drinking song from *Sleeping Beauty.* After Rachel had tired of teasing me for my guilty affection for Disney princesses freshman year at Emory, we'd started cheersing this way, and kept at it every weekend since. Now, in our late twenties, it was my way of retaining a through-line to Rachel, even with her fiancé and random people in our midst.

Rachel and I threw our heads back, throats undulating. Then she pulled me from the circle—and, thankfully, Young Professional—to dance. We thrust our hands skyward and grinned at each other through the haze of colored lights. Steadily, the vodka dulled the edges of the world. And I forgot to worry.

Rachel, Henry, and I took the next round of shots in to-go cups and spilled out onto the street. Henry held Rachel's waist. Together, we tromped through square after square. Colonial building façades peered down at us, blank and solemn. Laughing, I raced ahead of the couple, feeling the brickwork against the arches of my flats. I twisted my head around and watched the gas lamps smear by. Especially when I was intoxicated, historic Savannah had a strange way of unfurling in the night. I had yet to find anything that made me feel so gloriously untethered.

When we reached Chippewa Square outside of Rachel's apartment, I slowed, approaching the lion sculptures crouched on the platform in the center. I was panting. Exhilaration—or maybe the beginning of a stitch—glittered in my side. The beasts surrounded a statue of some general thrusting his sword into the ground behind his boot. But I much preferred the lions, all four of them, their paws draped over pointy medieval shields.

"Hi, little buddies," I whispered, reaching toward the stone manes.

Rachel came up behind me with a clobbering hug. "Slow *down*," she whined in my ear.

That's when I finally remembered: Dane's text. I shook Rachel off and ripped my phone from my bag, feeling my heartbeat in my neck.

Shit.

I'd forgotten to hit "Send" on the string of question marks, and so of course my brother hadn't texted back.

Sometimes, I wish it had stayed that way.

CHAPTER 1

Maura brought pomegranates to Dane's funeral reception. It was an odd choice and I mentioned this to Rachel, the hard pew edge biting into my thigh.

"What's wrong with pomegranates?" Rachel said.

I pictured a halved pomegranate. Those wreaths of slick, pink organs made my skin scuttle over my bones, just like when I looked too closely at a wasp's nest or a strawberry. I'd googled the sensation: trypophobia. Fear of holes and circle clusters. But this felt too exhausting to explain in a whisper.

"Haven't you heard of Persephone and Hades? Referencing eternal damnation to the underworld feels a tad insensitive, today of all days."

Rachel's cheek puffed. "Okay, Holly." Her eyes were fastened on the pulpit where Maura stood.

I had no choice but to look, too.

My brother's girlfriend was adjusting the stem of a tiny microphone. She had a face that made your mind itch as it tried to pinpoint what felt *off*. There was definitely something threading under the luminous skin. Inky princess tresses, black eyes, and sharp, birdlike bones that jutted at her clavicle. She wore a birdcage veil with pearled netting at an angle that fell a smidge short of jaunty. Seeing it—seeing her—gave me a jolt, like missing a step on my way down a staircase. Even speaking at my brother's funeral, Maura needed to enrapture.

Dane had brought his new girlfriend to meet the family over Easter brunch, five months ago now. Back then, the two of them had been dating only a few weeks. Maura complimented the plasterwork of my childhood home in that musical voice of hers; uncharacteristically, Mom had nothing critical to say afterward. *She has polish,* was all she provided. It was undeniable: Maura had dazzled both of my parents. I think, on some level, they'd doubted Dane's ability to land a girl like her.

As I sat in the pew, my fists fizzed with heat. We'd all doubted him, and now, here we were. How would things have turned out differently had we listened? It was a cruel game I often played during the long nights after his suicide when I knew sleep was futile. What if we'd tried a little harder? Rachel told me I couldn't get swept away in what-ifs, but really, who was she to tell me that? She wasn't the one fighting the riptide, feeling like the past was a puzzle. One that maybe, put together a different way, could have kept my little brother alive.

Maura slid a piece of paper over the podium.

Rachel put a hand on my knee as Maura started speaking. To my left, my mother's shoulders rounded under her cardigan. I noticed a tiny, slack space between my dad's lips. It reminded me of the way he'd looked when he'd told me what had happened to Dane two weeks ago—like he'd lost control of the bottom half of his face. It was the first time I'd seen his dad-armor slip, and I hated it.

The paper was, it turned out, an excerpt from *Charlotte's Web*. I had no idea why she'd chosen this. If we're talking animal books, Dane had much preferred *Jumanji*, leaning toward that edge of danger evident from the very first pages. Until his symptoms became evident a few months ago, he and I had been devastatingly close. I knew his taste in books.

Maura read from the paper with the voice of a jewelry-box ballerina. The quote she had chosen was from the spider's point of view. I dug my fingertips into my thighs. Every word drove another hairline crack through me, fault lines multiplying and branching like veins. Then Maura flicked her eyes up at me. *Saw* me. It made me feel naked, my every thought exposed, and my throat closed in response.

I surged to my feet and pushed past my family in the pew.

Rachel found me doubled over in a restroom stall. I stared at the toes of her Mary Janes under the door, seeing stars.

"Holly," she said. "Let me in."

"No."

"Come on. Open up."

I unlatched and cracked the door. Rachel handed me a cup of tepid water. I took it and wet my bristly tongue. "God, this is embarrassing," I said.

"What are you talking about? This is your brother's funeral. You're allowed to be upset."

She was right—not to mention the fact that I'd been on the opposite side of the bathroom stall for Rachel more than a few times back at Emory in Atlanta. After graduation, though, the scripts flipped. Rachel met Henry when she stayed on at Emory for grad school, and all too soon, she claimed that trifecta of adult accomplishments: a master's degree, an apartment, a fiancé. Thankfully Henry's family hailed from Savannah, too, so I'd jumped at the chance to reclaim my college roommate. These days, Rachel was the singular grounding force in my life. But sometimes I missed the feeling of her leaning on me, the way she had back in college.

My hand shook as I pulled the cup away from my mouth, slopping a bit onto the bathroom tile. I wanted to tell Rachel that there was something else bothering me, but I couldn't scrounge up the words. I set the empty cup on the back of the toilet and braced my palms on my thighs.

"I still don't get what happened to him, Rach. That time I visited him in his dorm room, I had no idea he was so sick—"

"I know." She let out a stream of air as her eyes jumped to the bathroom door. "I know."

Something molten leapt up my windpipe. Rachel seemed more concerned about someone walking in and witnessing my breakdown than comforting me. As a therapist, shouldn't she have been more adept at being—or at least appearing—present? I turned toward the toilet, feeling that heaving thing inside me. Somehow I'd managed to keep it at bay these past few days; I feared what might happen when I couldn't any longer.

Sure enough, the restroom door flapped open, making us spin. An usher with prominent marionette lines at her mouth glanced at us before turning on the sink. As she soaped her hands, I stared at Rachel, smoldering. The left side of my roommate's face jumped.

"I'm sorry," she said, when the usher left. "I know this is hard, and we can talk more about this later. Okay? You wouldn't want to miss what your brother's girlfriend has to say, right?"

"No," I relented, following Rachel out of the bathroom

stall. My breath and heartbeat had smoothed by now, but my legs still felt liquid. I paused at the mirror to swipe at the bruise-colored hollows beneath my eyes. Today, their gray shade looked like an absence of color, a photograph negative. "Of course not."

Mom, Dad, and I were the last to leave, just as the ushers descended on the tray of picked-over cucumber sandwiches. In line to exit the parking garage, Dad drummed his fingers on the steering wheel. It took him a few tries, inserting his parking slip into the stern metal machine mouth, until our fee registered.

"Third time's the charm," he said to the parking attendant who glared down at him from her glass tower. How would she feel if she knew this man had just left his son's funeral? Would she dare look at him like that?

Mom sat silently in the passenger seat, rubbing her temples like she did when she felt a migraine coming on. As Dad eased us onto the main road, streetlights slivered in through the windows, illuminating the half-empty backseat. Dane always sat to my left. When he was little, he'd kick the back of Dad's seat during long road trips. Dad would roar, threaten to pull over and make us change seats. These days, all I saw were the gashes that Dane had left in my life. I ran a finger around the rim of the cup holder between our seats, my throat thickening.

"Well," Dad said, "I thought some of those speeches were really heartfelt. That kid from his class—Jordan?"

"Jacob," Mom said. She didn't turn to face him.

"Jacob, that's right. Hope he'll be coming to Dane's showcase next month. But I didn't see Dane's friend Lauren. Did she make it?"

"I'm not sure."

Silence.

"Anyway," said Dad, trying again, "I thought the funeral home did a nice job putting everything on, didn't you, Holly?"

"Yeah," I said, at the same time that Mom said, "Hardly, Arthur. The food was mediocre and the sound system was unreliable. The floral arrangements were the only redeeming part of the event, and that's only because Maura graciously stepped in and offered her services."

Silence scorched the inside of the car again. I toyed with my split ends, made worse by the ombre dye job, and watched the road unroll in front of us like a black tarp. Soon I'd be back in my childhood bedroom. Mom and Dad hadn't explicitly asked me to stay with them, but since I sensed they needed me, I'd spent every night there since Dane's suicide. Each was more difficult than the last. I pictured lying in bed, looking at the asparagus-shaped shadows cast by my bedposts, feeling Dane's closed door across the hall. I knew what was inside. Immaculately rolled clothes that still smelled like him. A bookcase crammed with alphabetized spines. An army of figurines—wizards and winged beasts—that Dane had squinted at and painted with a minuscule brush. I hadn't set foot inside since he died, and the thought brought on that overflowing sensation again, something rising inside me like rancid dinner guts spewing past a jammed disposal.

"Hey," I said. My voice sounded tiny. "Would you mind dropping me off at the apartment tonight?"

Both Mom and Dad spun in their seats to look at me.

"Really, honey?" Mom's fingers fell from her temples.

"Yeah. I think I could use the change of scene. Being close to Rachel. You know."

"Of course," Dad said, but he was frowning.

My ribcage loosened with relief.

Dad drove into the heart of historic Savannah to deposit me at Chippewa Square. I tipped out of the car. After the over-air-conditioned funeral parlor, the September night felt lush, like a dream. A carpet of mist clung to the grass, obscuring the paving stones; oaks dripped Spanish moss from above. I brushed past the lion statues, night collecting in their open mouths.

As I approached Rachel's apartment, the begonias in the window boxes visible from the street, I felt a swell of affection. I'd never asked just how much their rent was, but I was convinced that Rachel and Henry cut me a deal. Otherwise, there was no way I'd be able to afford a room in the heart of historic Savannah by working at the public library.

I took the stairs to the fifth floor, my fingers trailing for memorized chips in the banister. At the door, I fumbled with my keys and took in a slow breath. Something had pulled me back to Rachel's apartment, but I still wasn't prepared for the delicate way she would try to gauge my mood. I couldn't even begin to fathom the small talk I'd have to suffer through with her fiancé. For now, all I wanted was to sidestep them both and burrow into the safety of my bed.

I opened the front door to an empty living room. Two stained wineglasses sat on the coffee table beside a crumpled bag of microwave popcorn. Instead of relief at the prospect of being alone, I felt another snip of rage. Had my roommate really come home from my brother's funeral—from seeing me unravel in the stall of a public restroom—to watch a movie and eat *popcorn?*

"Rach?" I called.

The silence of the apartment pressed against my eardrums. I threw my keys down next to the wineglasses and slunk into my room. There, I stripped down to a camisole and climbed into bed with my phone, itching for the grounding ritual of scrolling to distract myself from my grasping stomach.

At the funeral reception, I'd only managed half a deviled egg. I couldn't remember eating a full meal since Dane's death. I used to spend good chunks of time fantasizing about food: the juicy seasoned burgers in the pub around the corner from work, the silkiness of albacore nigiri on those nights I turned a blind eye to my bank balance. But these days, eating felt like an obligation. Today, I hadn't complied, and I was being punished.

I made the mistake of opening Facebook, only to see a couple posts about Dane's funeral jump to the top of my newsfeed. *RIP.* What a terrible, violent-sounding term. I stared at the screen, willing away the dam of tears behind my eyes. Sure, these people were probably well-meaning. They'd dressed up and made it to the ceremony, after all. But once they'd tapped out a status about Dane, off they'd gone, back to their sheltered lives.

I bet they all got to keep their siblings.

Muffled laughter sounded through the wall between my room and the master. A couple seconds later, a familiar rhythmic knocking started up, jostling the wire jewelry tree on my bureau. Then—I knew it was coming—Rachel's kitten-like sighs. I sank lower into my covers, burning with shame and rage. The popcorn had been bad enough. But *this?*

I pressed my eyes shut. I needed a distraction. Immediately.

I thumbed Maura's name into the search bar. A handful of common friends brought her name to the top of the list. Her Facebook page was underwhelming, so I navigated over to Instagram. *Better.* She had over a thousand photos, and I scrolled through, staring at her black eyes and sharp bones. Her prettiness felt wrong, jabbing at me like a needle.

It'd been a miracle I'd managed to evade her at the funeral. During the reception, I'd felt her presence on my neck. When she got too close, I found someone across the room to thank for coming and tore my eyes from her platter of halved pomegranates before my body could even register a shiver. Then I saw Maura approach my parents. I'd fled again to my stall in the restroom, my heart juddering against my ribs. I'd stayed there for a long time, until I was sure she'd be gone.

Presently, the sounds behind the wall quieted. I took a gulp of air, daring to wriggle free from my cocoon of blankets.

A minute or two later, Henry opened the door to his bedroom and stepped into the hallway. I could never make out the individual words that he and Rachel spoke in their room, only the cadence of their voices. But the hallway was another story.

"Hey," he called back to Rachel. "Check out the link I sent you to that one-bedroom condo. Killer terrace. I think it might be perfect."

My heartbeat doubled in tempo. *Condo?*

Back in the master, Rachel said something unintelligible.

Henry grunted. "I know. But we're going to be married next year, Rach. It's time to start building some equity."

I rolled over onto my side. Rachel had never mentioned anything about moving out. Or buying property.

A couple beats later, Rachel's voice joined Henry's in the hallway: ". . . literally the day of her brother's funeral. I think we're going to have to table this for the time being."

"The hell does that even mean?" Henry's frustration sliced in past the hinges of my door. "'The time being?' Yes, what happened to her brother is tragic, it's horrible. But we can't put our lives on hold indefinitely."

Rachel's voice was soft when she spoke next. "Babe, don't take this the wrong way, but you sound like a complete dick right now."

I turned the side of my face into the pillow as rage tore through me. Yes, Henry did sound like a dick. But also, it was mortifying to hear them talking about me in this way. Like I was a child, a nuisance, something holding them back from living the life they'd been planning.

I brushed the wetness off my face with the backs of my hands and returned to my phone, reaching for what had become habitual: the last text message chain with my brother. I'd been reviewing it nightly before bed. These past couple of weeks, it was the only way I could slough off the day before falling asleep. Dane's own phone had disappeared after his suicide, which didn't seem to surprise anyone, given his mental state back then. It still wasn't sitting quite right with me, though.

In hindsight, I realize Dane's symptoms likely started all the way back in March, but they didn't catch our attention until his graduation from Savannah College of Art and Design. Then he'd moved in with Maura, so my parents and I didn't get to see much of it firsthand. What we did see were glimpses of a gradual decline. Dane had always prided himself on his artful locks, but suddenly and without explanation, he stopped washing his hair. He fell silent, too, eyes vacant as empty nighttime homes—and it used to be near impossible to shut him up. Eventually, the paranoia began: a preoccupation with cameras in the corners of restaurants and on the sides of buildings. It wasn't until May that Dane had his first seizure one night when Maura was out meeting a client. Even now, when I imagine Dane jerking around, alone, it feels like there's a piece of driftwood skewering my heart. Dad finally convinced Dane to see a psychiatrist and a neurologist toward the end of the summer, but neither doctor had any definitive answers.

Thankfully, Dane's weird symptoms never bled into our text exchanges, which read like an extended inside joke. Take the thread three days before Easter:

Me

Easter bunny wants to know if lady-friend is attending brunch and, if so, how best to embarrass you. naked baby pics or LOTR elf costume?

Dane

Lady-friend will be in attendance. Will arrive in full Orc regalia (no need for elf cosplay)

Me

What about naked baby pics?

And that was that.

Then I scrolled down to the last chunk of texts, the last messages I ever sent and received from my brother. Even though I'd been looking at them every night, they still made my skin crawl.

The night I returned from the bar with Rachel and Henry—technically morning, at 4:42 A.M.—I was just sobering up when I got the call from my parents. Dane had been found in the townhouse he shared with his girlfriend with a steak knife cleaving the flesh from his clavicle to his navel. The investigating officers said it looked almost as if he had been trying to split himself in half. They couldn't believe he had gotten as far as he did.

That's when I'd seen the little red sun on my home screen, indicating an unread text.

Dane

Get it out get it out oh god get it out of me

Mom and Dad invited me over for dinner Thursday night, four days after the funeral. I didn't want to go, but then I remembered the way they'd looked when I'd blindsided them about wanting to spend the night at Rachel's apartment instead of with them.

I said yes.

Mom kissed me with the edge of her mouth when I arrived. She smelled like Pond's cold cream, like she always did. "Would you like to borrow some of my blush?" she asked, as she pulled away. "You're looking a little sallow, honey."

I put a hand to my face. "No, thanks. Where's Dad?"

Mom studied her manicure. Her nails were painted a slick nude shade. With her amethyst earrings, silky tunic, and camel-colored booties, she looked effortlessly moneyed—far wealthier than our family really was. I'd always marveled at her ability to create her own camouflage. "In the sitting room, watching TV. I'm not sure he's moved for the past week."

Since when had Mom talked about Dad with this disdain in

her voice? I bristled. "Easy, Mom. He's probably still shell-shocked."

"Well." Mom brushed her palms on her linen pants and reached toward a drooping calla lily on the foyer table. "You wouldn't believe the number of flower deliveries since the funeral. And they're all dead now. They need to be taken out." She marched the vase into the kitchen. Soon I heard the sloshing of water and leaves hitting the garbage bag. This was how Mom dealt with hardship: deep-cleaning the kitchen with brisk purpose, organizing junk drawers, and cooking elaborate meals snipped from *Good Housekeeping*. We were having roasted lamb and mint jelly that night.

"Need any help with dinner?" I called after her.

She told me she had it under control.

Dad was watching golf. He couldn't see me, so I stood at the entrance to the living room for a minute, watching the rise and fall of that little paunch of stomach that sat over his belt. My heart notched tight. "Hey, Dad."

His face brightened when he saw me. "Hey, darlin'." He patted the cushion next to him. "We're on the eighth hole."

"No *Duck Dynasty* today?"

"Would you believe me if I told you those clowns are starting to grate on me?"

I grinned. "Nope."

"You know me too well."

Someone onscreen sank a shot. Dad and I settled into a companionable silence. I could hear Mom clinking around in the kitchen as she readied dinner. Is this how the days since Dane's funeral had gone, then? Mom bustling about like a self-important whirlwind as Dad hid in the bowels of the house watching inane TV?

A commercial for Hardee's came on. Dad turned toward me. "How's the apartment?" It was the closest he dared to what I knew he really meant: *how are you?*

"Fine." I shifted on the couch. "How about you?"

"Oh, you know. The usual." Then Dad grabbed the remote and turned up the volume on the commercial. "It's been tense here since the funeral, to tell you the truth."

"I gathered."

"Your mother refuses to talk about it. Dane. The funeral. Any of it. She's whipped herself up into a tizzy waxing the floors, potting the hydrangeas. I told her, 'Di, we can hire people to do that. Relax.' She didn't want to hear it. She doesn't *want* to relax, because then she'll have to face what's happened."

"It's how she handles stuff like this, I guess." I shrugged. It was definitely Mom's style. Part of me hadn't been surprised to see how she'd thrown herself headlong into planning Dane's funeral. Finding the space, arranging for the readings, reaching out to Maura about the flowers. But another part of me had hoped she'd surface from her checklists long enough to talk with us about Dane.

Dad chuckled hollowly. "Very true." His hand migrated toward the remote, and I felt a flash of urgency. This was my chance to ask Dad for his perspective on what had happened to Dane, before we sat down for dinner as a family.

I took a breath. "Hey, Dad?"

"Yeah?"

I swallowed. "I've been going over and over things in my mind. Thinking about Dane and how quickly he . . . declined toward the end. It just seemed to happen so suddenly, you know? Have you ever thought about that?"

Dad ran a thumb along the buttons on the remote. "All the time."

"You were driving him to those psychiatrist appointments," I said quietly. "What did you see?"

Dad paused, as if he thought it was a bad idea to proceed. Then he notched up the volume on the TV another few bars. "Your brother wasn't well. Toward the end, he started saying some things that just had me scratching my head afterward."

"Like what?"

"Oh, just a lot of paranoid things. In July, he started telling me stuff about his girlfriend. That he didn't trust her. I tried to ask him, you know, 'What makes you think these things?' But there's really no reasoning with someone who's that sick."

I sat up straighter on the couch. "What—" I cleared my throat. "What did Dane say about his girlfriend?"

"Ludicrous things, I don't even remember. He painted her as some black widow, you know? Manipulating him, eating away at his soul day by day. It sounded like something straight out of a movie. And it couldn't have been more ridiculous. You've met Maura. That girl is as sweet as can be."

My hands curled into fists at my sides. It was no secret that Maura had a stronger personality than Dane. But then again, most people did. He'd showered Maura with attention in his own gentle way. There had been portrait sessions—many of them, in the early days. Once, I'd even asked Dane if he ever got tired of painting the same person over and over again. He'd only laughed, as if I couldn't possibly understand.

Dad went on. "So I asked him, 'If you're saying all these things about your girlfriend, then how come you're still with her? It's not like you're married, like me and your mother. Ha-ha.' He didn't have an answer for that. But here's what I can't understand." Dad's eyes glazed as he stared at the opposite wall. "Sure, Dane was sick with some mysterious goddamn illness. But he'd started seeing that psychiatrist in June, and he'd even been put on medication. He wasn't—suicidal. It wasn't like that."

I ran a finger down the break between cushions. Dad was right: my brother had been formally assessed. Dane had walked into Maura's house experiencing some mental health issues, yes, but never a desire to die.

And yet he'd left in a body bag.

"I know," I said. "Y'all would've told me if that was the case." Then I felt a blast of guilt. Though I'd largely avoided Dane since his graduation, unnerved by the emergence of his symptoms, Mom and Dad had been more attentive. Dad insisted on driving Dane to appointments with his new psychiatrist, and Mom invited the couple over for meals regularly. Dane rarely accepted, and Mom had grown frustrated that she'd never once been invited to Maura's, despite a litany of dropped hints.

"I keep going over things in my head. I don't understand what happened. I don't understand why my son would do something so goddamn horrific to himself." Dad looked from the wall to my face. When his eyes met mine, they held a rim of tears, and my stomach twisted.

I'd never seen my father cry before.

"Believe me when I say I'd do anything, Holly," he said. His voice was hoarse. "*Anything.* To understand what happened to my son."

Dinner was almost unbearable. Dad forced cheer to fill the silence while Mom sawed at her lamb and I actively avoided looking at Dane's empty chair. My brother had a magical way of defusing Mom's dark spells. The night of his sixth-grade open house, when a frazzled Mom had spilled the pan of burnt cookies on the tiles, Dane sprang to action, zigzagging across the floor with a broom and one of his newfound chocolate-walnut "pucks." I couldn't believe it—Mom had *spit* her laughter.

But Dane wasn't around anymore to rescue the night. At the table with my parents, I mumbled some excuse about seeing a movie with Rachel to leave early. The apartment was empty when I arrived, so I shut myself in my room and cried in peace. It was one of those painful cries that wring the snot from you, leaving you with an echoing headache. Afterward, my skull felt like an abandoned warehouse.

Exhausted and finally drifting off to sleep, I got to thinking again of Dane's decline. There had been hints here and there, but it wasn't until his graduation from SCAD that I finally admitted to myself something was very wrong with my brother. That day, Mom, Dad, and I met Dane at his dorm. He'd announced the previous week that he would be moving in with Maura, who'd recently purchased a townhouse.

"What kind of art student can afford a *townhouse* in Old Savannah?" I muttered as we approached Dane's dorm. A flock of students in caps and gowns spilled out from around the corner. I lowered my eyes, fixed a polite smile on my face.

"Student housing ain't cheap either," Dad said, at my side.

"I guess." I ran a hand along the tops of hedges as we approached the residence hall. "It's just—I'm sorry. *Two months?* They've been dating less time than it takes me to finish a series on Netflix. And now they're moving in together?"

Neither Mom nor Dad had time to react. We'd reached Dane's room, #103, and the door opened before we could knock. Dane stood there, his hair spiked with grease. Crescents of sweat darkened the underarms of his T-shirt. He looked like he hadn't showered—or shaved—in weeks.

The greeting I'd prepared shriveled in my mouth.

Mom was the first to find her voice. "Well!" she said brightly. "Congratulations!" She gave Dane a peck on the cheek before pushing past him into the room. What lay beyond Dane was even more distressing: take-out containers of rotting food, piles of shucked-off shirts and boxers, snarls of charging cables and wires, and a rumpled bed, sheets half-puddled on the floor. One of the curtain rods over Dane's window had even come apart in the center, causing the fabric to hang like a defeated flag.

My parents and I looked at one another with barely disguised panic. The last time I'd visited Dane's dorm, mere weeks earlier, it'd been immaculate. Even growing up in our childhood home, Dane had never so much as left a paper out of place.

I wanted to say something, but my mind had gone blank. It was the first time I'd ever struggled to communicate with my brother.

That's when Maura swept in. Little Maura, drowning in her school-commissioned graduation gown, delicate ankles strapped into gold stilettos. "Hello, hello," she sang, reaching out to hug my mother.

Her entrance shattered the tension in the room. Mom gave a delighted cry, accepting Maura's embrace and rocking her back and forth. Her manicure tangled in Maura's waterfall hair. "It's so nice to see you again, Maura. And congratulations."

When Maura drew away, she waved a hand at the disaster

that was Dane's room. "Such a pigsty, right? Don't you worry, Mr. and Mrs. Chambers, I'll make sure to whip Dane into shape once he moves in with me. I have a feeling all he needs is a . . . feminine touch." She glanced over at Dane with a wink.

Dane looked past her and made eye contact with me. Then he lifted the corner of his mouth in his signature expression of derision. It was so subtle, only I was able to see it.

Relieved, I smirked back at him. My brother was in there, after all. Maybe today he was eclipsed by an exuberant girlfriend, but he was there.

Mom sighed, her shoulders dropping visibly. "Good God, yes. What would we do without you, Maura? You were a godsend when Dane was sick, too."

I barely stifled an eye roll. Mom and Dad hadn't stopped gushing about how attentive Maura had been when Dane came down with the flu the previous month. Apparently, she'd pulled out all the stops: brought him homemade chicken soup and lotion-treated tissues, held cold compresses to his face, checked his temperature around the clock.

Dad glanced at Mom. "I'm not sure you've *ever* taken such good care of me," he said.

"Of course I have!"

"Hmm." Dad turned to Maura, dropping his voice to a whisper. "Secretly, I think she's disgusted whenever one of us is sick."

Maura dragged a toe over the carpet, with a small smile. "I don't know. I like taking care of people, I guess. It was the least I could do."

"So." Dad jangled the loose change in his pockets. "When's the big move-in day?"

Maura looked up from the ground. "Day after tomorrow," she said with a grin. "Tomorrow we've got to load all this into boxes. And then I promised Dane I'd go geocaching with him."

"Oh, no," Mom groaned. "Please tell me he hasn't roped you into that nonsense. Staggering through the streets of Savannah on an adult treasure-hunt? Come on, now."

"It's not all that bad," Maura said, linking an arm through Dane's. "We've gone together a couple times." She lowered her voice, affecting her own guilty whisper. "I actually think it's kind of cool."

". . . she says, utterly ashamed," Dane muttered.

I felt like throwing my arms around him. Dane was okay; he was acting like himself. And clearly, he saw how ridiculous this entire parental suck-up charade was.

Maura pouted. "Babe, I'm not ashamed of you. Quite the opposite!"

Babe? Ew.

My brother lifted one shoulder in admission.

"Once Dane's settled in to your new place, we'll have to finally have that coffee date," Mom said.

Maura winked at her. "And go to the plant nursery afterward. I haven't forgotten."

As Mom and Maura went on, I studied my brother's face, searching for more emotion. But he'd turned his attention to the carpet, his features impassive.

Sometimes, when we were little, Dane and I had tried to communicate telepathically. We'd heard twins could do it— why not us? We'd sat opposite each other, pressing our eyes shut, straining our brains. *Pancakes, pancakes, pancakes*, I'd think, as Dane worked to receive the message. Or, *gorilla, gorilla, gorilla*. That one he'd actually gotten, and we'd chalked it up to our incredible telepathic abilities, rather than the fact that we'd watched *King Kong* the night before.

That day in Dane's trashed dorm room, I tried to send him a telepathic message. *Dane, Dane, Dane. What's going on with you?*

But he didn't seem to hear me.

We had to part ways to prepare for the ceremony. Back outside the dorm with my parents, I drew a breath of summer air. I was free. My relief to be away from Dane was intoxicating, a drug that kept me running from him every day since.

CHAPTER 3

Our library database was down at work on Monday. Perched at the circulation desk, I clicked through listings for studios and one-bedrooms. It wasn't looking good.

"What're you looking at?" Esther, the head librarian, peered over my shoulder. It was my first day back since Dane's death, and I'd already rebuffed her attempt to "check in" with me that morning. Esther must have been resorting to gentle small talk to feel me out.

"Apartments." I swiveled a fraction in my chair, not wanting to face her head-on. "I overheard Rachel and Henry talking about buying a condo. I think my days are numbered."

Esther chewed the end of a croissant, so close I could smell the chocolate filling. I shrank away from her another degree. Especially when food was involved, I had to talk myself out of the reflexive recoil. After all, Esther was the first to believe in me those days after I'd slunk back to my parents in Savannah, the only one of my Emory friends without a grad school acceptance or a glittery job offer in Manhattan or with the UN. I'd tried hostessing at a restaurant near Emory for a few months, hoping something better would turn up. It never did. Driving back into Savannah, I'd numbed myself with a cherry slushie from Sonic and indulgent eighties ballads on the radio. To work in the same library I'd scoured as a kid for Animorphs books—it was a different kind of contentment. Some days, it was even enough.

Esther motioned to my computer screen, the puff of gray hair on her head wobbling. "Well, anything good on there?"

"No. It's depressing." I squinched up my face to let her know I was at least half joking. "Time for a raise?"

"Ha-ha." Esther swiped at the side of her mouth. "What have I been telling you for the past four years? Go get that master's in library sciences. Then we'll talk."

I folded my head over the keyboard in defeat.

Given recent developments and their implications for my bank account, I should have been packing my lunches. Instead, I went to the Chinese restaurant across the street. There I picked at the papery spring rolls and stared at the looping red dragon on the wall. The owner must have realized something was wrong because she was more attentive than usual in refilling my jasmine tea.

Dane and I had eaten Chinese food on my twenty-fifth birthday a year and a half ago—takeout, from a different restaurant I wouldn't be frequenting again. The issue must have been with the sesame chicken, because only Dane ate it and only he ended up locked in the apartment bathroom two hours later. Rachel, Henry, and I kept glancing at the closed door, wincing when the sound of running water failed to camouflage his retching. Dane had returned to the living room twenty minutes later with a gray face and took a valiant swig of his drink. "Ready to rally," he'd said, slamming it back down, even though all we'd been doing was playing Cards Against Humanity and trading cat memes. That had been typical Dane: throwing himself into even the most pathetic birthday celebration, food poisoning be damned.

In the restaurant now, I screwed up my eyes against the haze of tears, then trained them on the dragon. I forced myself to trace every undulation of its body like a maze, drawing in steady breaths through my nose.

When I looked down at my phone, Maura's face peered back at me, her chin buried in a mass of tissue paper–like blooms. Guess I'd never closed out of my Instagram stalking. As a florist, Maura was forever posting pictures of herself smoldering next to her flowers. She favored filmy slip-dresses and nude lips. I pinched apart the pixels of her face, zooming in on her dark eyes. Something about them was eerie. Unnatural. Were they too round? Missing tear ducts? I stared until my own eyes burned.

What game were you playing with my brother, Maura?

Dad had told me frustratingly little about Dane in his final weeks. And even though I'd pulled away from my brother—I'd own up to that crime—I'd seen enough to know Dane wasn't suicidal. Unfortunately, Maura was the only person who might have answers. Talking face-to-face with her would be the only way to figure out what she and my brother had been up to the night of his death—and if there was any merit at all to the statements he'd made about Maura being like some "black widow." Before I could register what I was doing, I was navigating to

Maura's business website, pulling up her email, and drafting a message.

> Hi Maura,
> I hope it's ok I looked you up online. I feel so bad about missing you at the funeral. How've you been? Would you ever want to meet up, maybe grab coffee or something?
> -Holly

I hesitated. Was I really about to *volunteer* to spend time with this girl? Something about Maura was just . . . off. She'd rubbed me the wrong way ever since I met her at Easter. But maybe I was being dramatic. What was a thirty-minute coffee date? I could handle that—especially if it meant uncovering critical intel.

Thumb shaking with adrenaline, I hit "Send."

I was jittery all the way back to the library. I kept pulling out my phone and checking to see if my message had been sent. Yes, there it was—no way to take it back now. But I couldn't expect Maura to respond anytime soon. She was a busy entrepreneur. There was the definite possibility that she'd *never* write back.

In the meantime, I had to get serious about a rental budget. Back at the circulation desk, I tore out a piece of notebook paper and began listing my monthly expenses. Groceries, phone, car insurance. Then I pulled up my bank balance on the desktop. Where the hell did all my money go? The deductions on the screen said it all: sushi, luscious eye shadow palettes from Sephora that I didn't even know how to use, hardcover books. There was absolutely no excuse for the latter. For God's sake, I worked at a *library*.

"Holly."

Shit, Esther. I minimized my bank account and flipped over my piece of notebook paper. "Yeah?"

"Someone's . . . here to see you?"

I glanced up. For a moment, I had the sensation of looking in a mirror. I had studied that face for so long it seemed absurd that it didn't belong to me.

"Hi." Maura wore a dust-colored slip and a narrow ribbon choker. She'd posed with the same necklace in one Instagram picture, I remembered, gazing into the center of a sunflower. She gave me a smile that sloped to one side. "I hope it's okay— I got your message and, as luck would have it, I was just around the corner. Dane told me you worked here, so . . ."

The pen I had been holding clattered against the desk and onto the carpet. Dane and Maura had discussed where I worked? And Maura had . . . *remembered*? In my peripheral vision, I saw Esther's neck snap in my direction. "Oh," I said. I bent to retrieve the pen, blood whooshing in my ears.

When I surfaced, Esther had drawn closer. "You knew Dane?" she asked Maura. Her eyes were wide.

"Esther," I protested.

Glossing over Esther's interruption, Maura offered me that lopsided grin again. "I hope this doesn't feel like an ambush."

"Ambush? Not at all! I'm the one who emailed you."

But I hadn't, you know, expected you to materialize at my place of work. During business hours. My lightheadedness from the funeral returned.

Breathe, Holly. Breathe.

"And I'm so glad you did." Maura's teeth flashed white in the fluorescent light. "I was so disappointed not to have the chance to talk with you the other night. And I'm just having a hard time . . . I mean, obviously. Nothing is sitting well with me. I'm so happy you reached out."

I clamped a smile on my own face, but internally, I was scrambling. Maura and I had exchanged scant words over Easter brunch and Dane's graduation—the only time I'd really spent with her. It surprised me to know she'd wanted to speak with me at the funeral, and that she'd been so excited by my email she'd come to meet me at my workplace.

"Of course," I said. "Sorry to hear you're having such a hard time."

"How . . . how are you holding up?"

I despised this question. I'd been asked it relentlessly during the funeral. But coming from Maura, it was even worse.

Well, Maura, I can't sleep. I don't have much of an appetite, beyond spring rolls and graham crackers. And for some reason, I can't stop looking at your Instagram.

Instead I said, "I've been better."

Another sad smile. "Me too."

Maura had a kernel-shaped beauty mark on her upper lip that I recognized from her pictures. I ripped my eyes away from her, my skin flushing hot.

"So, what do you think? Would you . . . do you want to grab a drink sometime?" Too late, I realized I'd proposed coffee in my email; I hadn't meant to promote our get-together to drinks. Hastily, I added, "Alcohol or caffeine. Or, you know, neither."

"Yes!" Maura clasped her hands together under her chin. "I would so love that, Holly. I'm free tonight, in fact. If you are."

"Oh." I looked down at the circulation desk. I wished I'd

had more time to plot my next move. I'd figured I'd have at least a day before Maura got back to my email, not to mention the luxury of distance to think through my response rather than having to craft it on the spot.

"Or another time," Maura said.

"No, no! Tonight works great, actually." Something about the tinge of disappointment in her voice had made me leap to offer reassurance. Suddenly, I couldn't stop the avalanche of words. "There's this cute wine bar on Taylor Street across from Monterey Square. It has the best cab sav—ugh, that came out more basic than I really am. Promise."

Maura grinned. "I hadn't even noticed."

"Okay, good. I get out at six—"

"Six works great." Maura's pure smile didn't falter as she tugged at her ribbon choker.

Startling relief sifted through me. "Great."

"I'll see you soon, then." Maura waggled her fingers as she turned and exited the library. Through the glass front door, I watched her glide down the sidewalk, her slip shifting like water over her thighs.

Esther cleared her throat, making me jump. I'd completely forgotten she was there.

My boss nodded toward the street. "Sounds like you have some fun plans lined up for later! Who knows? Maybe a night out on the town is just what you need."

Sure, Esther. One of these days, I really was going to have to call her out on her nosiness. For now, though, I was having enough trouble untangling my embarrassment from my suspicion from a foreign kind of excitement: a snarl of emotions like a knotted chain at the bottom of a jewelry box. I gave Esther a tight smile before turning back to my budget. It took adding at least three more line items in shaky script before the thudding in my ears quieted.

The afternoon limped by. At 5:55, I slipped into the library bathroom to press the static from my hair. Then I stared at myself in the mirror, biting my bottom lip feathered with dry skin. Something tugged in my belly.

Maura wants to play this weird-ass game.

She'd seemed so innocent, standing there in the library pulling at her ribbon necklace. Dad's voice rang back at me: *that girl is as sweet as can be.* Why, then, did I feel a dark dread uncoiling inside me as I walked out the heavy library doors headed for Taylor Street?

Maura sat at a small circular table facing the square. She already had a glass of red wine and had slicked a matching shade on her lips. Under the table, she was jiggling her espadrille, complete with milk-colored pedicure.

"Hello again," she said, looking up at me.

I slid into the wrought-iron chair across from her. The night air pressed, hot and insistent, against my hairline.

"I hope you don't mind I got a head start." She swilled the wine in the bottom of her glass.

"No, not at all." A waiter skated a laminated menu across the table for me. I scanned the meaningless jumble of letters. I'd forgotten the Dewey Decimal System earlier in the day; now, apparently, I'd forgotten how to read. "I'll just have what she has."

Maura smirked and sat back against her chair. "How was the rest of your day?"

"Fine. Yours?"

She shrugged with one shoulder. "Busy. I'm doing center-pieces for a benefit this weekend. It's been consuming my every waking moment."

I nodded and looked past Maura to the monument in the center of Monterey Square.

Maura made small talk about her work as I willed the waiter to return with my drink. When he finally did, I grasped the bowl of the glass with two hands, gulping down the wine, grateful for the shimmery warmth streaking through my innards. But that made me think of Dane. How the path I was illuminating with wine was the same he'd carved through his own body with a knife.

I set my glass down on the table.

"How are you sleeping?" Maura asked.

"Not well."

"Me neither. God, I hate sleeping with that empty spot next to me. Even in the summer, the sheets feel like ice."

I shifted in my chair. Was that weird of her to reference sharing a bed with my brother?

"I know what you mean. I've been trying to keep my parents company at their place, but it's so hard sleeping across the hall from Dane's room."

Maura held my eyes with her own and nodded. I reached for my wineglass again and glanced back at the monument.

The waiter came by to set a basket of bread and a bowl of olive oil between us. Slivers of orange bell pepper floated on top.

"Oh," Maura said, breaking off a tiny piece of bread. "Dane would have hated this."

"The bell pepper," I agreed. "He always used to vent about

how it would taint whatever food it touched. He was the pickiest eater in all the land." That last sentence felt awkward as soon as it landed, but Maura didn't seem to pick up on it. Or maybe she was being gracious, as she had with my *cab sav* comment.

"Yes!" she said. "Such a challenge to cook for. He'd stand behind me in the kitchen as I was preparing dinner, waiting to intercept any ingredient he didn't approve of. It was infuriating."

So Maura had cooked for my brother. An image flashed of Maura in an apron and I felt flushed and mortified, the same way I'd felt registering her beauty mark in the library. "You should know he subsisted on chicken nuggets and white rice for the first eighteen years of his life," I added, more to stabilize myself than anything else.

Maura giggled. "Oh, Dane." Then she sobered. "You'll be at his showcase, right?"

I nodded vigorously. Next month, SCAD would be exhibiting some of the work from his medical illustration portfolio in his honor. I'd promised to go with Mom and Dad, but I was secretly terrified of seeing a piece of art I wasn't prepared for. No one seemed to understand that managing my mind after Dane's death was a full-time job. I was forever smoothing down splinters of thoughts and memories that worried at the corners of my consciousness. The last thing I needed was to be blindsided by new material.

"Good." Maura smiled.

"Hey," I forced out, before I lost my nerve. "I want to ask you something. About that night."

The smile dropped away from Maura's face. I hadn't

thought her black eyes could grow any darker, but they did. "I'm not sure I'm ready to talk about that yet."

"Oh, I—no, of course—not any of the—" I swallowed, imagining asking Maura about finding him. The body. The blood. I finally choked out, "I don't want to talk about that, either."

Maura looked at me evenly across the table, but her face had a different, closed quality to it now.

"Dane mentioned something . . . odd to me." The cold knots of the chair thrust into my spine. I squirmed. "He said something about playing . . . a game? That night?"

Maura's brow knit together. "Game? I'm not sure what you're talking about."

"No? I figured he was into RPGs for a while in high school. And last Christmas, he *was* talking about that One Night game, but I don't know, it sounded kind of lame to me. Vampires? Werewolves?" I forced out a shaky laugh. I was babbling again.

This time, Maura didn't smile. "Dane and I had a quiet date night. We ate dinner together, watched *Dateline,* and took a walk through the neighborhood. Just like the police report said."

As she said that last line, I felt a cold front sweep in around our table. I stared at Maura's face and had that same sensation of seeing inside an open pomegranate. I didn't want to tell her about Dane's text.

Especially since it was clear to me now: she was lying.

"Okay," I said, hiding my face in my wine.

Silence descended. I drained my glass. When the waiter came by offering a refill, I shook my head. Maura chewed her bread, and I twisted the hem of my dress under the table, snapping a thread. Had I come on too strong? Ruined any chance I had to ply Maura for answers by rushing straight into the accusations? I'd screwed everything up.

"Holly," Maura spoke, surprising me. "I wonder. . . . Goodness, this is hard to ask."

My heart pricked. "Yes?"

"I'm finding it difficult to be home with so many of Dane's things around. Clothes. Books. Art supplies. Of course, some of them are a comfort, but it's overwhelming. Would you be able to come by and pick some of them up? Maybe . . . to have for yourself? And bring to your parents, of course."

I exhaled. "Sure." This was a double blessing: not only the opportunity to wring more intel out of Maura but also to reclaim some of Dane's belongings. The stuff he'd left at Mom and Dad's place hadn't been touched in years. Those figurines and report cards boxed in his closet were symbolic, yes, but they didn't hold Dane's essence anymore. I imagined drawing one of his soft hoodies to my nose, inhaling his cedar scent. My eyes stung, and I shoved a piece of bread in my mouth.

Maura gave me her phone and told me to enter my number. When I handed it back, I saw a telltale glimmer. I couldn't help myself; I actually grabbed her hand. "Is that—?"

Yes, it was—a pear-shaped diamond flanked by two emeralds. My ears felt stuffed.

Maura looked down at the ring as if seeing it for the first time. "Oh," she said, twisting the gems in the light. "Yeah, that happened. We'd been waiting until our next visit to your parents' to share the news."

"I—but—the two of you were only together for, like, five months!" My voice came out a childish whine. I'd been with my high school boyfriend, Eric, for nearly three years, and yet the prospect of marriage had never even occurred to me.

"Six, actually," Maura said smoothly.

I sat back in my chair, winded. How had my brother managed to afford *that* on a fledgling medical illustrator's salary? He'd only been graduated from SCAD for a few months. And how had I not noticed the ring before? I was *certain* Maura hadn't been wearing it at the funeral. I remembered the *Charlotte's Web* excerpt she'd read, the one from the point of view of the spider. Why had it taken me this long to realize how screwed up that was? Maura, going on about *weaving her web* as my brother's ashes sat in an urn beside her?

"Sorry!" Maura exclaimed, searching my face. "I didn't mean to shock you."

"No, it's okay."

It wasn't.

After splitting the check with Maura, I stepped away on wobbly legs. My eyes followed her slight frame down the darkening sidewalk until Maura disappeared around the corner. Then I settled onto a bench in Monterey Park, staring at the spot we'd just vacated.

Why had Maura denied playing a game with my brother on the night of his death? Was it possible trauma had wiped her memory, made her forget? Had Dane really been that far gone that he'd texted me in the throes of his psychosis? That's what everyone else thought. My parents hadn't even wanted me to take Dane's bizarre text messages to the police, insisting it would needlessly cast Maura in a negative light. I'd gone against their wishes and shared the texts anyway, but the police had brushed me off. Like my parents, the police insisted it was an open-and-shut suicide case. Nothing more.

But that explanation still wasn't sitting right with me. I put my chin in my hands. Why had Maura hidden her engagement to Dane? That one was really making my stomach roil. She claimed she'd been planning on telling my parents, but could I even believe that? Besides, what kind of girl got engaged without saying a peep on social media?

I stood up from the bench. Tonight had proven something was off about Maura; she knew more than she was letting on.

What the hell else was she hiding?

CHAPTER 4

After drinks with Maura, all I wanted to do was curl up in my room and play back our conversation in my head, but Rachel and Henry ambushed me when I arrived home. They'd prepared a giant strawberry and arugula salad and wanted me to join them for dinner. I forced myself to accept—maybe it would help me forget about the way they'd talked about me behind my back. So I helped them set the table, dancing to Rachel's playlist piped through the surround-sound system. I even asked them how the wedding planning was going, and this was a topic I usually avoided. I was overcompensating.

"I have to start looking for a dress," Rachel said, topping off our glasses of white wine.

"Wait, you haven't started yet? I thought Henry's already been fitted for his tux."

"Yes," Rachel said coolly, "Henry basically sprinted to the nearest tailor the second after he popped the question."

"That's kind of weird, Henry," I said.

Henry looked theatrically at me, to Rachel, and back to me

again. "What? Why?" he demanded. "I've been looking for an excuse to embrace my inner 007 for years. You girls don't get it. Tux rentals suck. I felt like a bulky penguin at my prom."

"Aw, but I'm sure you were the very *cutest* bulky penguin," Rachel said, snatching Henry's chin in her hands.

Bleugh. Spare me.

Journey came up on Rachel's playlist. Rachel and I dropped our forks to clasp hands and belt out the lyrics. Henry groaned into his arugula. He'd had to stomach nearly three years of this. Three years of throwbacks to our Emory days, when Rachel and I had screamed along to this very song between eye-watering Apple Bacardí shots. Even now, "Don't Stop Believin'" conjured the burnt smell of a heated curling rod, the thick promise of a Saturday night. Stop-motion frames of Rachel and me clutching each other as our heels caught in the gaps between paving stones on a race across campus.

All too soon, the song ended. Rachel looked down at her salad and gave a sad little sigh.

I bit the insides of my cheeks. "So," I said. "Y'all have any big plans for after the wedding? Turning into married drones and moving out to the 'burbs?" I failed to stick the landing; my attempt at playfulness sounded accusatory. Remembering their conversation I'd overheard still made me shaky with anger. I wondered if they'd cop to talking about moving.

"Actually, we'd like to buy a place downtown," Henry said, at the same time that Rachel said, "Not anytime soon." They looked at each other once, wildly, before their eyes dropped to their respective plates.

Self-pity surged inside me, syrupy and vile.

Rachel placed her hand over Henry's on the table. "Holly,"

she enunciated. "I want you to know, Henry and I aren't going anywhere anytime soon. Okay?"

Henry's eyebrows raised perceptibly. Clearly he did not agree.

Congratulations, Rachel. You are officially marrying a dick. My anger ballooned until it burst into humiliation. Here I was again, the child at the adults' table. And as for the adults? They were just humoring me.

"Okay," I whispered. I stabbed at my limp salad with my fork.

There was nothing more to say.

As I lay in bed that night, licking my wounds and listening to the cadence of Rachel's and Henry's voices through the wall, I found myself thinking of middle school. Those days, I'd clung to a circle of girls who'd turned their backs to me whenever I joined them by their lockers in between classes. Desperate, I organized a viewing party for the *Bachelor* premiere—for the past several weeks, these girls had talked of nothing but. I went with Mom to the grocery store, carefully selecting plastic champagne glasses and weighing the merits of Martinelli's sparkling apple versus apple-grape. I found a recipe on Pinterest and dipped strawberries in white and then milk chocolate, painting tiny tuxedos. Thirty minutes before the event, each one of the five girls cancelled, as if in a coordinated effort. Dane saw me receive the flurry of texts and sat in the living room with me eating the fussy strawberries off Mom's silver heirloom tray I'd polished earlier, pretending not to watch the show.

"This is stupid," he said. "I bet you every cent in my bank account that the next chick who walks in has fake boobs, too."

He accidentally ate a piece of strawberry leaf and gagged dramatically.

But he'd stayed until the very end.

Now, I blinked back tears against my pillowcase. I'd never felt so lonely living with Rachel and Henry before. So . . . *stranded*. And Dane wasn't even there to soften the blow.

It wasn't fair. He'd left me to weather this all alone.

On Sunday, I gasped awake at one P.M. from a nightmare about Dane. It was the same recurring dream that had been tormenting me ever since his death: Dane screaming, his mouth widening into an impossible black chasm. Each time, I was helpless, forced to watch my brother devour himself. I lurched upright in damp sheets and stared into the naked electrical outlet next to my bed. It, too, looked like a face in danger of expanding forever.

How was I supposed to start my day after that? How had I even entertained myself before Dane died? I still had a stack of overdue library books on my desk—I was sure to get a slap on the wrist from Esther about those—but whereas the prospect of cuddling up under the covers to read once would have been enticing, now I felt indifferent. I didn't want books. I didn't even want to be conscious.

It was three P.M. by the time I showered, dressed, and made it into the living room. Alone in the apartment, I sank into the couch, staring at my phone. All weekend, I'd been itching to text Maura, especially after the bomb she'd dropped on me about her and Dane being engaged. I needed more information, but I'd held off; I couldn't scare her away by coming on too strong.

Now it was finally time. I tapped out the message I'd been drafting in my head since our wine date.

> Hey Maura—I think I'll take you up on that offer
> to come by and pick up some of Dane's things.
> When works for you?

Then I tossed my phone on the couch and lurched to my feet in search of cleaning supplies. If I continued to be a burden to Rachel and Henry, the least I could do was make their appliances shine. I started on the oven, knowing it would be bad. The layers of burnt food sloughing off were sticky and acrid. Afterward, my wrists hurt, but my guilt stung less.

I moved on to the stovetop. Then the refrigerator. I emptied its contents onto the counters, sorted through the expired condiments, and attacked the plastic drawers with a sponge and all-purpose cleaner. A couple hours slid by as I cleaned, and I was grateful.

Still no reply from Maura.

Around dinnertime, a breeze filtered in through the open window facing Chippewa Square. A kid in a striped shirt was being pulled by his mother along the sidewalk. His feet flicked out along the curb, as if he were trying to tap out a pattern or a critical message before being dragged away.

Finally, my phone buzzed to life.

> **Maura**
> I'm free now

Seconds later, I was slipping on my shoes by the door.

Me
Great. Text me your address?

She must have typed it in wrong.

Twenty minutes later, I peered up at the building: an imposing stone structure with winged gargoyles clustered at the roofline and scrolled cast-iron balconies. A drainage pipe kissed the sidewalk, its spout shaped like a gasping fish. No one had alerted me to the fact that my brother had spent the summer living in a veritable castle. Even though he'd moved in with Maura as soon as classes had ended in May, a stunning two months after they'd started dating, I'd never visited.

I climbed a squat staircase, the banister green with age. Halfway up the steps, a silver cat pressed against my shins before flitting past.

Maura came to the door in a pair of terry-cloth shorts and a messy topknot. Dressed down, without the bold slashes of her choker and lipstick she'd worn at the wine bar, she seemed more vulnerable. She put a nail to her mouth. The inside of her wrist looked soft. "Come in," she said. "Sorry I look like a drowned rat."

For once, it wasn't Maura I was focused on. In the townhouse foyer, vaulted ceiling beams arched in the shape of an inverted bowl. Beyond that was a living room torn straight from the pages of *Better Homes and Gardens.* Crushed velvet settees in jewel tones, gossamer white drapery, and terrace doors flung wide. At the back of the living room were glass double doors to what appeared to be a greenhouse. And everywhere: flowers. Dusky succulents in terra-cotta bowls, vines tumbling from hanging pots, and bursts of pastel blossoms with moody dark centers.

"Wow," I said, following Maura inside. "Your place. It's so . . . grown-up."

"Ha." Maura moved into the living room, walking with that slight limp I'd noticed over Easter. The undersides of her highlighter-yellow socks were darkened with wear. I surprised myself by feeling a squeeze of sympathy.

"Please ignore the mess," she said, even though I didn't see a single item out of place. "My housekeeper quit, and I haven't gotten around to finding someone else." She splayed out across one of the settees and sighed. "I'd offer you a drink, but I'm a shitty hostess."

"I won't hold it against you." I sat down on the sapphire cushions beside her. Maura's fingernail went to her mouth again—I'd never noticed her being so fidgety before. "Hey, is something wrong?"

Maura reached for her phone. "I don't know how you're feeling these days, but I guess I hadn't expected to feel so . . . uneven. Some moments, Dane fades to the background, and I can focus on the task at hand, you know? Arranging flowers. Emailing clients. I think, 'Okay, I can do this. This is progress.' But then—suddenly—it just comes crashing back, obliterating everything. The fact that he's fucking *dead*."

I sat back against the firm pillows, picking at my own cuticle. I'd never heard anyone articulate so clearly what I'd been feeling.

Maura flicked through something on her phone. She held it out to me. I squinted until the blurry image took form: the mound of a body turned sideways under a plush comforter. A nest of dark hair against a pillow. It was Maura's sleeping body.

And, much blurrier in the foreground, the cut-off smirk of someone taking a stealth selfie. Full lips, just like mine. Two smudges of color that indicated my brother's mismatched eyes behind his Clark Kent glasses—one blue, one green. The starburst of Maura's phone was reflected in the lenses.

"He must've taken that the morning before he died. I just found it on my camera roll when I texted you back."

Oh, God. I was reeling. It was scary enough venturing into the minefield of Mom and Dad's house, knowing I could, at any moment, stumble upon something belonging to Dane, but to find a secret photo of him—an actual image of his face? I couldn't even imagine the horror. Would we ever be able to let our guard down again?

I folded my head into the bowl of my hands. "Shit."

We sat in silence. The sounds of the street below—a bicycle bell, a truck beeping in reverse—filled the living room.

"You know," I started. I cleared my throat, which felt sandy. "He was always doing mischievous things like that."

"I know."

"When he was a toddler, he'd come up with super creative ways to protest nap-time. One day, he climbed out of his crib, onto his changing table, and got ahold of the baby powder. He blanketed the entire room in the stuff. Bedsheets, bookshelves, floorboards—it looked like there had been a blizzard. Eventually, my parents saw the white stuff filtering out from under the door and rushed in, thinking he'd set the place on fire."

Maura smirked. "Sounds like Dane."

"It's rare you find a nerd with such an impish streak."

"It really is."

Our silences were becoming more tolerable, I realized. Longer, too.

"Okay, I think I'll actually offer you a drink now," Maura said.

I followed her into the kitchen. I guessed she'd serve me wine or some other form of alcohol, considering the heaviness of our conversation, but instead, Maura set a teapot to boil. I hugged myself as I looked around the space. It was a true chef's kitchen—Viking stove with blood-red knobs and an imposing stainless hood. Green tendrils spilled over the windowsills, herbs and spices vying for the light. Over the bar was a framed diagram of a human heart. I recognized the style instantly, and my breath stuck in my throat. I hadn't seen this one before. It was a cross-section, as many of Dane's illustrations were, leading the viewer through cavities and chambers like an intricate network of underwater caves.

"Dane's?" I asked.

"Of course. He had this uncanny ability—"

"I know. That precision."

"Well, yes, that. But he had this way of taking flesh and organs and extracting the humanity from them. Reducing them to . . . these soulless machines. It was masterful."

I rubbed my palms along my forearms. Dane had received a lot of positive feedback on his work, but never stated quite like that.

The kettle screeched. Maura reached on her tiptoes and pulled a tin canister from a cabinet above the stove. "These really do the trick whenever I'm feeling anxious," she said. Using a pair of miniature tongs, she extracted what looked like a purple rosebud from the tin, dropped it into a teacup, and poured the steaming water over it. She glanced at me. "Want one?"

"Sure." Was she insinuating that I might be feeling anxious, too?

Was it that obvious?

Maura poured again. I watched violet bleed into the water like ink.

"Let's go back to the sitting room," she said.

Who under the age of sixty-five even used the term "sitting room"? I couldn't tell if Maura's stilted language was old-fashioned or simply the mark of fine breeding, like her spindly racehorse ankles. After all, Dane had mentioned she'd grown up relatively wealthy on the East Coast. I gripped my elbows behind my back as I followed Maura and the tray of tea out of the kitchen.

Back on the couches, Maura handed me a cup and asked me about growing up in Savannah.

"I don't really have anything to compare it to," I said. "Dane and I were born and raised here, as you know."

"Well, what was it like being little-Holly? What were your parents like?"

I hesitated. "I'm not sure what you mean."

"Sure you do." Maura looked at me, her head tilted with amusement. Then she rolled her eyes, as if she were doing me a gratuitous favor. "*For instance . . .* which one did you gravitate toward? Who was the disciplinarian? Did you feel like you could confide in them?"

"I . . ." My face warmed. I couldn't remember the last time anyone had taken such an intense interest in my past. People only asked where I was from to make small talk, or else to gauge how established my family was in Savannah. But Maura was interested in something else, something meatier.

"I . . . I guess I've always been closer to my father?" I'd

never said it out loud before. The words left behind a bitter residue, like gunpowder.

"And Dane . . . he was closer with your mother, wasn't he?"

I nodded.

Maura leaned her elbows on her thighs, inclining toward me. Her eyes were dark globes. "How come, do you think?"

I laughed, too loudly. "Geez, Maura, I don't know! You going to have me lie down on this couch and tell you about my dreams, too?"

Maura looked down at her lap. "Only if you want."

My stomach promptly collapsed with guilt. What was wrong with me? The girl was only trying to get to know me, albeit in her own strange way. I made sure my next words came out soft. "How about you, Maura? Tell me about your family."

Maura's elbows slid off her thighs and her shoulders dipped, opening grooves beneath the straps of her tank top. I caught myself following the lines of her skin against the edges of fabric and looked away quickly.

"Not much to say. I grew up in Connecticut."

"And?"

"And my parents were great. My mom is my best friend—truly. How many girls get to say that and mean it?" Maura gave a dreamy smile. Then she rushed on to tell me about the lush garden off the terrace of their family home. "That's where I started learning about plants. I'd learn some more from professors at SCAD—that was mostly about creating and selling fragrances, though. Really, I'd say the bulk of my education happened outside the classroom."

I sipped my tea. Maura was right—it did seem to be loosening the molecules in my core.

"In fact . . ." Maura put her teacup down and pressed her palms together, looking gleeful. "I'll show you something I just ordered. I think you'll like it."

She disappeared and returned with a small clouded Tupperware and a tray of six plants, each about the size of a human hand. I peered closer. They were bowl-shaped with pointed lips and odd red veins. Their scalloped collars made them look like miniature dragons.

"Pitcher plants. From the rainforest." Maura placed the tray over her knees. "Want to touch?"

They skeeved me out. "No, thanks."

Maura laughed. "You're cute. Come on, I promise they won't bite. Not you, anyway."

"Really, I'm good." My tongue felt too thick in my mouth.

"In the rainforest," Maura explained, "this red rim here draws in flies." She indicated the crimson lip on one of her plants with her own dark nail. "It's moistened by dew and when the flies hit it, they're immobilized. Sucked inside. Then they're drowned, their bodies liquefied." Maura unscrewed the Tupperware. With a pair of tweezers, she extracted a tiny worm.

What the hell was she doing? Live insects? I glanced away, gripping at the couch armrest to steady myself.

This seemed to delight Maura. "What? It's just a little mealworm! Pitcher plants like their meat. Can you blame them?" Maura dropped the worm into one of the open mouths. There was an audible sizzle.

Wetness sprouted under my arms. "Charming," I managed.

"I think they're beautiful."

"Actually . . ." I set my teacup down on the coffee table, reaching out with a hand to steady the movement. The cup wobbled a bit, refusing to nest right in the saucer. "I have this thing about holes. The way those plants look like open mouths . . . it kind of freaks me out."

Maura looked up. "What do you mean, a 'thing about holes'?"

"I don't know. It's weird. Whenever I see clusters of holes, or circular patterns, I get wigged out."

"Oh." Maura set the tweezers down on the coffee table. "Trypophobia, you mean."

My brows crunched together with surprise. "Yeah. You've heard of it? I didn't realize other people—"

"Yeah, sure." Then she winked at me. "I know things, Holly."

I pushed my shoulder blades into the tufted pillows, feeling like I had the moment Maura caught my eye while reading at my brother's funeral. Exposed. I didn't like it.

Maura dropped another few worms into the gaping red mouths. I couldn't figure out which was more unsettling—the way she lovingly dispensed the mealworms or the sound of the carnivorous plants dissolving them on impact.

Outside the terrace doors, the sun was setting, the diaphanous curtains stirring gently. The street below was so quiet I could hear the rushing of the fountain in Forsyth Park. Where had all the traffic gone? I had the sudden, intense urge to pee. But as I pried myself off the settee, exhaustion crashed over me. Maybe it was because I hadn't been sleeping well; maybe my triggered trypophobia had left me drained. In any case, I needed a rest.

"Can I lie down here for a minute?"

"Of course."

I slipped off my shoes and curled up on the cushions, my

eyes tracing the intricate crown molding along the ceiling. Here I was, lying down on Maura's couch like I had quipped to her. I hadn't realized it would feel like such a relief. I riffled through my memory for the excuse I'd given Maura for coming over. *Right—to pick up Dane's things.*

It could wait.

"Speaking of holes, I've been having nightmares about Dane." My voice sounded lazy. "That he's screaming, and his mouth just keeps getting wider and wider until he's practically devouring himself."

"My goodness," Maura said. "That sounds horrific." She screwed the lid back onto the Tupperware and moved the tray of pitcher plants to the coffee table. Then she lay down across her own couch. "I've been dreaming about him, too. Last night I dreamt that Dane was next to me in bed, coughing up a leech."

I felt my heart beat faintly in my wrists. "Look at us," I said. "We're wrecks."

"I suppose we are."

"Also, my roommates are leaving me. So I'm probably going to be homeless soon." I wasn't sure why I was telling Maura this; the words seemed to float out of my body.

"Why?"

"They're getting married and buying their own place."

"Those bitches."

I closed my eyes. For a while, I enjoyed the delicious sensation of melding into velvet, listening to the fountain spray outside. "Yeah," I said. "The worst part is . . ." I trailed off. "Never mind."

"What?" Maura prompted, gently.

I passed a hand over my face. "Well, one of my roommates, she's my best friend. We roomed together all of college. I get that she wants to have her own place with her soon-to-be-husband, but I guess I hadn't realized how much it would actually sting when it happened, you know?"

"Damn," Maura said. "That really sucks."

I sighed. It felt good to finally say these things aloud.

"I'm glad you emailed me the other day, Holly."

"Mhmm."

"You're good at being vulnerable. Most people aren't."

Maura's eyes were on the ceiling. She'd pulled out her top knot, and her long hair was now swept up over a pillow, exposing the curve of her neck to me. Under my exhaustion, I felt a flicker of attraction. What would happen if I wedged my body against hers on the cushions? The second the thought occurred, I rushed to snuff it out.

"You're welcome to spend the night," Maura said, and for a single stomach-bending moment, I was sure she'd read my mind. "I'd understand if you didn't want to be walking all the way back in the dark, alone."

I don't remember if I ever replied.

CHAPTER 5

I woke early the next morning to a dog barking outside. My mouth felt caked with a familiar bitter, gunpowder-like scum. Where was I? Buttery morning light sifted through the lushness of overflowing leaves and petals. I lurched upright on the velvet couch, memories from the previous night crashing over me. Had I really fallen asleep here unloading my vulnerabilities to Maura? What had I been thinking?

The couch Maura had been lying on was empty now. I grasped for my phone and purse on the coffee table, stuffed on my shoes, and made a mad dash to the front door.

Walking briskly through the gray morning, I passed a couple old trolleys—all glossy paint and ornate wood—parked in preparation for the day's tours of the city. In an hour or two they'd grind to life, along with the horse-drawn carriages and the stenciled hearses boasting ghost tours through historic Savannah. But for now, the streets were still.

I was hoping to arrive home early enough to avoid detection, but Rachel was rooting in the fridge when I walked in. She looked pointedly at my rumpled T-shirt.

"Where were you last night?"

"I stayed at my parents'."

"Where's your stuff?"

"Left it there. I got lazy."

Rachel turned back to the fridge and I felt a stab of remorse. Why was I lying to her?

I never would have guessed it would come so easily.

I closed myself in my bedroom and shook out a couple Advil into my palm. My head pounded and my eyelids felt gummy. Fortunately, I still had an hour before I needed to get ready for work, so I set my alarm and flopped face-first onto my bed.

Maybe that was all I needed. More sleep.

That week, I couldn't stop thinking about Maura. I moved through my routine like a sleepwalker: going to work, doing my laundry, and continuing to scroll online for available apartments. But Maura was invading my mind, curling into its furthest reaches like an unrolling carpet of fog. It was swiftly becoming clear that my brother had been dating—no, *engaged to*—quite a character. I combed through all the tidbits I knew about her. Those strange black eyes, that nibbled index nail, the sizzling pitcher plants, and the way she'd described Dane. *He had this way of taking flesh and organs and extracting the humanity from them. Reducing them to . . . these soulless machines.*

Why did all these details fit together in such an eerie, discordant way? I had to be missing something.

On Friday, I took a detour on my way home from work to

stroll through Forsyth Park with a latte. A woman sat on a bench to my right, making a basket out of palm fronds. I smiled at her, watched a glass-colored dragonfly sputtering on its back on the concrete. I bent down and used a dried leaf to flip it over. Then I straightened and tried to pick out Maura's townhouse from where I stood. There it was—with the gargoyles at the roofline and a sharp iron fence of fleur-de-lis. I remembered lying across from Maura on our matching jewel-tone settees, and something like longing shot through me. I needed to talk with her again. But I couldn't just show up at Maura's place unannounced.

Could I?

A minute later, Maura opened the door in a red kimono-style robe. "Holly!" she exclaimed.

"Sorry to surprise you like this. I was just passing by and realized I never even picked up any of Dane's stuff that we talked about. Are you free right now?"

Maura glanced behind her. "Actually, I'm so sorry, but I'm getting ready for an event tonight."

"Oh!" Immediately I felt sheepish. Stopping by Maura's out of the blue on a Friday afternoon? *Of course* she had plans. Despite my shame, I hungered to know more. "What kind of event? Are you hosting?"

"No, not this time. It's at a client's place." The edge of Maura's mouth lifted. She looked like she was about to say something, but didn't.

"That's cool." I looked down at the bristly doormat.

Maura cleared her throat. "What are you up to tonight?"

"Actually . . . nothing!" Was that a subtle invitation? If I could go with Maura to this party, it'd be an opportunity to peel back another layer of her secrecy. To see and talk to whoever

Maura rubbed shoulders with. Excitement built in me like champagne fizz, making my words come out in a rush. "Gosh, I haven't been to a party in . . . forever! Is it one of those parties that's open to the public?"

"Hmm." Maura adjusted the tie at her waist. "Not really."

"Oh." Even I was mortified by the depth of disappointment that came through that single syllable.

But to my shock and delight, Maura only laughed. "Holly," she said, taking me by the elbow. "Why don't you come with me?"

Maura offered to lend me a dress so I wouldn't have to walk back home and change.

"It's no problem," she insisted, leading me down the hallway and into her master bedroom. "I have so many dresses I don't even know what to do with them."

As Maura riffled through her closet, I took in her bedroom. So this is where Dane had slept. Exposed beams overhead, a yawning fireplace with tiles featuring aristocratic-looking women in profile, and a small sitting area occupied by a champagne-colored sofa. Vibrant orchids and irises nestled in moss-laden slings hung from the rafters. I dragged a fingertip over Maura's dresser, searching frantically for any signs of Dane. All I saw was a framed photo of him and Maura. Maura's head was tipped back as she laughed, spilling dark tresses across Dane's slight chest. Dane looked at her in the way a little kid waking from a bad dream might regard a nightlight. He looked handsome.

But there were none of Dane's illustrations in this room. None of his art supplies or his immaculately painted figurines.

Had Maura scrubbed every trace of my brother from her place after his death? Or had she never even given him the opportunity to leave his mark?

"Hmm." Maura stepped out of her closet, holding an ivory silk sheath with a pronounced slit up the side. "Try this."

I thought of protesting that it wouldn't fit, but the words died on my lips: Maura and I had very similar builds. I clutched the garment to my chest.

Maura looked at me, expectant. Then a languid smile crossed her face. "Oh, aren't you a doll? I promise not to look."

She clapped her hands over her eyes in an exaggerated manner, as if playing hide-and-seek with a child. Even so, I hunched into the closet, shedding my tweed skirt in a heap and awkwardly pulling on the ivory sheath. The silk slid against my skin like oil.

"Want me to get the zipper for you?" Maura approached and I turned, giving her access to the pull at the back. Her knuckles brushed the skin above the lace trim of my underwear, and I felt a frisson run through me, cold and electric.

"There." Maura assessed me.

My cheeks flamed under her scrutiny. I hoped she wouldn't notice.

"Goodness," she said, turning away at last. "Sometimes it freaks me out how clearly I see his beauty in you."

Maura wore a violet gown with a back that left her sharp spine naked. The bones rippled under her skin as she filled a couple flasks in the kitchen. Then we stole outside, cutting back across Forsyth Park. It'd taken two hours for Maura to help me with my hair and makeup and to do her own, so the park was almost empty now, save for some tourists with bulky cameras around their necks and a wizened man playing "Pop! Goes the Weasel" on a clarinet. The moon was a rind sitting high in the sky. We stopped to admire the fountain, ringed in a bed of blue flowers. Water spurted from the statues within: egrets and mermen holding conch shells. A gust of wind blew spray at us, numbing the skin at my neckline.

Maura giggled, took a pull of her flask, and then motioned to me. "Come on!"

Our heels clunked over the zigzagging bricks, perilously—often, the brickwork buckled around massive oak roots. I widened my stride to keep up with Maura. We passed a boutique with red walls and antlers mounted upon them; galleries and gift shops displaying jewelry, handbags, and soap in the lit windows; SCAD buildings boasting the school's intricate crest. After a few blocks, I started to grumble. "I had no idea we'd be walking for this long. I would've worn flats. Or called an Uber."

"Come on," Maura said again, making no move to slow her gait. "Flats would've ruined your outfit, and I would've rejected the idea of an Uber. What's the point of living in Savannah if not to walk through it at night? You know . . ." Maura smiled in an unfamiliar way. "In a few days, my mother is coming to visit for the first time."

"Oh, wow." I stopped, using Maura's borrowed stiletto to scratch at my shin. A horse-drawn carriage rolled past us, the horse's eyes looking tired in its blinders. "She's never been here before?"

Maura kept walking, forcing me to jog to keep up. "Nope. Never seen the city, never seen my place."

"You're kidding." I thought back to the first day I'd entered

Maura's townhouse, the way my shock and confusion had given way to awe in the soaring foyer. "She's going to be so blown away."

"I hope so. I have a whole itinerary planned for us. See?" Maura swiped at her phone and held it out to me. It looked like she'd created a color-coded Excel sheet. She scrolled through it. "We're going to do all the tourist things. Pralines on River Street. A walking ghost tour. And, of course, she's coming right in time for Dane's showcase. You're still planning on going, right?"

"Of course."

"Yay! I'll have to introduce you. Since I'll be showing Mom around Savannah, let me practice being a tour guide on you, okay? Behold." She tilted her head up to the building to our right, a stately, black-shuttered three-story with an ornate iron balcony.

"Yes, the 17Hundred90 Inn," I said impatiently. I noticed she hadn't actually given me time to consent to getting a tour. I took a swig from my own flask and shifted my weight to one foot to relieve my aching sole.

"Do you *know* about the 17Hundred90 Inn?"

"Of course I do. I grew up here."

Maura crossed her arms over her chest. "Okay, tell me what you know."

"Well . . . just the basics. Some girl fell in love with a sailor who didn't love her back and, like, flung herself off the balcony in despair."

Maura made the sound of a game-show buzzer. "Holly, if there's one thing you've got to get right in Savannah, it's the ghost lore. How many other cities can claim to be steeped in history like we are? It's an honor. We must take it seriously."

"Must we, now?"

"Don't be fresh with me. Let's get this story straight. 'Some girl,' as you said, was named Anna Powell. She was sixteen years old—do you remember being sixteen? What was that, ten years ago for you? Not quite as long ago for me."

The alcohol was burning a neat little patch in my stomach. "Watch it, Maura."

"Okay, now imagine being married to a man thirty years your senior. See? Much older than you, don't feel bad. Steel White built the inn. He had a lot of money, but Anna wasn't feeling it. She pined for someone younger, someone with an impetuous spirit, like hers. She found that in a German sailor who arrived into port one day."

"Okay, I got that part right."

"You did. But what you missed is that this fetching lad left Anna with an unwanted gift: a baby. And when Steel found out, he was livid. He locked his young bride in room 204. And there she was trapped, for days and days on end. Each day, Steel would come to deposit a slice of almond cake and a glass of water at the door. Then he would leave, even as Anna pawed at him and begged him to let her out."

"Almond cake? That's kind of random."

Maura ignored me. "To keep herself sane, Anna ripped the pages from the Bible in the room, found a pair of sewing scissors, and fashioned these lovely, intricate paper dolls. She probably could have sold them for a handsome price, had she been out in the world. This is how she occupied her time, day in and day out—making paper dolls and agonizing that she couldn't see the harbor from her prison window."

I glanced over at Maura. The way her eyes shone made her look almost febrile.

"Eventually," she went on, "Anna's hands took on a life of their own, cutting these dolls in a frenzy. She didn't even need to look down at them anymore. This might have been when she went mad and attacked her own face with the scissors, dripping blood all over the snowy bedsheets.

"One day, sitting in her pile of blood-streaked paper dolls, Anna could feel it happening, even if she couldn't see it: her beloved sailor leaving the harbor, the sails of his ship shrinking to thumbnails against the horizon. That's when Anna opened the window, climbed out onto the balcony, and flung herself over it, into the brick courtyard below."

"Eek." I looked at the curlicue balcony again, a chill groping its way over my spine.

"'Eek' is right. But of course you've heard the accounts of guests staying at the inn? How Anna's spirit will visit them in their beds at night, gazing down at them and caressing their cheeks before diving out the hotel window?"

"Yes," I said, gripping my elbows. "That sounds familiar." Was Maura really going to tell this extended tale to her mother when she visited?

"Good." Maura readjusted the strap of her beaded purse on her shoulder. Then she looked up at the façade of the inn, lighting on a wooden trellis choked with blossoms. It was impossible to tell their true color in the night.

Maura's arm snaked out, and she broke off a flower head with an audible snap. She rotated the bloom slowly in her fingers. It reminded me of something I couldn't quite place, maybe a puzzle or a toy that had entranced me as a kid. I ran my tongue over dry lips, unable to look away.

"*Petunia atkinsiana*," Maura said, still contemplating the hypnotic flower. "Part of the nightshade family. Petunias are harmless, though their cousins are known for all kinds of unsavory behavior. Causing hallucinations, paralysis. Blindness." She reached out and tucked the flower behind my ear.

"Whoa." I flinched, feeling the cold petal press against my scalp. "Do you promise this one is harmless?"

Maura gave me a gentle smile. "I promise. Besides, that shouldn't be what you're worried about." Then she looked back up at the façade of the old inn. "Never underestimate the power of grief, Holly," she said, quieter now. "It may be one of the deadliest poisons of all."

I couldn't stop touching the petunia in my hair during the rest of our walk to the party. But Maura acted as if the entire bizarre conversation hadn't happened. She chatted with me about silly things, like how the squirrels in a particular square had gotten brazen enough to snatch food out of tourists' hands. Even her tone had turned bouncy and light. She'd reverted back to a normal twenty-two-year-old girl, and I forced myself to relax.

We turned onto Oglethorpe Avenue, past the station with the firemen loitering on the street. A group of SCAD girls clomped past us in skimpy dresses, giggling, their long hair flaring out in the night. When we stopped in front of one of the mansions, I forgot all about the petunia.

"Here?" I demanded.

Maura looked at me, almost crossly. "Yes."

We'd be entering through the massive wrought-iron gate. The black tines thrust toward the sky like daggers; they matched the ironwork on the mansion's widow's walk. Elaborate cream-colored scrolls were carved above each window and door.

"And this is one of your *clients*, you said?"

She laughed and touched a hand to my elbow. "Come on."

A man in uniform heaved the gate open for us; it emitted a slight groan. "'Evening, Ms. Rossi."

"Good evening, Jeffrey. How're the boys?"

"Feisty as ever, God love 'em."

"I'm glad to hear it."

Down a short paved walkway and past a wall of hedges stood a grand entryway flanked by columns. Maura opened the door as if it were her own home and motioned me inside. An imposing staircase swept up the center of the room, splitting to either side on the second floor. The amber glow from the sconces on the wall was just enough to illuminate the curve of the banister, carved into a swollen blossom at the base of the staircase. There sat a mirrored table with a smirking cherub statue poised upon it. The ceiling itself was a masterpiece, edged in gold leaf and intricate plaster vines. A behemoth chandelier hung from the center of it all. Its crystals made me think of human eyes.

"They'll be out in the courtyard," Maura said, leading me back.

The courtyard was even bigger than the room we had exited, inlaid with dizzying brickwork and blurred by the lushness of hedges, ivy, and dripping Spanish moss. Stars peeked from behind the blackened foliage. Delicate sounds echoed against the stone: the clinking of cutlery, laughter, and the steady trickle of a tiered fountain.

"Maura!" A woman rose from the full banquet table in the center of the courtyard. She looked to be in her late fifties, with a statuesque face and an iridescent green mantle draped over her shoulders.

"Odette, thank you for having us." The two exchanged kisses before Maura turned to indicate me. "Meet my friend, Holly."

"A pleasure." Odette kissed either side of my face and I followed suit. Her skin was smooth and icy.

Maura touched Odette's elbow. "How's your mother? Will she be coming down to join us?"

Odette shook her head. "She's well. But perhaps tonight would not be wise."

"I understand."

Odette considered us both. "I must admit, we've already started eating, but I did save you a couple seats near the head of the table."

Said table was a riot of color. Heaping flower arrangements. Tureens of liquid with blossoms floating on top like skins. Exquisite Cornish game hens with bits of twine at the legs and vibrant, diced vegetables—everything from filigree-like frisée to slivered, violet roots arranged in whorls. A platter of open-mouthed mussels clotted with salt, surrounded by electric-blue coral. And then—it couldn't be—three gasping fish heads rising out of a glossy pie. At my place setting, my empty plate shone like a moon.

"You need to try this," Maura said, sliding a glistening wafer onto my plate. "Honeycomb cake. And this! Dragonfruit parfait. My favorite."

The parfait was packed into a slender flute of mouthwatering sunset colors. "I guess we've started with the dessert course, then," I said, taking the long-stemmed spoon that Maura handed me. Then I scooped a bit of cream off the top of the confection and rolled the cold sweetness around in my mouth.

"Dessert always comes first at Odette's." The young man

sitting next to Odette winked at me. He wore an impeccably tailored, red velvet dinner jacket and horn-rimmed glasses.

Maura waved a delicate hand toward me. "Holly, Matias. Matias, meet my friend Holly."

"Charmed. Now tell me, Holly." The end of Matias's brow lifted as he assessed me. "How did *you* manage to worm your way into Maura's inner circle? It's such a rare and coveted position."

I gave a brittle laugh and looked down at the wafer on my plate. "Well."

After a moment, Maura said, "Holly is Dane's sister."

The trickle of the fountain expanded to fill the sudden silence. Someone pushed away from the table farther down, where I couldn't see them. The scrape of their chair against the bricks made me flinch.

"Did you know Dane?" I ventured, to no one in particular.

The table remained silent, until Odette cleared her throat. "Holly, can I interest you in a honey-cardamom cocktail? Or perhaps some lavender mint julep?" A server in uniform swept in with a tray full of drinks, and I grabbed the first one I saw: a martini glass topped with a bed of white froth. Nestled in the center of the foam was a spur-like seedpod. Eight canoe-shaped holes stared up at me. Quickly, I fished the seedpod out of the glass with my spoon and shoved it inside my napkin.

"Star anise," Matias stage-whispered, and I flushed, realizing he'd seen my little freak-out. "Good thinking. I wouldn't recommend popping the whole thing in your mouth, unless you're looking for a shock to the system."

"And who among us is not?" Odette murmured, sipping from her goblet. Then she raised her glass. "To Holly. Welcome."

The table toasted me.

A swirl of conversation closed over us. They were talking about things I didn't recognize, politicians and galas and art installations. Eventually, I finished my drink, so I grabbed another from a proffered tray. Mint sang up through my sinuses. Time collapsed as I sipped my drink and moved the vibrant food around my plate. I used the side of my fork to break the honeycomb cake into glittering fragments. Then I shifted the miniature prisms to catch the candlelight, stuck them to the moistened tines of my fork, and lifted them to dissolve on my tongue. It was the first dish I could remember tasting— *enjoying*—since Dane's death. Maybe there *was* something magical about it.

At some point, I must have taken another drink. And another.

The conversation around me built to a crescendo. Were they talking louder as the night wore on? Gesturing more? Or perhaps it was just all this talk of things I couldn't understand. A young woman next to Matias with a fox-like face joined in. She had immaculate white-blond hair down to her waist. Sometimes she murmured her addition to the conversation, but mostly she just listened with shiny, pursed lips.

I served myself a Cornish game hen. The skin was crisp, delicious. But no sooner had I made it past that, my knife hit bone. I felt queasy and put my utensils down.

"You're pigheaded," Matias was saying to Maura.

"I am not!"

"You are. And I think it's part of what makes you so wildly successful. Holly, are you aware of how successful your new friend Maura is?"

The sound of my name pierced the fog around me. "I . . . what?"

For the second time that evening, Matias quirked a perfectly shaped brow at me. "I said, 'Are you aware of how successful your new friend Maura is?'"

It seemed an unfair question. "I mean, I've seen her place. Is that what you're asking?"

Matias and Odette exchanged a look before bursting into laughter. I felt a surge of overfullness, of nausea. I wasn't sure I liked Matias very much anymore.

"I'm only trying to do you a favor, lovebug," he said. "Maura may very well be one of the most powerful women in Savannah."

"Oh, Matias, for Heaven's sake." Now it was Maura's turn to roll her eyes. She looked sidelong at me. "Don't listen to him."

I ignored her. "What do you mean?" I pressed Matias.

"Let me make one thing clear, Holly." Matias leaned forward, causing his chair to squeak. I looked at him, even as my body flattened itself against the back of my chair. His pupils were magnified through his lenses, owllike. "Maura has dedicated her life to helping others. And she'll do whatever it takes to keep pursuing her noble mission. We should be bowing at her feet."

"You devil," Odette crowed, throwing her head back.

Bowing at her feet? Was he serious? Maura spent her days clipping flowers and making bouquets, not eradicating malaria or homelessness. Suddenly, I remembered Maura telling me about the centerpieces she'd labored over for the benefit. Could that have been what Matias was referencing? Good for her, but pro bono work didn't exactly make her a deity. I felt like laughing along with Odette, but was too afraid to indulge in the tickle in my throat. Sudden iciness danced across my vertebrae. I spun in my chair, half expecting to find a snickering dinner guest behind me.

"Thank you kindly for the unsolicited advice," Maura told Matias coldly.

"Hey, now." Matias raised his hands in mock surrender. "I'm just helping a girl out. Heavens, Maura, you know I've sent you after my fair share of exes. God rest their souls."

Odette giggled into her goblet of wine. The fox-faced girl laughed along.

"Hey," Maura said sternly, setting down her drink. "That's not funny. Those men were suffering—deeply—and you were there to help them."

"Sure thing," Matias said, a smile flickering at the edge of his mouth.

"Wait a second." I was struggling to track the conversation. "Suffering? How do you mean?"

"It's in the past," Matias assured me. "More mussels, Holly?"

I shook my head. "How do y'all know each other, anyway?"

"Matias was one of my first clients here in Savannah," Maura said. "I was fortunate to meet him shortly after I graduated."

Matias wagged a finger at Maura. "Please, darling," he scolded. "*I'm* the lucky one."

I frowned, fought down a wave of dizziness.

Maura was watching my face carefully. "You okay?"

"Yeah." I shivered. "I think a spider just crawled across my neck or something."

Maura looked at the collection of martini glasses next to my plate. She had the decency to remain silent, but her eyes telegraphed it: *How many of those have you had?*

I put the heel of my hand to my forehead. I didn't know, and the night was starting to tilt away from me.

Maura's face was impassive. "We should get going. Holly isn't yet accustomed to your heavy pours, Odette."

"All in due time." Odette smiled.

Maura slipped her hand into mine and pulled me to my feet. I smoothed the creases out of the silk sheath at my hips with whatever traces of my dignity remained. As I took in the spoils of dinner strewn across the table, nausea washed over me again: hen carcasses, ribcages split and pooling pink blood; lustrous, pried-open mussels and clusters of those elegant parfait flutes, smeared with a film of cream and jam.

We said our goodbyes. There were more fragrant kisses, a couple whispered exchanges I couldn't make out.

As I turned away from them, I could feel the heat of the guests' eyes on my back.

The insides of our car slid around like marbles. Apparently, I was so wasted that Maura had broken her own no-Uber rule. I kept my gaze anchored to the dark fringe of oak trees visible through the windshield, playing back Matias's words in my head. *Maura has dedicated her life to helping others. And she'll do whatever it takes to keep pursuing her noble mission.*

What the hell was he talking about?

In a slurred voice, I tried to give the Uber driver my address.

"Nice try, sweetie," Maura interrupted me. To the driver, she said, "She's coming home with me. She can barely sit up right now, let alone put herself to bed."

My voice emerged a childish whine. "I can put myself to bed!"

Maura smiled at the Uber driver in the rearview mirror, as if to say, *See?* "You're wasted, Holly," she said to me. "Don't worry, though. I'll take care of you."

Back in the townhouse, Maura guided me into the guest room and I lurched toward the bed. I didn't even care when she unzipped the back of my dress and shucked it off me, cool fingertips ghosting along my hips. Then I dove under the covers.

Maura left the room and came back. "Here." She set a glass of water on my nightstand. "You need to finish this before you pass out."

I groaned, burying my face in the pillow.

"This is nonnegotiable. Drink."

I struggled to sit up and sip the lukewarm water. Maura folded two tablets of Advil into my fist. "And take these," she said. "I'm putting a little dish by the bed here so you can take a couple more when you wake up. I'll make you my top-secret hangover remedy in the morning." After I'd drained the glass of water, she tucked the cool coverlet up around my chin.

"Mhmm," I said, settling into the bedding. "Thanks for taking care of me."

"My pleasure. It's what I do."

I paused, fighting my leaden eyelids. "Maura, I have a question."

"Yes?"

I'd wanted badly to ply Maura for information, but the way she'd shut down at the wine bar—when I'd asked about that "game" Dane had referenced—made me hesitate. Until now, emboldened as I was with alcohol. "Why was Matias saying those things about you?"

"Because he's a jackass who likes to stir the pot. Don't pay any mind to it."

"What did he mean when he said we should be bowing at your feet? I mean, isn't that kind of over-the-top?"

Maura heaved a giant sigh. She looked up at the ceiling. Then she said, "Move over."

My stomach crunched. Still, I did as she asked. Maura lifted the hem of her dress and climbed into bed behind me. She left a pocket of space between our bodies, but I could feel her there, depressing the mattress. I remembered her naked spine, and my heart began to rabbit in my ribcage.

"So you're a right-side-of-the-bed sleeper, huh?" she said, settling behind me.

What did that matter? I said nothing.

"Here's the thing, Holly." Maura pushed aside my hair, and I flinched as her fingertip began to draw languid circles on my back. "We're at home now. And I don't particularly want to talk about people like Matias anymore. They're fine and dandy in small doses and with sufficient alcohol, but really, Matias and Odette and all of them are superficial people. I can't connect with them the way I've found I can with you."

My heartbeat had moved into the back of my mouth. I swallowed, considered turning around to face her. Even the thought of it paralyzed me.

"I've given it some thought," she continued, and I could feel the timbre of her voice. "I'm still not sure exactly why that is. Do you have any ideas?"

"Any ideas about . . . what?" My own voice came out hoarse.

"Why I feel so strongly that I can connect with you."

"I . . . I don't know."

"Hmm." Maura lifted her finger. The sudden absence of the small circles on my back was marked, as if she'd drawn some of my warmth away with her. "I mentioned it earlier tonight, but there are moments when you angle your head a certain way and I just *see him*. So clearly. It's thrilling and unnerving at the same time. Thrilling because—well, wouldn't we both kill to have Dane back with us, at least in some form? Unnerving, because it feels like I'm convening with the dead."

I stiffened.

"I miss him so much." She must have drawn closer, because her breath stirred the baby hairs around my ear.

I pressed my eyes shut. I wasn't sure if I was trying to push thoughts of her out or pull memories of him in. Maybe both. "Me too," I whispered.

I waited until Maura's breath turned rhythmic, indicating she'd fallen asleep behind me. Then I released a breath and forced myself to sink into the mattress.

When I finally drifted off, I was still gripping the sheets.

CHAPTER 6

That night, I dreamed of the first time I saw Maura. I'll admit it: Easter brunch may have been the first time we met, but it wasn't the first time I'd laid eyes on her. Two weeks before Easter, after visiting Dane one afternoon, I ducked into a CVS near campus. I had a bad habit of resting my chin in my hand at work, conjuring a constellation of pimples along my jawline. So I went straight to the skin-care aisle and picked up a tube of acne treatment.

Even in my dream, I heard the beep of the cashier passing items across the red scanner beam. The girl ahead of me in the checkout line had already opened the bottle of Coke she'd taken from the refrigerated case.

Bold move.

As she tipped her head to take a swig, I watched her dark hair cascade down her back. My eyes followed the shiny waves down to a tiny waist, lower still to faded cutoffs and a peek of pert butt-cheek below.

The girl must have felt my eyes, because she turned and

looked at me over her shoulder. I rushed to hide the acne cream behind my back, mortified. It didn't seem fair that someone with such a perfect body should be graced with such a striking, feline face. But alas, there we were, and she wasn't looking away. I gulped, dropping my gaze to the carpet, but not before seeing the girl's lips part infinitesimally. Then the cashier called her to the register and I was spared.

The dream ended and I woke up feeling hollow. Maura wasn't next to me in bed anymore. It was still dark.

I stared up at the ceiling. Two weeks after the CVS incident, when Dane introduced Maura as his girlfriend, I'd recognized her immediately. My humiliation that afternoon in CVS had seared her face and body into my memory. It wasn't only that I'd been caught checking her out—I couldn't remember *ever* checking out a girl before. In her Easter dress, Maura had reached for my hand and I'd fought to keep my heart from bursting out of my mouth. I remembered the perfect curve of her butt under her cutoffs, and my face flamed. Did she remember me, the pimply creeper who'd stared at her ass in line at the drugstore? Was her smile friendly or knowing?

It was impossible to tell.

I drifted off again and woke late with a pounding in my skull, wondering if the entire evening at Odette's had been a dream, too. My neck felt leaden as I raised my head to look around the bedroom. The ivory sheath dress was gone. Maura must have removed it after taking care of me, and I tried my hardest not to interpret that as a slight.

I swiped for the Advil that Maura had left me on the bedside table and chased them with a swig of water. Then I padded into the hallway bathroom. As I swept my hair out of my eyes, preparing to wash my face, my hand brushed against something cool and damp. Somehow, the petunia that Maura had plucked from the inn's trellis was still behind my ear, looking as fresh as the moment she'd picked it. How was that even possible? I'd been lolling around like a drunken fool in the Uber. And, from what I could recall, I'd slept fitfully last night in the guest room bed.

I pulled the flower out from behind my ear and laid it on the sink. The tender skin where it had rested revealed two strange red marks, each about the size of a staple. I leaned in closer to the mirror to inspect them. Rubbed a fingertip over them. They were sore. I could feel the indentations in my skin, see the way the flesh puckered around them. They called to mind the angry puncture wounds I'd once gotten after stepping on a blue crab's thorny carcass on the beach.

Unnerved, I knocked the flower off the edge of the sink and into the trash.

I found Maura in the sun-drenched kitchen, standing over a sizzling griddle. "Oh!" she exclaimed when she saw me. "I was just about to check on you. How are you feeling?"

I put a hand to my forehead. "I've got a headache, but I just took the Advil you left me, so hopefully I'll be feeling better soon."

"Sit," Maura instructed, pointing to the kitchen table. Then she began flitting around, pulling items from the cabinets and the refrigerator. A minute later, she set a plate in front of me—whole-wheat toast crowned with two sunny-side-up eggs, half an avocado, and a side of glistening blackberries and raspberries—as well as a tall glass of orange juice.

I looked up at her in surprise. "You didn't have to do all this."

But Maura only waved my comment away. "Did you still want my hangover remedy?"

I indicated the beautiful plate in front of me. "You mean this isn't it?"

Maura went to the windowsill over the sink and came back holding a small glass vial filled with a dark substance. As she unscrewed the top, she told me, "I don't just do flower arrangements, you know. I also make herbal remedies on the side. Tinctures and such."

I frowned, thinking back to my extensive Instagram stalking of Maura's account. She posted a lot about her floral business, but never about any kind of herbal remedies. "Oh," I said, trying to sound casual. "Is that what Matias was talking about at dinner?" Would *that* side hustle make her worthy of worship, like Matias described? Saving the world, one hangover at a time?

A slight smile. "Kind of." Maura approached me with the dropper. "This tincture is the best after a night of heavy drinking—chamomile and elderberry, among other delightful ingredients. Now stick out your tongue."

I hesitated, then barked out an awkward laugh. "What?"

"You heard me. It'll only take a drop or two. It tastes intense, I'll admit, but you can chase it with your orange juice."

The stuff inside that vial did not look appetizing, but Maura's face was so earnest I indulged her and opened my mouth. She placed a couple beads of the tincture on my tongue. Maura must have soaked the herbs in vinegar, because it stung my tastebuds, filling my mouth with medicinal intensity. I snatched my glass of orange juice and took a giant gulp. "Whoa," I said afterward.

"Give it an hour or two, and I guarantee you'll start to feel a difference." Maura sat down opposite me at the kitchen table, resting her chin in her hands. "So, did you have fun last night?"

"Mhmm." I said it around a mouthful of eggs and toast that I'd stuffed in my mouth to absorb the vinegar. Though the tincture hadn't been the most delicious, Maura's breakfast was another story.

"Me too." Maura looked past me, her eyes unfocused. "Gosh, I can't even tell you how nice it is having someone around. It's been so difficult—so *lonely*—living in this big townhouse by myself after Dane's death."

I took a satisfying bite of toast. By now, the butter Maura had applied was liquid. "I bet," I said.

Maura sighed. "Sometimes I forget that he isn't here anymore, you know? And I'll feel like he's in the next room over and have the urge to call his name . . . those are the worst moments. It makes me feel that much more alone."

"I'm sorry," I said, setting down my glass of orange juice. I could relate to Maura about feeling Dane's energy in the house. I felt it every time I stayed with Mom and Dad, across the hallway from my brother's old room, and it was beyond unnerving.

Maura seemed to perk up. "Hey. Have your roommates found a new place yet?"

"Not that I know of. I heard them talking about a certain condo they found online, but I'm not sure if they've even looked at it."

"Oh." Maura swiped at the tabletop with the finger she often nibbled—it was the only finger whose nail polish was chipped. "That must be stressful for you, not knowing when they're going to move out and leave you homeless."

I shrugged, playing it off, but Maura's remark elicited a

sinking sensation within me. With all the excitement of Odette's party, I'd forgotten about my impending housing dilemma.

"Do you think . . ." Maura spoke haltingly, as if chewing her way through a new idea. "I don't know . . . would it be totally absurd if . . . ?"

I popped a blackberry in my mouth. "What?"

But Maura only shook her head. "No. That would be unfair of me to even ask."

Ask what? I wanted to blurt.

But before I could clarify, Maura's eyes had refocused and she pasted a giant smile on her face. "Oh! I almost forgot. Let me rustle up Dane's things before you head out."

I'd almost forgotten, too. Maura left me in the kitchen, where I had the chance to polish off the eggs and drain my glass of juice. As I ate, I mulled over Maura's words. Had she been about to . . . ask me to move in with her? Surely not—that would be ludicrous—but the very thought made me breathless.

A few minutes later, Maura returned with a single cardboard box. "Here." She looked triumphant as she set it on the table next to my plate. The hollow sound it made against the tabletop indicated it wasn't even full.

I glanced at her with peaked eyebrows; Maura only nodded in encouragement. It seemed she expected me to go through Dane's things in front of her, which seemed a tad presumptuous, but I relented—she had, after all, been going out of her way for me lately. Gingerly, I undid the flaps on the top of the box and pulled out the items inside: a stack of clothes, a leather toiletry bag, a compact white-noise maker, and several glossy coffee-table books.

I let out my breath. "That's it?"

Maura smiled brightly. "Yep!"

"But . . ." I was speechless. How had the entirety of Dane's belongings boiled down to half a cardboard box?

Maura stared at me.

"I mean, I knew Dane had a . . . sparse aesthetic," I managed finally, "but I guess I was just expecting more. I mean, he *lived* here. This was his home."

Maura shrugged. "I've combed the house, but if I find anything more, I promise to let you know." She gave me another dazzling smile and lifted her chin at my empty plate pooled with grease. "So. How'd those eggs treat you?"

I carried Dane's box back to the apartment without too much difficulty. It was light, and that made everything that much more depressing—the fact that my brother's entire life had been culled down to a stack of generic items. T-shirts and coffee-table books. They could have belonged to anyone.

Back at Rachel's, I spread the items over the living-room floor. I smoothed the worn knees of Dane's jeans, unpacked every toiletry item from the leather bag and lined them up in neat rows, like soldiers preparing for battle. There were a few wiry beard hairs caught on the padded lip of his razor, and I touched a fingertip to them, fighting down a swell of tears. Then I turned on the white-noise maker and listened to the last setting he'd had it on. Shushing rain sounds interwoven with peeping frogs. A rainforest? My heart burrowed into the soles of my shoes.

How could this be it?

Presently, I packed the items away and stowed them in my bedroom closet. Then I forced myself to dive into my weekend chores. To Maura's credit, her tincture did, in fact, seem to be kicking in—my headache had fallen away and I felt a burst of energy. Mere hours later, I looked down at my stacks of folded laundry and packed Tupperwares on the gleaming kitchen counter and felt a rush of gratitude.

Thank you, Maura, for salvaging my day.

But my mind kept wandering back to our conversation over breakfast. What, exactly, had Maura been alluding to when she'd asked me those questions about Rachel and Henry? Had she really been thinking about the possibility of my moving in with her?

It's been so difficult—so lonely—*living in this big townhouse by myself.*

My heart squeezed, surprising me. I remembered the way Maura had looked answering the door in her messy topknot and no makeup a while back. Vulnerable. Such a small girl in such an echoing, expansive estate. But the notion of us rooming together was definitely off-the-wall; no wonder Maura hadn't spoken it aloud.

Would it be totally absurd if . . . ?

Yes, it would be totally absurd. But then again, living with Maura would mean 24/7 access to her place and her belongings. Going through Dane's items had been so enormously underwhelming—clearly it was going to take more to figure things out. In fact, the more I thought about that stupid white-noise maker, the more frantic I became. It felt like an army of insect legs were trampling beneath my skin.

That couldn't be all my brother had left behind.

Maybe if I had the opportunity to do some digging through Maura's townhouse on my own, I could piece together Dane's mental state toward the end of his life. Dad was right—Dane's sudden decline, mentally and physically, just didn't make sense. And for my brother to have chosen such a grisly way to go . . .

I'd do anything, Holly. Anything. *To understand what happened to my son.*

I couldn't banish the image of my father's shaky rim of tears. He hadn't cried at Dane's funeral, but his façade had finally crumbled. In front of *me*.

I closed my eyes, drew in a deep breath. If I lived with Maura, I'd be poised to figure out exactly what "game" she'd been playing with Dane. And why she refused to tell me about it.

I picked up my phone and set it down again.

I did this three times before finally working up the nerve to text Maura.

"So, I have some news. I'm . . . well, I'm moving out."

We were sitting in the living room after dinner, Rachel's legs sprawled over Henry's lap. They were both on their phones. This is usually how it went—Rachel and Henry on one couch, me on another. It hadn't bothered me before, but I'd gotten touchy since overhearing Henry talking about moving. Ever since, instances like this only seemed to highlight my role as third wheel. *There's Holly the leper. Best she stay on her own couch so as not to infect the others with her terminal loneliness.*

Rachel's head jerked up from her phone. "*What?* Why?"

I twisted my fingers in my lap. Maura had responded to my text within the hour with a string of delighted emojis. "Well, I don't know, I guess I decided it was time. Y'all are getting married . . . it's a new chapter. For all of us."

"Holly," Rachel said. Her mouth was slightly agape. "That's completely unnecessary."

"Well," Henry said, glancing up from his phone. "I, for one, think that's great."

I felt a punch of venom. *Of course you would. Dick.*

Rachel glared at him before looking back at me. "I mean, if that's really what you want?" She paused. "Are you getting a place for yourself?"

"No, I have a roommate. I'm excited."

Rachel's hands tightened on her phone case. "So, what's her deal? Please tell me it's a her."

"Yep, it's a her."

"Did you vet her?"

"Sure."

"Make sure she's not an axe-murderer?"

Well. My fingertips migrated, reflexively, to the sore indentations left by the petunia behind my ear. "Rach, it'll be fine. She's sweet and she's got a beautiful townhouse right on Forsyth Park. I couldn't believe I could afford the room."

"Beautiful townhouse on Forsyth Park." Rachel's eyes narrowed. "What's the catch?"

I didn't want to think about that part. "Seriously, I'll be fine. And if I don't like it, the lease is month-to-month, so I can leave whenever." It wasn't a lie.

Rachel exhaled. "Okay. That's good." I could see her guilt surfacing, and I fought back a twinge of my own sadness. Rachel was the best friend I'd had in my adult life. Back in college, we'd roamed campus together late at night when she was feeling restless and homesick; she'd stocked our mini fridge with my favorite smoothies on days I felt especially low. Once, I'd woken Rachel in the middle of the night, convinced there was a saber-tooth tiger under my lofted bed. Her reaction? To leap out of her own bed with her phone light on, raring to investigate.

After graduation, I'd flailed without her. It was a cringeworthy time for me: trying to make that horrible hostessing job work, ultimately slinking back home to live with my parents. I'd always assumed I'd lost Rachel to the real world, so when she announced she'd be moving to my hometown—coincidentally the hometown of her new boyfriend—it was the ultimate relief.

It meant getting my best friend back.

"What are you up to Friday night, Rach? Maybe we can go out to dinner? My treat—to celebrate the end of an era." Even as I spoke the words aloud, I realized Rachel and I hadn't made plans outside the house since the night of Dane's death. Maybe she was trying to give me space to grieve, and that was thoughtful, but the fact remained: the only time I really spent with Rachel anymore was at the kitchen table or on the couch, as we scrolled through our phones.

Rachel winced. "Friday? Oof, we have a meeting with the wedding coordinator, and then we promised Henry's parents we'd come by . . ."

"No worries." I forced a smile. "Just because I'm not living here doesn't mean we won't see each other!"

"Obviously." Rachel nodded hard.

I tried to convince myself this wasn't a lie.

t was raining the Saturday I arranged to move into Maura's place. Restlessness had been worming through me all week. It hit early in the mornings, when I woke with an edge of something between anxiety and anticipation. I'd stare at the naked outlet next to my bed, and the feeling would expand to fill my chest. The only time I felt relief was at night, when I reached for Dane's text message chain. I'd gotten in the habit of addressing him in my head as I cradled my phone in the dark.

Getting there, buddy. I'm doing everything I can.

The fish-headed pipe gushed water in front of Maura's townhouse. Rachel and Henry had helped me load the car the night before—I'd dropped off much of my stuff at my parents' house, since living with Maura would be a very temporary arrangement. I'd told them I'd found a new roommate online and dodged follow-up questions. Now I hefted one of my rolling suitcases up the stairs and knocked on the door. Maura answered in a midnight-colored romper with silver snaps running down the middle. She was barefoot, her toenails painted lime green now.

"Hi, roomie," she said, reaching for the handle of my suitcase.

Inside the townhouse, the sound of the rain was amplified. Even though I'd already been inside Maura's home twice, the sheer expansiveness was still shocking. It made me feel insignificant. The jewel tones of the furniture, combined with the crowding of flowers and indoor trees, created a sumptuous, dizzying palette. Maura's terrace doors were still flung open, the terrace itself packed full of tumbling plants—Maura must have moved them out there to collect rainwater. Above the fireplace, she'd hung a garland of cardboard diamonds spelling out "Welcome" in red letters. Had she really bought that just for me?

"Wow," I said. "I wasn't expecting such a reception."

"You mean your old roommate didn't hang up any decorations for you when you moved in?"

I thought back to the day I'd shown up at Rachel and Henry's apartment, thrilled to be moving back in with my college roommate and out of my parents' house.

"Not that I remember," I admitted.

Maura smirked at me over her shoulder. "Old roomie: zero. Maura: one."

I followed Maura into the guest room I'd slept in the night of Odette's party. I hadn't gotten the opportunity to fully appreciate it then. It was bigger than my bedroom at Rachel's, with a queen-size canopy bed piled high with plump pillows. An antique oval cheval mirror stood in the corner of the room. To the right of the bed was a small, soot-stained fireplace inlaid with cerulean mosaic tiles. Two terra-cotta pots sat on either side, overflowing with ivy and cream-colored blossoms.

Maura set my suitcase next to the bed. "Welcome back to your room. Let me give you the grand tour."

Down a hallway, where a chandelier shivered overhead, there were more rooms. Maura took me into a study filled with dark wood and wall-to-wall bookcases. There was even a rolling ladder slotted into the shelves. I inhaled and smelled something spicy, peppery. Sure enough, there was an angular tree leaning out of a planter by the window, its narrow trunk prickly and bent to one side. Its scent filled the room, mingling with that of leather.

"Okay," I said, "it's official. Ten-year-old Holly would've wet herself with excitement to move in here."

"Hope you've learned some bladder control since then."

I blushed. "Don't worry, your floors are safe. Seriously, though." I spun around once, slowly, taking in the space. "I feel like I'm Belle, straight out of *Beauty and the Beast*."

Maura shrugged. "I thought you might like this, working at the library and all. If you're not sick of books by the time you come home from work, you're always welcome to hang out here."

I followed Maura's sightline to a solid desk in the corner of the room, covered with a slew of papers and fine-tipped pens. It was the first indication of clutter I'd seen in her townhouse. I drew closer and took in a sharp breath. On the papers were various drawings of human lungs, intestines, and something that might have been a bladder or a stomach.

Dane's work.

"Oh," Maura said, rushing over. "I'm so sorry. I couldn't bring myself to put them away and—I apologize, Holly. I wasn't thinking."

"No, no. It's okay." A haze of confusion settled over me.

Why hadn't Maura included these drawings and supplies in the box of Dane's stuff? I swallowed, trying to figure out a polite way to raise the issue. "Do you think there could be more of Dane's stuff around the townhouse, then? Because I thought you said you'd combed the place . . ."

"No. No. This is definitely it." Maura crossed her arms over her body, looking cold. "I'm really sorry. I totally forgot these were still out here."

Did I believe her? She'd already lied to me once. I searched Maura's face for signs of deceit, but saw only that naked hopefulness, so earnest it made my throat tighten. I leaned over to pick up the lung illustration off the desk. It was exquisite, saturated and red, veins straining against the tissue like worms. Which had been the last drawing Dane had touched? I thought of the skittery feeling I always got when my feet slipped into existing footprints on the beach. Was there any chance of my fingerprints overlapping with Dane's? I stared at the red lung. What had Dane been thinking when he'd drawn this? How far had his illness progressed by that point? The technicality of the illustration frustrated me: it didn't provide any clues as to how my brother might have been feeling.

"Come on," Maura said. She was in full-on tour-guide mode—I noticed she spoke differently as she took me around her house. Louder, with a bit of a flourish, like she had the night of Odette's party. I followed, still thinking about Dane's illustrations.

"The master," Maura announced, pushing a door open. "But of course, you've already been in here."

It wasn't any less impressive than the first time I'd seen it. Even though the tones were more muted here than in the living room, the combination of those creamy white orchids in the hanging baskets and the rich material of the drapery and bedding was nothing short of lush.

I had to say it. "Are you sure you're a *florist*?"

That cracked Maura up. "I told you, I've done well with my business. I managed to find a loyal client base here in Savannah. I consider myself very fortunate."

"Do you mean your floral business, or your medicinal herb one?"

Maura paused, looking thrown. "Both."

The bed in the center of the room had a coverlet that matched the sofa. I had the urge to run my hands through the sheets. Had Maura washed them since Dane slept there? She must have. And yet—how could she?

"Now, I've got some bad news," Maura said.

"What? Your scullery maid is on vacation?"

"Ha-ha. No, I'm afraid, given our current circumstances, that we'll have to share a bathroom. It will only be in the mornings, for showering. Otherwise I can use the powder room down the hall."

"Sure. I don't care."

"Good." She nodded toward a closed door off the master bedroom. "There's an en suite, but I haven't been in there since . . ."

A trapdoor opened in my stomach when I realized what Maura was saying. It took a second or two. Then I licked my lips, which had gone papery. "Oh. Right."

She nodded once, solemn. "Yes. He did it in there, in that bathtub." She added quickly, "Of course, it's been cleaned since. I wouldn't want you to think—"

My heart slammed against my breastbone. "Oh, God, yes, no—"

"I just wouldn't want you to—"

"It's no problem, really, I get it."

We both looked down at the floorboards. I curled my hands into fists at my sides, coaching myself through three deep breaths. *One. Two. Three. Hold it.*

"Would you like me to help you with the rest of your things?" Maura asked after a minute, in a small voice.

I looked up, forcing a smile. "You know, I just got hit by this tsunami of exhaustion. I think I'm going to lie down."

"Sure," Maura said, whisking us out of the master bedroom. "I can show you the upstairs another day. I hardly use the rooms up there, anyway."

I kept my gaze anchored to the floorboards passing below, the grains of wood standing out in harsh relief. In the hallway off the kitchen, I caught a whiff of something treacly, like glazed donuts, and had to fight down nausea.

What the hell had I been thinking, agreeing to move in here? Only fifteen minutes into my tour and I'd already had to see Dane's abandoned artwork and stand outside the room where he had killed himself. It was all too much. I was emotionally exhausted and, suddenly, violently furious with myself. I'd been impulsive. I hadn't weighed the consequences or really considered what living here would entail. Instead, I'd rushed to get answers for myself and my dad. Or maybe I'd been charmed by Maura tucking me in at night and fixing me such a resplendent breakfast. Either way, I was a fool.

And now I was in over my head.

CHAPTER 8

Maura and I soon settled into a rhythm. Mornings, we shuffled politely around each other in line for the bathroom. Then we'd sip coffee at the breakfast bar, rubbing grainy sleep from our eyes. When I got home from the library, I'd hear Maura working in her greenhouse off the living room, playing lazy, ambient music through her phone. Our paths wouldn't cross again until dinnertime, when we might both vie for the stove. Then we'd flash apologetic smiles. We were sniffing each other out gently. Besides, I sensed Maura was afraid of overwhelming me again.

On the third morning after move-in, while sipping coffee together, Maura held out a textured, iridescent box. "Look," she said, popping the top off.

Inside were rows of what appeared to be exquisitely crafted candies shaped as miniature bottles. The details—tiny paper labels, tiny metallic bottle tops—were immaculate. "Whoa," I exclaimed. "Are these—"

"Cream soda chocolates," Maura said. Her voice wavered

with excitement. "I had them specially ordered for my mom when she visits—it's her favorite drink of all time. Aren't they adorable? They really taste like cream soda, too."

"So cute! I bet she'll love them."

Maura flushed as she carefully tucked the top back on the pretty box and retied the satin ribbon.

"By the way." I cleared my throat. I'd been growing impatient to investigate the townhouse and had been trying to work up the courage to ask Maura about her schedule. If I didn't pounce now, I worried I'd lose my opening. "What have you got going on today?"

"Client meeting in the afternoon," she said, rising to set her mug in the sink.

I affected nonchalance. "Like, late afternoon?"

She gave me a strange look.

"I have an extra pork chop in the fridge and thought I'd cook both up for us tonight." The lie came out seamlessly, despite the fact that in the days I'd lived with Maura, we'd never once eaten dinner together.

Maura made an expression somewhere between a grimace and a smile. "Oh," she said. "I don't really do red meat. Besides, who knows when I'll even be home? Definitely not before six. This client is especially . . . high-maintenance." She licked the side of her thumb, where she must have gotten a drop of coffee. "Guess you'll have to try to enjoy that pork chop without me."

As I walked to work that morning, I made some quick calculations. The library closed at five that day, and, if I walked fast, I could probably make it back to the townhouse in twenty minutes—which left forty glorious minutes for snooping.

Mercifully, the workday passed quickly. By four-thirty, I had my lunch Tupperware rinsed out and packed away, and all the holds pulled for the day. I watched the clock at the top of my computer screen.

Soon.

Esther's face materialized above my monitor. "Holly, hey. Are you busy right now?"

I bit back a wince. "What's up?"

She'd fallen behind cataloging new inventory and was set on finishing before the end of the day.

Of course.

I glanced again at the time on my computer. "I can help, I just—have somewhere I have to be at six . . ."

Esther waved away my concern. "With the two of us working together, it shouldn't take us longer than twenty minutes. Promise."

It did—forty-eight minutes, to be exact. When the clock on the wall passed five, my stomach dipped.

At 5:15, sweat prickled along my forehead.

Finally, at 5:18, Esther pronounced us done. I grabbed my purse and power-walked out of the library, calling a hasty "bye" over my shoulder. My pace accelerated as I made it onto the sidewalk. Was it even worth trying to salvage my plans at this point? Was twenty minutes enough time? What if Maura came back from her client meeting right at six? Or *early?*

No, I couldn't wait for Maura to have another meeting. It'd been torture waiting just three days.

By the time I arrived back at the townhouse, my ponytail had come loose and I had a stitch in my side. I jiggled my key impatiently in the front door. Finally, I was granted entry; Maura's palatial home swallowed me up into the foyer. As usual, the perfume of flowers was like a brick to the head. When would it stop making me so goddamn *dizzy?*

I threw my purse on the ground. Then I crossed the living room and took a tentative step into the greenhouse, nudging open the glass door. Humidity pressed against my skin; it smelled like rain-soaked soil. A few stems lay scattered on what looked like a wooden prep table along with a discarded pair of clippers. The rest of the space was orderly: rows of flowers in trays and, closer to the worktable, tall canisters of cut stems wrapped in cellophane.

But no Maura—yet.

I bolted.

I dropped my stuff in my room and went straight to Maura's study. Even though the sunlight outside was vicious, the library was a dark cocoon, all cocoa-colored wood and leather. I sat down at Dane's desk, still cluttered with his medical illustrations. They appeared untouched since the day I'd moved in. I flipped through them, turned them over. No secret inscriptions, not even a single signature. I turned the illustrations back over, forcing myself to take them in. Lungs, intestines, stomach. Sacs of flesh running their mysterious processes in concert to keep our bodies alive. Dane had interrupted all of that with a steak knife ripped up through his gut. Didn't he know how tenuous everything had been? It enraged me. Sometimes I fantasized about taking him by the shoulders and screaming at him for everything he'd ruined. The delicate machinery of his own body. The precarious balance of our family. Had he been thinking at all about these things that night in the bathtub?

Fighting back tears, I darted into the hallway in the direction of Maura's room. She'd left the door ajar, and I pushed it open with my fingertips. The bed was made, the champagne comforter pulled taut. I approached her wardrobe. Just a shallow ceramic dish with a few gemstone earrings, a tiny spined succulent, and that framed photo of Maura and Dane.

I opened Maura's drawers. Inside were silky camisoles in every jewel tone imaginable. T-shirts folded into triangles, velvet to the touch. I couldn't resist running my fingers through the fabric, so different from the scratch of polyester blends living in my own dresser.

So this was what wealth felt like.

I opened a drawer at the top of the dresser. Satchels of dried rose petals. And then—nested bras with filigree straps. Delicate piles of lace thongs.

I slammed the door shut, my pulse hammering.

Maura kept her makeup in a lacquered black box with a pink silk lining and a mirrored inlay. Would I really find any clues about Dane here? Probably not. But my hands riffled through her cosmetics on their own agenda. Here were the powders and palettes that painted that perfect Instagram face. What a thrill it was to see the secret mechanics behind it all. I unscrewed a jar of translucent powder. It smelled like her. I uncapped a stick of gloss, twisting the end—*click, click, click*— until a perfect, pink bead thrust past the bristles on the other side. I stared at it. Then I swiped the brush over my bottom lip. It tasted like cinnamon, sticky and alien on my mouth as if calling attention to my trespass. I caught a glimpse of myself in the mirror and couldn't resist shifting my face to one side to admire the new sheen. It made the very architecture of my lips look different somehow.

More like Maura's.

There was a faint rattle of the doorframe. My shoulders leapt to my ears. Paralyzed, I listened for the turn of Maura's key in the front door. It didn't sound. Once my heart rate smoothed out, I dropped the lip gloss back in the lacquered box and put it away where I'd found it.

Focus, Holly. Focus.

I approached the bed. There was a tiny scar of foundation on Maura's pillow. I looked over at the opposite side of the bed. Could I? My hands tingled. I grabbed the other pillow and held it to my nose, breathing deeply, taking care to fold my glossed lips into my mouth to avoid marking the pillowcase. Dane's woodsy scent slammed into me like a jackhammer.

My lash line prickled. I used to smell that scent walking into Dane's room, before I even saw him doing whatever he was doing. Penning intricate doodles at his desk. Playing *Mario Kart*, the only video game he deemed worthwhile. How could someone so real—someone I could still smell—be *dead*?

I replaced the pillow and dug through Maura's bedside table. Maybe this was where she'd stowed traces of Dane. Or maybe—could it be a hiding place for the "game" she and Dane had played on his last night alive?

I ripped the drawers open. But there weren't any games inside—card, dice, or otherwise. Instead, I found an ancient-looking silver-backed hairbrush with a few dark threads of Maura's hair snared in the bristles. A scrap of black lace. A tube of ibuprofen tablets and a blister pack of birth-control pills. I dropped the latter as if I'd been scalded.

On the top of the bedside table stood a fogged cup with about an inch of water in it. Behind it was a bell jar, displaying my own distorted reflection, with three black flowers under the glass. Roses, each in varying stages of bloom. Their stems were black, too, except for the bone-colored spot where they'd been snipped. There seemed to be some kind of vapor rising off the petals, but it was probably just a trick of the light on the glass.

Curious, I extended a finger and immediately yanked my hand away from the bell jar, shocked.

In ninth grade, my deranged physics teacher—the same one who had karate-chopped a block of wood in front of the class to demonstrate the power of inertia—had us gather in a circle holding hands. He'd cranked some apparatus and a current had ripped through us, jangling my bones. I'd tried to pull away, but the guy holding my right hand had crushed it in his sweaty grip, forcing me to endure the torture.

Touching the bell jar had felt just like that, which didn't make any sense. There was no source of electricity, at least none that I could see. Had the glass somehow picked up a current from the wall socket?

I paced back and forth in front of the bed. I still hadn't made it into the bathroom. My resolve welled and trickled away. Could I do it? Did I have a choice? No. I owed it to myself—to my family. I wasn't sure I would find any clues, though it struck me as cowardly to search everywhere but there. I needed to see where my brother had died.

Cramming my fists into my pockets, I strode to the closed bathroom door, revving my courage. The doorknob was a gold curlicue, like the handle of a genie's lamp.

One. Two. Three.

I shoved it open.

It was a lovely bathroom. What had I expected? Green granite counters. Black-and-white diamond tiles. Wainscotting. Old-fashioned vanity lights around the mirror. A vase of fresh orange tulips sat between the double sinks. I peered closer. Surely, Maura must have been watering them? But she'd told me she hadn't set foot in her en suite since Dane's suicide. Just like she'd told me she'd packed up all of Dane's things.

Lie number two.

I rolled my shoulders and dared to look at the tub. It was a gorgeous claw-footed number, deep and gleaming. The kind of tub you'd dream of sinking into one winter evening with a bath bomb and a good book. I moved closer to look into the drain, grazing the faucet with shaking fingers.

Shiny, circular wells gaped up at me. Holes. My pulse quickened, revulsion clambering over my skin.

Some nights when I couldn't sleep, I tried conjuring up the horror that must have driven my brother to rip a knife through his own body. That night, the dark wells in the tub drain must have filled with blood. The act of imagining usually set panic simmering in my own gut, but never enough for me to understand what Dane had experienced. Of course, I would never truly know—especially since I'd made it my personal mission to flee from my brother at the first signs of his suffering.

When I was twelve, we had a mouse problem at home. Mom set out sticky traps in the cupboards and beneath the refrigerator where vents blew warm air onto the tiles. One day, while grabbing the milk carton, I saw it: a bulging, furred body smeared into the adhesive. I turned to run, but Dane was there. He surprised me by blocking the doorway.

"No," he said, his voice stony. "Look at it. You owe it that much before it dies." And he pushed me toward the pad. This time my eyes met the frantic dark marbles on that triangular face. I saw a naked, straining paw—toes spread—before Mom swept in and disposed of it all.

Fourteen years later and I hadn't gotten any better at fighting my impulse to run. That was another way I flagellated myself in the middle of the night: by imagining all the things I should have done with Dane instead of abandoning him. There were so many options. Movie marathons at Rachel's—enough spins through this fantasy and I could smell the popcorn butter on my fingers. Diner pancakes—I could feel the red vinyl of the booth sticking to the backs of my legs. So many unspoken words that, who knows, might have unlocked a different reality.

There was a rumble somewhere deep in the townhouse. Unmistakable, now, the sound of Maura's key turning in the lock.

I froze.

"Honey, I'm home!"

I twisted to look at the bathroom once more. In the mirror, I caught a second glimpse of my foreign, swollen lips—Maura's lips—and swiped the back of my hand across my mouth in a rush.

As I turned back, I could have sworn I saw a flash of red in the tub, clawed down the porcelain lip.

I fled.

CHAPTER 9

Over the next few days, I started taking walks during lunch to clear my head. Maura's townhouse had me overwhelmed. Had I imagined the blood in the bathtub? I must have—it'd been clean seconds earlier. The marked absence of Dane's things still unsettled me, too. I knew Maura kept a pristine house, but wouldn't it have been a comfort for her to see an item of Dane's out? A stick of deodorant? A sock? *Something?*

And what was with those roses under the bell jar? Yes, okay—Maura was a florist, so I could understand the flowers. They were kind of pretty, in their own dark way. But why put flowers under glass? And why the hell had I felt that shock of electricity when touching it? Did this have something to do with Maura's medicinal side hustle?

Nothing was adding up.

On a whim, I stopped into an antique bookstore. Usually, the scent of books calmed me. And while I did smell sheaves of yellowing paper—that delicious concoction of dust and aged ink—there was something else in this cramped, dimly lit store. A sharper, unfamiliar scent. I wedged my body between stacks of wooden crates. In addition to books, the store sold hundreds of old maps and prints in plastic sleeves. I reached out to flip through a couple.

Botanical prints.

I almost laughed out loud. *Of course.* And surely Maura would have loved these intricate, vivid diagrams of dahlia, white honeysuckle, and chokeberry.

"Looking for anything in particular?" The shopkeeper, a plump woman in an embroidered tunic, peered over at me.

Yeah. Got any pictures of creepy black roses that shock you when you touch them?

I shook my head. I'd been detected; it was time to leave.

Back on the street, I squinted as my eyes adjusted to the light. In July, a month before his death, Dane and I met at a bistro right on this corner. I'd been relieved to see him wearing a clean shirt. He'd even shaved. I'd thought maybe Mom was right, that living with his girlfriend would be good for him.

That day, Dane had ordered a plain hamburger. "No onions, no lettuce, no pickles, no mushrooms, no mayo, no nothing. Ketchup on the side," he said. The waitress—a pretty girl with a diamond stud in her nose—gave him a flirtatious smile, as if to say, *Really?* But Dane avoided her eyes, flipping his menu shut and letting his signature curtain of hair fall over his face.

"Ooh, so cold," I teased him, as the waitress walked away. "But I guess it serves her right for judging you."

Dane said nothing. He seemed to be picking at something—his napkin or fingers—under the table.

"How does it feel to be done with school?" I asked.

He shrugged, not looking up. Dad had mentioned earlier that week that Dane had an intake appointment with a psychiatrist. Dad hadn't elaborated, and I hadn't asked for more information. I didn't want to know; I'd had to force myself just to get lunch with Dane today. I was hoping the psychiatrist could hook him up with some medication and I'd never have to see that side of my brother again. Wasn't that how it worked? I had a couple friends in college who swore by their antidepressants.

The waitress came by with a basket of fries and set it between us. I grabbed one and stuffed it in my mouth, letting out a groan. "Ugh, I'm pretty sure these are seasoned with crack."

My brother hesitated. As kids, we'd fought over who got to dig into the main course first, to the point where Mom had been forced to establish a rule: Dane and I would switch off. Monday night, I got to serve myself a gooey square of lasagna first. Tuesday night, Dane got first dibs on the chicken parts, going straight for the prized wings. Ridiculously, this rule lasted until I left for college.

After I'd had at least a handful of fries, Dane finally reached a shaking hand out toward the basket. I gasped. My brother's nails were crusted with blood, a grisly interpretation of a French manicure.

"Dane! Oh my God. What happened to your hands?"

They flew back under the table. "Nothing." His hair fell over his face. "They've just been bothering me, I guess." He started picking at them again under the table.

"Well, Jesus, don't keep messing with them!" I pushed the basket of fries away, my appetite disintegrated.

Dane slid his hands under his thighs and gave me an eerie, too-big smile. "May I be excused, sister dearest?"

I was too unsettled to sass him back. Instead, I watched my brother walk to the restroom at the back of the restaurant, avoiding the waitress's eyes as he passed. I remember thinking that maybe it was time to have a conversation with Mom and Dad about what they'd learned from Dane's intake appointment. Did they know that he was picking at his hands so intensely he was drawing blood? The psychiatrist must have noticed. I hoped that was something that could be addressed with medication. I didn't want to see my brother's hands looking like that ever again.

Dane wanted to leave almost as soon as he returned from the restroom. I couldn't help feeling guilty—had I pushed him too far by commenting on his nails? Made him feel self-conscious? Ashamed, I'd asked for the check. The waitress brought over to-go containers for our unfinished meals.

Now, I wished I'd insisted on staying. Asked Dane some more questions. I wished I'd provided support, even just *listened*, instead of rushing to chastise him.

That day with my brother, I'd only added to his problems.

The rest of the workday dragged. Around three, Rachel texted me wanting to get pizza, but I felt too overwhelmed by the thought of even stringing together a reply. Instead, I focused on the crumbs lodged between keys of the front-desk keyboard. There was a really big one nestled against the space bar— maybe I could fish it out with a paper clip? I glanced down at my phone screen. The red circle on my message icon stared back at me, an accusatory boil.

I took the long way home that evening to brainstorm my next move. I passed a courtyard with a stone birdbath and little pump-kins marching up the stairs to the house. I gnawed my lip, thinking. Clearly, I'd have to get a better sense of Maura's schedule to plan when I'd search the other rooms in the townhouse, but I didn't want to arouse suspicion by asking again too soon. I paused, admiring the statues carved into the base of the house in front of me: a winged woman with almond-shaped eyes and a languid-looking sphinx. They, too, looked like they were harboring secrets.

The townhouse was silent when I arrived home. But the air was charged. I wasn't alone.

"Maura?"

Sure enough, there she was, her small body wedged into the corner of the blue settee. Her shoulders were pulled up toward her ears, hands cradling the iridescent box of bottle-shaped chocolates. She didn't look up at me.

"Hey. What's going on?" I sat on the opposite side of the couch. Never before had the points of Maura's body—her shoulders, kneecaps, and wrists—looked so brittle. I felt a surge of protectiveness.

"I don't know," she said, her voice monotone.

"Wow, that's a lie. Spill."

Maura tugged at the silky ribbon on the box, still refusing to look at me. "My mom cancelled her trip to Savannah."

"What? Why?"

"Because my sister's kids got the flu and she needs help taking care of them." She picked up her phone and tossed it to the opposite side of the couch. It grazed my thigh before lodging beneath the armrest.

"And what about Dane's showcase?"

Maura finally looked up at me. "If Natalie says she needs our mother's help, none of that matters. It just confirms what I already knew."

"What's that?"

Her face went blank. "That I'm invisible."

I thought back to the unfamiliar smile I'd seen on Maura's face when she'd brought up her mother's visit. It hadn't been the alcohol, after all—it had been Maura allowing herself to indulge in a very thin hope.

Maura picked up a glass on the coffee table. Her sip was soundless, but she set the cup back down with an angry crack. Her mouth left a petallike smear on the glass.

I couldn't believe it. I'd never met Maura's mother, but already I hated her. If only she could have seen her daughter's smile contemplating the upcoming visit. And the way her face was crumpling now that her plans had been dashed. My fury made my words come out in a rush.

"I'm sorry," I said, "but that's absolutely ridiculous. This is a showcase honoring your dead fiancé. Your mom should be here." I braced myself for Maura to react. When she didn't, I plowed on. "You know, my mom has her moments, too. She isn't always the most . . . touchy-feely. Not the most maternal."

"No," Maura said. Hanks of her dark hair hung down the sides of her face. "You don't know what you're talking about, Holly. You have no right to compare your situation to mine. No fucking right."

She raised the box of cream soda chocolates and smashed it against the floor. An army of foil-decorated miniature bottles spilled out from the crushed corner, skittering against the hardwood. Then Maura snatched her phone out of the side of the couch and swept out of the living room. I stared at the rolling chocolates as my heartbeat expanded to fill my body. I wished I could go after her, fold her into a hug, but I knew it never would have worked. Even if I'd had the courage, I wouldn't have known how to comfort her.

That night, once again, I couldn't sleep. Maura's woes made me think about Dane's showcase, wondering what images I'd see framed on the walls. I tried to imagine the kinds of drawings that would upset me the most, but my mind came up blank, and that scared me even more.

Restless, I threw the comforter off my body and stole into the hallway. Light from the street shot in through the terrace doors, slicing a ghostly film down the center of the living room. Maura's empty glass still sat on the coffee table. I picked it up, shifting it in my hand to study the faint, smeared crescent she'd left behind. Slowly, I brought the glass to my mouth and settled my own lips over Maura's imprint. I smelled, rather than tasted, the traces of iced coffee. Instead of stoking a thrill, the contact left me feeling profoundly sad.

Past the living room, Maura's dark greenhouse beckoned. That had been one room Maura left off the tour, which was interesting, considering how much time she spent there. Was that the part of her work that attracted the likes of Odette? Why had Matias said we should be bowing at her feet? I'd been hoping to get some degree of closure living with Maura, but the opposite was proving true. The longer I lived with her, the more questions accumulated. There had to be something I was missing, something that might even connect to Dane when all was said and done.

Glancing behind me, I darted inside the greenhouse.

I flipped on the overhead lights. There was something eerie about being in a greenhouse without any sun. The three walls of dark windows made me feel exposed, with the glare preventing me from seeing out. *Glass houses indeed.* I threaded through the rows of boxed flowers toward the back of the room, the concrete shocking against my bare feet. Maura seemed to grow it all—everything from tropical birds of paradise and hibiscus to the more standard fare of mums and baby's breath . . . plus, of course, a slew of others I didn't recognize. As I wandered, grazing petals and stamens with a knuckle, I could smell the leaves.

I approached Maura's workstation, a long wooden table next to an industrial metal sink. She'd since cleaned up the stems I'd glimpsed scattered there. On wire racks hanging from the wall she'd arranged skeins of twine and ribbon and an assortment of different containers—cylinders, cubes, and mason jars in glass, ceramic, and terra-cotta. Several different sizes of clipping shears hung from hooks. There was a black rubber mat in front of the sink. A few whiskers of cracked concrete peeked out from under it. I glanced in the silver basin. A single glossy leaf sat overturned next to the drain.

Maura's bedroom had been far more interesting.

I crouched to run my hands through the canisters of cut flowers wrapped in cellophane beneath the workbench. The burst of pollen-heavy fragrance sprang a headache behind my eyebrows. Gingerly, I pulled a stem from the metal container. The center of the yellow flower was a black cone; the end of the stem dripped with water. There were roses, lilacs, something else with petals like tissue paper. My hands slowed on the fourth metal canister, barely visible and wedged against the corner of the wall. I dragged it toward me. The top was covered with a gauzy white shroud cinched in by a black ribbon. I touched a finger to the material and felt the springy response of leaves and blossoms underneath.

Screw it.

I untied the ribbon and ripped off the shroud in one motion, tossing it under the workbench. Underneath were roses with ink-colored petals. I stared at them, transfixed. This had to be the same kind of flower I'd seen in Maura's room.

As I studied the black roses, I noticed movement on the outside of the metal canister. Condensation gathered near my hands. I touched the pad of my index finger to one of the beads of water. It scalded me. I ripped my hand away and gasped, remembering the same electric current that had leapt from the bell jar on Maura's bedside table.

Heart hammering, I walked to the center of the greenhouse and paced in between the rows of flowers. Goosebumps stood up on my forearms. Why did I keep getting shocked by these weird black flowers? There was no carpet underfoot to have rustled up static electricity. Could it really just have been a coincidence? The current felt far stronger than any static I'd ever experienced, shooting straight through my muscle and into the marrow of my bone. Rubbing my forearms, I stepped into the living room, sure someone must be watching.

Empty. But I didn't trust the silence.

I rushed back into the greenhouse. This time, I lifted a rose out of the canister, gritting my teeth against the pain. Its stem was coated in a slick, red-black substance. Droplets converged on the end and dripped into the depths of the container. Shaking, I placed a fingertip against a coated leaf near the base of the plant. The syrupy warmth that came away on my skin was familiar in a way I wished it wasn't.

Blood.

"What the hell are you doing?"

Maura stood in the entrance to the greenhouse, her eyes

like flecks of black mica. The next moment, she was beside me, snatching the rose out of my hand. Then she lunged for the white shroud and forced it back over the canister.

"I—I was just—" I backed away from the workbench, watching as Maura took the dark ribbon and slung it back around the container.

She rounded on me. When she spoke, I didn't recognize the gravelly tone. "What the fuck were you *thinking*?"

I looked down at the concrete, blood thundering in my ears. God, she was pissed. I'd thought Maura was livid earlier that day, when she'd learned her mother had cancelled her trip to Savannah. But that didn't compare to what I saw now, the snarl across her raised cheekbones.

An excruciating quiet stretched. Neither one of us moved.

"Why would you go through my personal things like that?"

"I'm really sorry, Maura."

"Are you? And after I'd told you how close I felt to you, too. That's quite the slap in the face."

I finally dared to look at her. I'd never seen her mouth set this way, in a violent kind of slash. My gulp was audible. "Maura, what were those flowers? And what were they"—my voice snagged on the word—"drinking?"

Maura laughed humorlessly. "You'll have to work quite a bit harder to regain my trust if you ever expect me to answer questions like that."

Another serrated silence.

"You could hurt yourself in here," Maura said. "You could hurt us both."

Giddy with terror, I thought of the shears hanging up on the wall and actually stifled a giggle. This happened to me sometimes. Overwhelmed by intense emotion—terror, sorrow—I'd suddenly find myself fighting the impulse to laugh. When my parents and I had visited the police station and the detective began briefing us on what they'd encountered at the scene of Dane's suicide, I'd had to excuse myself from the room, horrified to be choking down ugly laughter. That day especially, it felt as if my emotional circuit board had been fried.

As I clamped down on the inappropriate laughter now, Maura's eyes narrowed.

"You have my word, Maura," I said, sobering. I swallowed, balled my hands into fists behind my back. "From here on out, I'll stay out of your workspace. Promise."

CHAPTER 10

For the next couple days, Maura and I circled each other like wild animals, leaving wide berths. I noticed that Maura had closed the double doors to the greenhouse on Monday. This was strange—she usually worked with them open.

When I came home that evening, I saw she'd hung a sheet over the glass.

I couldn't stop thinking about the black roses I'd found. I tried googling the phenomenon late at night, hoping to find some shred of information that would explain it away. Maybe what I'd seen wasn't blood, but some kind of red liquid fertilizer. I searched every possibility I could think of: nothing.

At work, I combed the inter-library database and requested the most promising botanical titles I could find. The books arrived later in the week, and I forced myself to wait until I got home to crack them open. With Maura occupied in her greenhouse, I grabbed a bag of pita chips from the kitchen and shut myself in her study with my new library books. *Encyclopedia of*

Flowers and Herbs. The Physiology of Flowers. The Secrets of Flora. I even pulled a few tomes from Maura's shelves. Then I sat cross-legged on the carpet and spread the books around me.

It was overwhelming: glossy spreads of veined leaves and zoomed-in stamens. Intricate cross-sections that looked like Dane's work, like the vivid diagrams I'd stumbled across in the antique bookstore. Extensive indices filled with unfamiliar terms. I ran my finger down the index in the physiology book. No entry on "black rose." Returning to the front of the book, I paged through, stopping short on a description of plant nutrients.

> Iron functions as a micronutrient, shuttling oxygen through the circulatory system. Without sufficient iron, a plant cannot produce chlorophyll, and chlorosis occurs—a condition wherein a plant's leaves turn yellow while its veins remain green.

My fingernail underscored the word "iron" in the book. Could that explain why Maura was soaking her plants in blood? Was she trying to super-charge her roses by feeding them elevated levels of iron? Maybe that's why the petals had turned black.

I flipped slowly through botanical photos, as if in a trance, until I reached a familiar image. It was, undeniably, the flower Maura had plucked from the inn trellis and stuck behind my ear, the one that had somehow created those puncture wounds. I shivered, ran my finger along the Latin name. Just as Maura said it, *Petunia atkinsiana.*

> Petunias are among the more innocuous members of the nightshade clan. This family of plants has a sinister

reputation—many contain alkaloids capable of sparking seizures, hallucinations, and death.

Yikes. Maura hadn't been kidding, then. I flipped through a couple more pages of nightshades, surprised to find that the infamous "deadly nightshade" featured lovely purple blooms and luscious-looking black berries. Even the Latin name was pretty: *Atropa belladonna*. Allegedly, it referred to the use of nightshade tinctures by Italian women long ago to dilate their pupils and achieve a doe-eyed look. Angel's trumpet, on the opposite page, was also deceptively pretty, a frilly-edged blossom lolling from the plant's elegant neck.

If absorbed into the skin or eyes, the alkaloids from angel's trumpet can enlarge the human pupil until it fills the iris, causing vision problems.

I blinked and pressed a finger to the corner of my own eye, feeling squeamish.

Back to the black roses. I searched the index for mention of blood. Nothing, nothing . . . until I checked the index in *The Secrets of Flora*. It brought me straight to the introduction of the book.

Man has always harbored a fascination with flora, and for good reason: tangled within earth's root systems are a multitude of secrets. Many have taken liberties in exploring, and pushing the boundaries, of botany. Legend has it, for instance, that a sect of botanists during the Middle Ages engaged in the dark practice of steeping pea tendrils in their own blood—if only to see what would result.

My eyes jerked toward the ceiling. *What the hell?* But when I looked back at the text, the next paragraph resumed without further mention of the vampiric botanists. I flipped forward and backward in the book, certain I was missing something, but there was nothing more.

I pushed *The Secrets of Flora* away, feeling faintly ill. Was I to believe that was *Maura's* blood I'd seen on the ends of those black roses, then? What had she done? Slit her wrist and filled a bucket? Used some kind of IV equipment swiped from a hospital? I shuddered. Perversely, it would almost comfort me to know that Maura had been using her own blood to feed her roses.

It would mean she wasn't using someone else's.

On Friday morning, I woke to a dream about Lenten roses. I recognized the apricot-colored blooms from Mom's planting beds. When I opened my eyes, ghosts of the vivid flowers lingered for a moment in the stillness of my bedroom, dancing across the surface of my dresser.

It was fitting that I should dream this on the day I had plans to help Mom in her garden—and coax out information about Maura. During the time Maura and Dane were together, Mom and Maura had gone on more outings than I had with Mom in months. They'd gone on coffee dates, gotten mani-pedis together, browsed flowers at local nurseries. Though I was sure Mom would never say anything critical about Maura, there was a good chance she knew something I didn't.

And so after work that day, I donned a pair of gardening gloves and got to work in my childhood backyard. I much preferred hanging out with Mom when our hands were occupied.

It took the pressure off. Mom explained to me how the acidity of the soil affected the hydrangea petal colors, and I lapsed into the comfort of listening, just as I had as a child when she'd taught me the names of the plants in this very garden.

"Did Maura ever come over and help you out here?" I ventured when she'd finished.

Mom used the back of her glove to push hair from her brow. "No. I didn't want to inconvenience her by asking her to come all the way out here. She had a really busy schedule."

"Yeah? Didn't Dane mention that she had, like, multiple jobs?"

Mom frowned. "I'm not sure. I only ever knew about the floral arranging."

Visions of those blood-soaked black roses filled my head; I struggled to craft what I could only hope sounded like an unassuming question. "Do you know if she ever grew any plants of her own? Didn't she have a greenhouse?"

"I believe so. I never saw it for myself, though."

"Don't you think it's a little odd that Dane and Maura never had you over to their place? Were they super secretive about their relationship or something?"

Mom sighed. "I don't know, Holly. I don't think so. Dane was so proud to have Maura as his girlfriend. He told me once he felt lucky that he was the one she seemed to pluck out of their class at SCAD, that she could've had any guy."

"But why *is* that?" I had the distinct sense I was pushing Mom too far, but I couldn't stop. "If Maura could've had anyone, why pick Dane? Don't get me wrong, Dane was amazing. But he was sensitive. Not at all like Maura. Do you think she liked being idolized by him or something?"

I was right—I had gone too far. Mom shot me a look.

"These questions are coming out of nowhere, Holly. If I didn't know better, I'd think you were trying to drag Maura's name through the dirt."

Face flaming, I attacked the ground to start on another hole. Mom saw straight through me, and it made me irrationally furious. It was Dane's job to cajole Mom, not mine. I didn't have the skills, hadn't inherited Dane's little case of emotional lock-picking tools. The wave of anger redoubled in strength, but this time, it had a different target: my brother. How could he have done this? How could Dane have left me stranded, knowing he was the only one with access to our mother?

"You know." Mom looked at me sidelong. "I have some news."

I could tell that she could barely contain herself from the way her skin jumped around her mouth. How like her, to keep some scintillating nugget of information tucked deep in her fist only to surface it an hour into our time together.

"What?"

"Eric Monroe is back in Savannah."

My neck felt hot. I lifted my hair off it with the back of my arm. "Oh?"

"He started working at his father's law firm. Somehow I always knew he'd end up back here."

"That's nice," I said, peeling off a gardening glove. There was a rim of soil inside the furrowed wrist.

"'That's nice'? Surely you have something more to say on the matter."

"Not really."

"I can get his address for you, if you'd like to stop by and say hello."

"No, thanks."

Mom gave me a stern look.

"What?" I pulled off the other glove, suddenly repulsed by the grittiness on my arms. "I'm going to wash up now. I can feel the dirt under my nails."

After my shower, I sat in a towel on my childhood bed. Even now, at twenty-six, coming home was like entering a state of suspended animation. I remembered returning after graduation—this room had felt like a preserved crypt. It was creepy, but also ridiculous, as if my parents were treating my childhood tchotchkes with the reverence of museum docents. The same overlapping configuration of hair-ties I'd scattered on my desk over winter break had sat untouched, like crop circles.

If my room was a crypt after six months, what would Dane's become?

I dug in my dresser for a fresh top and jeans. As I eased the drawer shut, something clattered. There was a mason jar at the far end of the bureau, the petals of a dried blossom pressed against the glass.

Anger and desire clanged in my chest. This hadn't been out the last time I'd been in my old room. I snatched the mason jar and sat back down on my bed. Unscrewing the top, I gingerly lifted out the rose from my senior prom bouquet and dug my fingers inside the jar. Yes, there they were—the slips of paper Eric had folded in half and given to me before we'd left Savannah for college. We'd both agreed it didn't make sense to try to force a long-distance relationship. At least, I had *thought* we were on the same page, until I'd started unfolding these pieces of paper one lonely night in my Emory dorm room when Rachel had been out.

I removed a sandwich of paper now.

Do you remember eating raspberries in the cemetery?

That was a cute way of putting it. *Yes, Eric, I remember taking fistfuls of the soft berries out of the paper bag from the farmers market. But more vivid in my memory is the taste of berries on your mouth, my hands under the waistband of your jeans, and the way my body arched to meet yours.* We'd crept in after dark and spread our picnic blanket behind a stone angel with eyes pitted by the elements.

We'd been mere feet from dead people and hadn't given a shit.

That part made me cringe. Who did we think we were? (Sixteen-year-olds with raging libidos, that's who.) Even so, sitting on my childhood bed remembering, I felt a thrum between my legs. No, Eric and I hadn't been soulmates, but we'd still had fun. I put the slip of paper back in the mason jar with the dried rose and returned it to the top of the bureau.

"Holly?" Mom called up the stairs.

"Yep!" I hung my towel in the bathroom and headed to the door. At the last minute, I turned and snatched the jar to take with me.

CHAPTER 11

The smell of onion and garlic greeted me back at the townhouse. As I entered the hallway, I heard the telltale sizzle of a hot saucepan. I was hungry, but I'd have to hide out in my bedroom until Maura was done making dinner. I'd made the mistake of walking into the kitchen two nights ago, when Maura had been stirring a cup of tea. She'd taken one frigid look at me and I'd bolted from the room.

I closed myself in the guest room and stretched out across the bed. This was not what I signed up for when I'd agreed to live with Maura. I still hadn't found any clues about Dane, and now I was being iced out.

"What are you doing, hiding in here?"

I jumped. Maura looked in through the crack in my door, a glass of red wine in hand.

"I was—I just—"

"Get your ass into the kitchen. I made shrimp and cassava chowder."

Maura disappeared down the hall, and I got to my feet,

feeling woozy. When had she forgiven me for going through her greenhouse? *Had* she even?

The bright kitchen lights were a shock after the dimness of my room. Maura had already poured me a glass of wine at the breakfast bar. Now she ladled a pumpkin-colored stew into a bowl.

"Here," she said, handing it to me. Her warm knuckle brushed my hand in the process.

I sat down at the bar. "Thanks." The chowder smelled divine. Full shrimp curled in the bottom of my bowl. We sat side by side, eating without speaking. I debated apologizing again for going through her workshop but lost my courage.

"This was my favorite dish growing up," Maura said, taking a sip from her wine. "I ate it for two weeks straight after getting my wisdom teeth out."

"It's delicious."

"Thanks, but I'm not sure I quite nailed my mother's recipe. She didn't make it often. I told you I was one of four girls, right? Whenever one liked a particular dish, there was always another who professed her vehement hatred for it. There was no pleasing us all."

I tried to imagine Maura sharing the limelight with three siblings. I couldn't.

"My childhood was one big scrabble for attention," Maura said, as if reading my mind. "Our house was a loud one, as you might expect. It was hard to stand out. The only time that really happened was when one of us did something *so spectacular*. Once my oldest sister started riding equestrian and cleaning up at regional competitions, though, I didn't stand a chance."

I licked my spoon, setting it down next to my bowl of chowder. "Really?" I said. "Horses?" It wasn't adding up. I couldn't imagine how anyone could see Maura and look away.

"Really. Keep in mind, I'm not telling you all this to get your pity. I think I turned out okay. But I do think those years left their mark on me." Maura's eyes went far away. "Then, when I was in high school, my dad was diagnosed with stomach cancer. I dropped out of school to help Mom take care of him for a year, but I kind of ended up taking the lead on that."

"Oh, God." I hadn't been expecting this turn in the story. "Maura, I'm so sorry."

She shrugged. "Don't feel sorry for me. The year spent taking care of my dad was the most fulfilling of my life. It was an honor to be there for him, especially through his last days. I'd never felt closer to him."

I stared into my bowl, stunned. Maura, dropping out of high school to tend to her dying father? I'd been so self-centered at that age I'd thrown a fit if—God forbid—I heard my friends went to see a movie without me.

"Gosh," I said again. "That really is heartbreaking. I'm so sorry."

"Thank you." Maura gave me a gentle smile. "What about you and Dane? What were your sibling dynamics like?"

I scraped my bowl clean with my spoon. It seemed safe to assume that we weren't going to be discussing the greenhouse incident, but it unsettled me, those barbs lurking under the surface of our polite conversation. "Why?" I asked. "How much did Dane tell you?"

Maura's face was unreadable. "Not much, actually."

I swallowed, unsure whether to feel relieved or insulted. "Oh, I don't know. We were normal, I guess."

"No." When I looked up at Maura, her black eyes were blazing. "That's a cop-out, and you don't get to pull that card, Holly. Not here, not with me."

My heart stuttered. When had we veered off course again? "I—well—"

A knock at the front door rescued me from the moment.

Maura jumped. "I completely forgot. Matias said he was coming by to pick up some supplies."

"Supplies?"

"Herbal remedies. Sit tight." Maura left the kitchen, emerging in the hallway a minute later with a shallow cardboard box clinking with glass jars and vials. I listened to the murmur of her and Matias's conversation in the foyer, staring into the depths of my empty bowl. Had Maura made Matias a hangover remedy, too? I surprised myself by feeling a flash of protectiveness. I didn't like the idea of her giving that to anyone else.

A few minutes later, the front door shut, and Maura reappeared in the mouth of the kitchen. "Come on," she said. "Let's go sit down in the other room, okay?"

Maura picked up her glass and half-finished bowl of chowder and carried them out of the kitchen. I poured myself a couple fingers more of wine before following her into the living room. There Maura patted the cushion next to her. I joined her on the couch, feeling disoriented. The wine had darkened Maura's lips and painted a lacy flush along her collarbone. I was having more trouble than usual looking away.

Maura sat back against the cushions, cradling her wine. "Now, what were you saying?"

"Just that Dane and I . . . I don't know. Things were normal. Good." I paused, knowing this wouldn't be an adequate explanation. She looked back at me, expectantly, so I went on. "We were both in our heads as little kids. In our own imaginary worlds, creating characters we'd slip on and off like costumes.

Most of the time, our worlds converged, and we'd get lost in these elaborate storylines. We'd feed off of each other."

One of our favorite games had revolved around the sundial in the backyard. It was decorated with the classic sun face: large hooded eyes, a cloak of pointed flames. We'd race to draw an imaginary line past the shadow it cast and into the garden. Then we'd bury our "treasures"—acorns, berries, pebbles—in the corresponding areas. I liked to think that's where Dane's obsession with geocaching was born.

"Most of the time," Maura echoed.

I glanced back at her. "Well, not always, of course. We were separate people, obviously, each with our own mind."

"Of course."

I stared at the rim of dark bubbles around my wine. Against all odds, I was keeping my balance—if I wasn't careful, I was going to fall.

Maura was quiet for a long time. Then she said, "I feel like there's another part to this story."

I wasn't ready to go there yet. "Did you ever see Dane's ashes?" I asked instead.

"I—what?"

"Dane's ashes." My throat had turned gritty, and I cleared it. "The first time I saw them, I was shocked. I didn't realize I had expectations about what ashes would look like, but I totally did. I guess I'd been expecting those fluffy campfire ashes, you know? But the ashes in his urn looked more like sand." I didn't mention that I'd dared to sniff them, hoping that maybe, just maybe, I'd be rewarded by a jolt of my brother's cedar scent. I'd picked up nothing but the lingering traces of metal, and something had twisted violently inside me in response.

Maura set her drink on the coffee table. Then she got up to

open the terrace doors. Night air swirled in, raising bumps on my arms. I thought about getting a cardigan from my room, but moving from the couch seemed, once again, impossible.

"I'll tell you something, Holly," Maura said, sitting back down. This time she angled her body so she was facing me. Her weak ankle—the one with the limp—was crossed under her knee. "Sometimes I wonder whether I can even live now that Dane is gone."

Were we finally here? My heart accelerated. "Why would you say that?"

"Because." Maura's face was so close to mine that I had to glance away. "The way that your brother looked at me . . . Sorry, is that weird for me to be saying to you?"

"No, no." I waved at her to continue, even though a knowing, dark feeling was beginning to sift through me.

Maura shrugged, took another sip from her wine. "There are some people that, when you talk, their eyes just seem to drink you all in. Every molecule of you. Your brother was like that."

I nodded, chills racing across the back of my neck. She wasn't wrong.

"And it just isn't fair," Maura went on. "How can I keep living on this earth—flossing my teeth, dreaming, eating peanut butter out of the jar—when his body has been incinerated in a furnace? When he's been turned to dust?"

I flinched.

"I'm sorry. I didn't mean to be crass. I only wanted to express how ludicrous it all is. That he's gone and everything just . . . continues."

"It feels wrong because it is." I braced my hands on my thighs, dug my nails into my skin. Once again, Maura had articulated a feeling I'd harbored myself but never had the courage to express. When I found my voice, I spoke haltingly. "Dane and I went to sleepaway camp up until we were teenagers. Did he ever tell you that?"

"He might have mentioned it," Maura murmured, running her fingertips over her thighs. For a disorienting second, my body registered a delighted shiver, as if it were my legs Maura was trailing her fingers over.

I was too self-conscious to give her context to my story, to explain how I'd struggled to make friends at camp—there was no way she'd relate. Especially during those hellish middle-school years, I'd spent most of my days elbowing into rigid circles of girls with perky ponytails and glitter-laced sunscreen. Mealtimes were even worse, because they meant sitting on the end of a picnic table to grasp at the scraps of conversation that floated my way. Dane never had this problem in his own unit. Sometimes I caught him looking over at me during lunch, securely buckled into his own throng of buddies. He never said anything, but I sensed he worried about me.

"Well," I said, "it was tradition that on the last day of camp, we all took our sleeping bags under the stars. The year I was fourteen—which means Dane must've been ten—I woke up in the middle of the night." I pressed my eyes shut. I could still hear the shrieking crickets, smell the remnants of the smoldering campfire.

Maura's eyebrows lifted. She said nothing.

"Then I saw it." I felt a jolt of fear just remembering. "This hunched thing smelling the sleeping bags. A coyote!"

"Uh-oh," Maura said.

"I started to scream but stopped at the last second. Super slowly, I craned my neck to see who else might be awake. Hoping it wasn't just me."

I'd never seen Maura clinging to my words like this; usually, the roles were reversed. "Was it just you?" she whispered.

I looked down into my lap. "At first, I thought so. But then I turned around. Even though he was in a different unit, Dane had somehow moved his sleeping bag behind mine, and I hadn't noticed until that moment. We looked at each other." I swallowed past a lump.

Maura's soft face made the lump balloon in size.

I didn't trust my voice to convey the rest of the details. The way Dane had mouthed to me, "It's okay." The way I'd stared, heart pounding, at his mismatched eyes—they matched in the night—until the coyote stalked away and I sagged against my pillow.

I made myself look back up at Maura. "It wasn't just me," I said.

The beautiful living room swam. My brother had made sure it was *never* just me. The night my friends had bailed on me for the *Bachelor* viewing, all those times my mother had worked herself into a panic and Dane had swept in to calm her in a way no one else could. How many older sisters could say the same thing of their sibling?

"Oh, Holly," Maura said.

I blinked rapidly, forcing back tears. "It's more than that, though."

I could feel the heat of Maura's eyes on my face. But I wouldn't look up.

"Dane and I were super close all the way through high school. Barring the usual sibling rivalry, of course. Even when I went off to Emory, we texted constantly." I smiled, remembering the way I'd been distracted studying for finals because Dane was blowing up my phone with memes of corpulent seals after

I'd complained about feeling bloated from the stress. But just as quickly, my smile crumbled. "All of that changed once his symptoms started."

I paused, but Maura wasn't jumping in to say anything. I took my bottom lip between my teeth. "I mean, you know how it went. He started having his weird seizure-things and lashing out and having those 'delusions.' And I suddenly—I couldn't bring myself to see him." My voice cracked. "His mind and body were disintegrating, and I couldn't bear to watch him falling apart in real time. So I just avoided him, as if it would make everything go away." There was, of course, another part I couldn't say aloud: that watching Maura swoop in to care for my brother when I couldn't had felt like stomping barefoot through broken glass.

Just like that, I'd lost my balance. Guilt and grief rushed up with the suddenness of a swimming pool floor tilting into the deep end. Maura gave me space to cry in a way most people wouldn't. Eventually, her arms encircled me, pulling me to her shoulder. I melted into her. The cool fabric of her shirt felt like a salve on my eyelids.

"Holly," she said, smoothing down my hair. "Your brother left this giant hole in all our lives. But please—don't make things worse by feeling guilty about what you did or didn't do. Okay? You reacted as any sibling might. You were afraid. It isn't easy to watch an illness like that take hold of someone you love."

"It isn't," I whispered.

"I know. And Dane knew, too. Dane knew that you loved him and that you were there for him. Even if you weren't answering his every text."

I pulled away from Maura, a shiver running through me. What had she just said?

Suddenly, Maura's hand *was* on my thigh—I wasn't imagining it this time. Sensation ricocheted up and down my body, scattering my thoughts. I realized I had been waiting for this moment ever since I'd laid eyes upon Maura at CVS, however delusional that might have been.

Maura's hand flickered to my face. There she used her thumb to swipe tears off my cheekbones and notched her first two fingers under my chin, raising my eyes to hers. I was sure she could see my thighs quaking at her intimate touch. Then her lips settled on my bottom one, sharing in my salt.

CHAPTER 12

Well, well. Look who decided to wake up."

Maura smiled down at me, caught in a dusty shaft of morning light. Backlit by the sun, her face was dark. "My God," she breathed, reverent. "You look just like him when you sleep, the way your mouth settles. Did you know that?"

I jerked up to a seated position, scrabbling to figure out where I was. Then a couple frames from the night before flashed in my mind—Maura's hand on my thigh, her lips on mine— and my stomach cinched into a knot. It had really happened.

I'd really done this.

My shoulders burrowed into the padding of Maura's headboard as I backed away from her. "How long have you been watching me?"

That musical laugh. "Oh, I don't know. Can you blame me for losing track of time?"

I squinted against the harsh light. "What time is it?"

"Hmph. Not telling." Maura thrust her arms out behind

her in bed, leaning her weight onto them. The posture emphasized the exquisite skin bared by her negligee. The grooves along her clavicle and between her breasts invited my touch, and a familiar ache began to spread through me. I wrenched the covers to my chin.

Maybe if I didn't speak, I could keep it all from being real.

"Oh, I see, are you all shy now?" Maura pushed off the mattress and leaned over me. Then she slid a hand under the covers and drew an electric trail from my bottom lip down past my navel. When, against my will, my body lifted to meet her, she laughed softly and pressed herself against me.

At some point last night, I'd turned off my thoughts like a spigot. But this was proving harder to do as daylight streamed onto the bed my brother had shared with Maura. Maura kissed me, and her 1,227 Instagram photos strobed against my eyelids. Those eerie, beautiful eyes. The sharp bird bones and kernel-shaped birthmark on her mouth. Part of me had hoped she'd be less hypnotic once I finally touched her, but unfortunately, the opposite was proving true. I turned my face away from her, groaning into the pillow.

"Good morning to you, too," Maura sighed and rolled back onto her side of the bed. "So, what do you want to do today?"

The faucet inside me opened to a torrent of panic. This—this was the kind of question someone asked her partner. We had never spent a weekend together. For a while, Maura hadn't even been *talking* to me. I took in mouthfuls of the bedroom air, heavily perfumed from the moss-laden baskets of irises and orchids hanging from the rafters. I felt dizzy. What had I *done*? My brother hadn't even been dead for two months, and somehow I'd managed to commit the unthinkable. It would have been bad enough to sleep with my brother's fiancée when Dane had been living. But after his funeral? Maura and I had both been there. This surpassed anything I could have invented in my mind, even in periods when my thoughts veered into the darkest of territories.

"Oh, I don't know." That was a lie. I course-corrected, my brain slowly coming online. "There's Dane's showcase tonight, and I promised my parents I'd go with them, so." I pulled the comforter tighter around my chest. I could still feel the ghost trails of Maura's fingertips on me.

"You don't have to remind me, silly. I'm going, too. Obviously. And that's fine if you're going with your parents—I'll meet y'all there. But that isn't until tonight. We've got plenty of time to sip coffee and plan our day." Maura stretched luxuriously, hair spilling everywhere. Then she swung her legs over the side of the bed, tossed me a sly smile, and padded out of the room.

I waited until I heard Maura clattering about in the kitchen before I dared spring out of bed and down the hall. Then I locked myself in the hallway bathroom, my back against the wall, breathing rapidly.

"Okay, you're okay, you're okay," I chanted. I didn't know where the mantra was coming from, but it seemed the only acceptable response to the horror unfolding around me.

The tips of my fingers tingled into numbness. I lurched toward the sink, filling my cupped hands with cold water and splashing it over my face. Then I dotted some on my neck and wrists, sinking onto the closed toilet seat.

I'd never so much as kissed a girl before. Sure, I'd watched my college girlfriends titillate male onlookers by snaking their arms around each other on the dance floor, pressing soft girl lips against soft girl lips. But all the while I'd told myself that wasn't for me. Maybe I'd just resented the idea of doing it for the sake of performance; maybe it was something I'd wanted all along. Though I'd never contemplated being with a woman before, something about Maura—her magnetism, combined with that raw vulnerability—made our coupling inevitable. The truth? Sleeping with Maura had been electrifying.

I worried, if given the opportunity to do it again, I wouldn't be able to resist.

My God. Had I really just slept with my dead brother's fiancée? Woken to her admiring how I looked like him in my sleep? With my fingertips, I stretched the skin on my temples to the margins of my face until I winced from the pain.

A tiny splinter of my consciousness believed the worst: that Maura had something to do with Dane's death. But the rest of my mind rushed to smother the thought. Despite rooming with Maura, I still hadn't found anything suggesting she'd played a part.

"Holly?"

Her voice was a jumpstart to my heart. The pounding turned erratic, nausea coursing through me.

"Be right there," I called.

Back in her bedroom, Maura held a wooden tray with two steaming mugs of coffee, a plate of scones, and an unfamiliar maroon case with snaps along the side. She smiled when she saw me. Then she set the tray down on her bedside table and reached for the case.

"Want to play a game?" she asked.

I froze in the doorway.

So Maura wants to play this weird-ass game . . .

"Holly! My goodness!" Maura rushed to my side and placed the back of her hand along my cheek. "You look like you've seen a ghost. Did you have some traumatic experience playing dominoes or something?"

"Dominoes?" My voice was a feeble scratch.

"Yeah, dominoes." Maura lifted the maroon case and unsnapped the side, exposing stacks of slick, spotted tiles. "Never mind. Let's just stick with the coffee. Come on, get back in here." She closed the case, set it on the wooden tray, and herded me under the covers. Shaking, I leaned back against the elaborate, tufted headboard, accepting the mug of coffee Maura offered.

"I checked while I was in the kitchen, and there's a farmers market going on in the park," Maura said, settling beside me. "There's a woman there who sells the most darling handmade wreaths. Want to go?"

I stared into my coffee, immobilized.

"Holly?"

"I . . ." To my humiliation, I felt wetness streaking my face.

"What's wrong?" Maura set her mug on the bedside table and grabbed mine out of my hands. Coffee sloshed over the side, staining her bedspread, as she rushed to wrap her arms around me. "What is it? What's going on?"

How had things spiraled so out of control last night? My teeth knocked together. "You—me. What we did. Jesus, Maura, Dane hasn't even been dead two months . . ." Mentally, I flipped through scenes from the night before. Bowls of that colorful chowder, Maura and I cradling glasses of red wine . . . Somehow we'd started the evening indulging in our grief over Dane's death, only to turn around and send my brother the biggest *fuck you* of all. We were terrible human beings.

I was a despicable sister.

Maura pressed her face into my shoulder. "Shhh. Don't do that. Don't do that to yourself."

I felt a scream building inside me. "What do you mean, don't do that to myself? You're saying it like there's an option! Like I can just—turn it off!" Imagine that: an "off" switch to my guilt. It had been so insidious since Dane's death, I would've done anything to make it go away. The fury rushed in then, blotting out my confusion. How *was* Maura able to flip off her conscience like a light? How the hell could she forget my brother so conveniently? It didn't seem fair. Or right.

Maura was rocking me back and forth now, pressing her face so hard into my shoulder I could feel the edges of her teeth through her lips. "Don't go there, Holly. Don't torture yourself." She drew away from me and glanced over at the bedside table. "If it helps, think of last night as bringing us both closer to Dane."

My stomach curdled. God, could Maura have said anything more twisted? What was *wrong* with this girl? I followed her sightline to the black roses under the bell jar and my heart jolted, as if running over a pothole. Yes, it had to be those same black roses I'd uncovered in her greenhouse, drinking from a pail of blood.

"What are those things?" I quavered.

"These?" Maura tapped her nail against the glass. "Oh, just something I keep around to remind me of your brother. Pretty, aren't they?"

My mouth went gummy and dry. That wasn't the adjective I would have used.

"Come on." Maura swiped hair out of her face, then swung

a leg over the side of the bed. "Finish up your coffee. Let's get showered. We've got a whole glorious weekend ahead of us."

It was an overcast day in the park. Summer was fading. Feeling nauseous, I trailed behind Maura, who darted in and out of stalls with a wicker basket slung over one arm. In it, she piled a mass of fruit and vegetables: purple onions, sweet potatoes, carrots with bits of soil clinging to their spidery roots. The wares in each tent—jars of honey with garish labels, spotted eggs, swollen nectarines—crowded me. Everything felt menacing and oversized.

What the actual fuck.

Here was Maura, gallivanting through a farmers market as if she hadn't a care in the world, mere hours after sleeping with her dead fiancé's sister. This girl was sick. I dug my nails into my palms, watching her.

Maura lingered in a tent with terrariums, studying the tiny jewellike plants inside. Despite my rage, I felt a flare of interest. I never got to see Maura interact with her plants—that happened only in the privacy of her greenhouse. She blushed with a childish energy now, pushing out her lips as she touched leaves and petals.

"I can't not have this," Maura said, holding up one terrarium with a single brooding bloom inside. It was a wash of purples and deep greens, like dusk condensed into a glass the size of her fist.

I shrugged as if to say, *It's yours.*

As the woman wrapped the glass bulb in tissue paper, Maura reached over and brushed the inside of my wrist with the back of her nail. It was the one she always chewed, just rough enough to catch, and it sent a thrill across my forearms. I glanced at her, a question, but her eyes were on the flower, alight with the pleasure of having purchased it. It was hers. Then her fingers laced in mine. I felt the press of her engagement ring against my own fingers, and it called the nausea back.

I slept with my dead brother's fiancée.

We wound through the farmers market stalls, still hunting for the woman selling the wreaths that Maura had promised. She bought a paper boat of powdered sugar donut holes, and we found a bench where we could sit down to eat. I managed a single bite before my stomach rioted. Then I set the remains in the grease-stained paper. Maura snatched it up without pause and popped it in her mouth, pink tongue flicking over her lips.

Dane had known that tongue. Now, so did I.

As we exited the park, I forced myself to inhale deeply, scanning my body for lingering trails of Maura's touch. Could I still feel them? What would happen when they faded? But just as soon as I conjured up the scintillating path of her mouth and fingers, I felt that lurch again.

Holy fuck, I slept with my dead brother's fiancée.

"Ooh," Maura said, pausing at the periphery of the park. She pointed to a nest-like tangle of undergrowth near us. Her eyes lifted to mine. "Do you know what this is?"

I was too distracted to reply. Was Maura seriously launching into another botany lesson? *Now?*

"Dodder," Maura said, extending a finger to pluck at a wispy, yellow stem. The tangle looked like a gargantuan mass of Silly String, eclipsing any trace of life beneath it. "Otherwise known as devil's thread. Isn't it magnificent?"

I rammed my bottom lip between my teeth, refusing to engage. I was in no mood for her little plant riddles today.

"You see," Maura said, running a thumb over a white petal, "after germinating, these beauties shoot out tiny little tendrils that latch onto their host plant—see these chrysanthemums below? Devil's threads feed on water and nutrients through their host. Some people would call it parasitism, I suppose, but I like to think these flowers are getting something out of the relationship, too. After all, isn't it an honor, being able to cede yourself to something greater?"

I dared to peer closer, and flinched. Tiny white buds gaped like miniature mouths. I hadn't known something like this was even possible. These devil's threads had actually wound themselves around the stems of the chrysanthemums, choking them in knots of yellow-green coils.

It didn't look like an honor to me. It looked like a violent takeover.

Maura let go of the plant and grinned. "God, I'm *famished*. What do you feel like having for lunch?"

CHAPTER 13

The walk back from the park dragged on for an eternity, Maura chatting animatedly and touching my arm every so often. I'd worried she would try dragging us to a restaurant for lunch, but fortunately, she remembered she had leftover Thai in the fridge. We arrived home and Maura went straight into the greenhouse after getting her food. The clunk of the glass doors closing sent relief billowing through my body.

When it was time to leave for Dane's showcase, I was still reeling. For once, it was a relief to meet up with my parents, even if it was for an event that I was dreading. It meant escaping the townhouse. SCAD had cleared the desks out of a lecture hall and set up tables of wine, crudités, and bruschetta. It occurred to me that someone had been responsible for thinking this through. As in, *What's the appropriate food to serve at a showcase honoring a student after his brutal suicide? Cupcakes? Too glib?*

I didn't know what I had been expecting, but the twenty or so students milling around the space felt simultaneously like too many and too few. They flickered in front of me like holograms.

Mom called to me from the back of the room, and I rushed to meet my parents. When Mom offered her side hug, the smell of her Pond's cold cream called up tears.

"You okay, Holls?" Dad asked. He'd dressed up tonight in slacks and a belt—still paired with his tennis shoes. The fresh wave of affection gutted me; I thought of how he'd been suffering. Why we were here.

"Yeah, of course." I dragged the back of my hand under my nose and reached for a glass of white wine on a nearby table. If I was finally looking at Dane's work, I was going to need all the fortitude I could muster. I nodded up at the framed illustration my parents had been regarding. "Wow," I said, gulping my wine.

Even before Dane had gotten a job as a medical illustrator, he'd been fascinated by complex machinery, natural and man-made. Here was a cross-section of a shell, its spiraled innards crunching tighter and tighter until they vanished altogether. I couldn't help feeling a buzzing frenzy as my eyes traced the contracting spiral to the end.

There were more cross-sections to see, of course, unfurling flower buds and animal skulls. My parents and I took them all in. But by the sixth or seventh picture, my awe of Dane's precision started to give way to frustration. Everything was so technical. Perhaps this was why I had been afraid of coming to this showcase—because I'd been hoping to find some indication of Dane's emotions and psychology in the days leading up to his suicide. But clearly, there was none to be found.

Dad was bursting with praise about Dane's work, but Mom stayed silent, peering at the illustrations and then back into her wine. Maybe she was trying to find clues in the meticulous work, too. Then she craned her neck. "Let's say hello to Maura," she said, looking over my head.

The wine in my mouth turned to battery acid. I'd been dreading Dane's showcase for so long I hadn't even stopped to consider what else it would entail: the inevitable collision of my worlds. The shame I felt imagining telling Rachel about Maura was rivaled only by imagining doing the same with Mom and Dad.

Oh, wait, I never told y'all that Maura and I were living together? Silly me! You know what else? She and Dane weren't just dating; they were engaged! Funny, huh? Why didn't I tell you any of this? Oh, I don't know. Maybe because I think my new roommate might have had something to do with Dane's descent into madness and consequent death.

Maybe because Maura and I slept together last night.

I slammed my wineglass down on a nearby table and put my fingertips to my damp hairline. For a terrible, tense minute, Mom, Dad, and I scanned the room for signs of Maura. I was frantic. Maybe if I saw her first, I could stave off a meeting.

"There she is!" Mom nodded past a clump of students. Maura stood in a tasteful belted dress, talking with a couple girls her age.

I grabbed Mom's wrist. "Not now. She's in the middle of a conversation."

Mom frowned at me. "Well, honey, that's sort of the point of these things. I'm sure she'll introduce us. Come on."

Mom started on a beeline toward Maura, and I scrambled to keep up with her. Dread pulsed like a heartbeat within me.

No, no, no. Please, God, no. My mind spun through potential explanations to address what Maura might or might not say to my parents. Would she assume my parents knew we were rooming together? Or did she feel weird about it, like I did? Judging from our conversation in bed that morning, Maura didn't seem to have any qualms. What if she gave me a flirtatious look in front of my parents? What if she—God forbid—*touched* me?

My hand shot out to grab my mother's wrist again.

"Mr. and Mrs. Chambers."

I nearly doubled over in relief. It was one of Dane's professors, a woman with a severe black bob and a pea-colored tunic, intercepting us just in time. When it was my turn to be introduced, she took one of my hands between two of her gnarled ones. They felt like warm bark.

"Your brother was a master," she told me.

"Thank you. I can see that." I smiled, swallowing my panic, then looked past the professor's shoulder at Maura. I could only make out one of her friends through the crowd—aquiline nose, red beaded necklace.

"SCAD's done an incredible job setting this up," Dad was saying.

The professor tilted her head to one side with a smile. "In all honesty, there wasn't much to be done. Dane was prolific. I'm not sure you knew this, but he was so dedicated to his work that he continued coming to the studio into the summer, even after he'd graduated." A twisted smile. "And of course, none of us had the heart to turn him away."

I offered a vague smile of my own. "Dane was such a skilled artist, there's no denying that. I'm just wondering if he had any work that was more . . . I don't know. Expressive?"

That tilt of the head again. "I can't speak for Dane," she said after a beat, "but what I do know? It's nearly impossible to create without expressing."

"Very true," Dad said, even though the professor's statement couldn't have been less helpful. I glanced over at Mom. She'd mentally detached from the conversation and—I could tell—was preparing to engage Maura. I was running out of time.

I ground my molars in frustration. "Do you see any of Dane's friends here tonight?" I asked the professor. "Besides his girlfriend, of course. I want to make sure I talk to them, thank them for coming."

The professor frowned. "Hmm. When Dane wasn't with Maura, he really tended to keep to himself. Let me think . . ."

I watched her eyes sweep the space and hastily calculated my next move. If I could just speak to one of Dane's friends and ask them about their take on Dane and Maura's relationship . . .

The professor gave me a sad smile. "I'm not sure," she said. "I'd hate to direct you to the wrong person."

A thought clicked into place. "What about . . . was there a Lauren in Dane's class?" I turned to Dad. "Didn't you mention Dane being friends with a Lauren?"

"Yep," Dad said, with a decisive nod. "Lauren and Jordan."

"Jacob," Mom sighed.

"Hmm." The professor was back to scanning the room. "I'm afraid I don't see Jacob, and I can guarantee you won't see Lauren here tonight."

My heart jolted. "Why? Did she and Dane have a falling out or something?"

She shook her head, dropped her voice. "Lauren fell very ill after graduation. I don't really know the details."

Mom's hand clamped over my wrist: my time was up. Sure enough, she put on a strained smile for the professor. "Thank you again for the lovely evening. If you'll excuse us."

Then Mom was leading us toward Maura again. Maura, who was now alone, holding a vegetable skewer on a wilted napkin. The way she stood with one leg crossed over the other made her look like an awkward marsh bird. This confounded me. The only real social situations in which I had seen her—Easter brunch, SCAD's graduation, Odette's party, and even, to some extent, my brother's funeral—had placed Maura at their center. I had assumed this was always the case, likely because I had so much trouble tearing my own eyes away from her. Surely, middle school Maura had never been shouldered out of a circle of girls. And yet here she was, standing at the periphery. Alone.

When I looked back at Maura, her eyes found mine.

"Hey," she mouthed.

No, no, no. Maura wasn't allowed to look at me like that. Not here, not in front of my parents. This was going to be a disaster. I needed to find the restroom, somewhere I could breathe. Anywhere but here.

"Maura!" Mom was the first to bridge the distance, gathering Maura into an embrace. I marveled at the easy way they hugged. I never fit that comfortably against Mom. All I ever felt were wrists and elbows. I studied Maura's hand gently rubbing my mother's back.

No engagement ring.

Dad and Maura hugged next. My heart pounded out an erratic rhythm, and I looked down at the floor.

Mom regarded Maura, beaming. "It's just so wonderful to see you," she said. Almost as an afterthought, she added, "And you remember Holly?"

Then Maura looked at me—really looked at me—and it punched the air from my chest.

"Yes," she said, refusing to look away. "I think I do."

So this was how Maura was going to play the evening. I shouldn't have been surprised. She was going to make me squirm; at this rate, I wouldn't last two minutes.

"This is a lot, isn't it?" Dad gestured at the milling students, Dane's work on display. "How're you taking it all?"

Maura raised one shoulder. "It is a lot. I'm feeling overwhelmed by . . . well, by how much I'm missing him, I guess. How are y'all holding up?"

Dad and I both waited for Mom's reply. "We're just feeling so fortunate for SCAD's generosity," she said.

"Totally." Looking at the ground, I felt, rather than saw, Maura's eyes light on me. "Actually, I'm feeling a lot better now that you're here."

"Anytime you need us, Maura, you know where to find us," Dad said. "You have my wife's number?"

"Of course, yes. We're getting our nails done next week!" Maura gripped hands with my mother, grinning, before switching her attention back to me. "Actually, Holly, I was wondering if I could have a quick word?"

Drumbeats in my ears. What was she doing? Mom and Dad stared at me, waiting. Could they feel the heat of panic radiating off me?

"Okay," I managed.

Maura led me out of the lecture hall. As soon as we rounded the corner into a linoleum hallway, her hand closed over mine. She gave me a yank and I stumbled after her.

"Maura! Where are you taking me?"

Eventually she found the door she was looking for—one with a rectangular darkened window—and hastened me into a classroom that smelled of tempera paint.

"Maura—" I started again, but then her lips were on mine, her body pressing me against the wall.

I melted into her soft mouth with a moan, my fingers tangling in her hair. Maura's taunting hand slid up my thigh.

"You have to promise me," she said, breaking away suddenly.

I was breathing hard. "Promise you what?"

"That you won't move out. Don't leave all of a sudden." Another deep kiss. "Okay?"

"I mean, I wasn't . . . planning on it?"

"Good." That sleepy smile crossed Maura's face. Then her thumb grazed my jaw, and I flinched with anticipation of unraveling again at her touch. "We need each other, Holly. You get that, right? I can help you. I promise I can make you feel better. And I need you, too. Because without you—without Dane"—her voice dropped in pitch—"who will even see me?"

A shudder rippled through my body. Here it was again. *Without you—without Dane.* Why did she keep connecting us like that?

"Maura," I said. My voice was wobbly, so I tried again, infusing it with resolve I didn't feel. "When you say things like that, it really makes me worry."

She drew back, as if I'd scalded her. "What? Please. You don't have anything to worry about."

"Don't I?" I swallowed, looking from Maura's full lashes to the beauty mark perched on her lip. What was it she'd said to me this morning as she'd looked down at my face on the pillow? *You look just like him when you sleep, the way your mouth settles. Did you know that?*

I said the next part quietly. "I am not Dane. Okay?"

"Of course!" Maura laughed, touching my face again.

"Don't be silly. Of course you aren't." Then she pressed her lips back to mine, but the urgency was gone.

Back at the reception, Maura and I went our separate ways. This was better off—I needed to recover from our encounter. I snatched another glass of wine from the table and gulped at it, scanning the room. Had Maura really flirted with me in front of my parents and then pulled me into a deserted classroom to seduce me? To tell me I needed her? That part was laughable. I chose to keep living with Maura because I needed answers, not because I needed *her*.

And what about those chilling words? They rang in my head even now.

Without you—without Dane—who will even see me?

For starters, it was a ridiculous notion. Maura had a face like a model or a newscaster, one that eyes couldn't help but devour. But it wasn't just the way she looked. It was the way she spoke, moved through spaces, commanding attention, *enchanting*. Hell, she had Odette's entire bevy of Savannah elites nearly worshipping her. She had to be playing me. People like her couldn't possibly feel insecure.

That wasn't the most disturbing part, though. There was the matter of Maura equating me with Dane. Was I functioning as some kind of sick stand-in for Dane after his death? Who exactly was she picturing when she closed her eyes and touched me?

I shivered, downing the rest of my wine, and made a last circuit around the showcase on my own. Dane's precise cross-sections were beginning to turn my stomach. Why was every illustration here so . . . clean? I remembered my brother picking at his bloodied nails under the bistro table. These meticulous illustrations *couldn't* have been inked by the same person who'd stopped showering and started fixating on the cameras in the corners of restaurants.

I thought of the illustrations I'd stumbled across in Maura's library. The way she'd crossed her arms over her body, feigning surprise. *I totally forgot these were still out here.*

Bullshit. I was sure of it now: there was something I wasn't seeing.

Before Mom, Dad, or Maura could notice, I slipped out of the lecture hall and into the night.

CHAPTER 14

The last time I saw Dane was in early August. I'd been avoiding him for weeks, turning down multiple invitations in a row. Finally, my guilt got the better of me, so I decided to have him over to the apartment. Lunch seemed circumscribed enough for me to handle. I was prepping a beautiful summer salad for us with snap peas, mushrooms, and carrots.

After I let him into the apartment, Dane followed me into the kitchen, a sheaf of his dark hair obscuring half his face. He had a way of looking uncomfortable whenever he entered a new space. Usually, it was endearing, but that day it felt different. He wore a plain white undershirt; one of the cuffs was flipped up at a rakish angle. He looked pale, but otherwise good.

"Hi," I said, giving him a side hug. Dane and I weren't big into hugging—no one in the family was—but I forced myself to make an effort. I wasn't sure why. Maybe it was to counteract my guilt for my shitty communication. Maybe I wanted to show Dane that his new, terrifying symptoms didn't faze me.

Me? Never.

Dane's arm felt limp across my back. "What're you making?"

"What does it look like, nincompoop?"

Dane narrowed his eyes. "I don't know about this. Mushrooms?"

"Chill, you'll like it. Trust me."

He settled on a stool at the bar, hooking one foot on the bottom rung. I snuck a glance at his fingers—no sign of blood anymore—and relief unfurled inside me. Thank God, he even seemed to be acting more like himself, unlike that terrible day back at the bistro a month ago. Maybe the new medication had finally kicked in.

"I don't know, sister dearest," Dane said. "Remember playing Manhunt, when you told me to trust you? I ended up with a split lip and a face full of mud."

"It's not my fault your little eight-year-old chicken legs couldn't clear that tree branch. *I* didn't have any trouble, as I recall." I'd been twelve, racing after my own friends in the empty lot across the street. Dane had felt like a nuisance that day; I'd been annoyed he couldn't keep up.

"Yes, but you should've known. Big-sisterly duty, and all that."

I sank my teeth into my bottom lip. *Twist the blade, why don't you, Dane? I'm trying here.* My knife slid off the onion I'd been chopping, veering onto the cutting board and narrowly missing my fingers. "Shit."

Dane perked up. "Want some help?"

"No, relax. You're my guest. Can I get you anything to drink? I was going to open a bottle of white—" The words were out of my mouth before I could snatch them back. *His medication.*

"I, uh." Dane poked at the grout between tiles on the breakfast bar. "I'm not supposed to drink, you know."

"Of course, of course. I've got juice. Water? Rachel's militant about the whole no-soda-in-the-house thing, but—"

"Water's fine. I'll get myself a glass."

Dane loped into the kitchen behind me, got some water from the filter on the front of the refrigerator, and settled back onto his stool. I glanced up at him from my heap of diced vegetables, burning with shame. Dad had mentioned that Dane's psychiatrist had put him on some medication. It had a name that sounded alien. Thorazine? *No, that's what they inject into asylum patients in the movies.*

Dane started telling me about one of his clients then, and the tension dissipated. I offered my condolences and threw in a few stories about Esther and patrons I'd encountered at the library. Dane ran a finger around the lip of his glass as I spoke. I could tell he was really listening by the set of his body and the questions he asked. Not many people did that; I felt a flare of affection for my brother.

When that conversation petered out, Dane said, "Look, I can't stand watching you massacre that carrot anymore. Someone needs to take control in here." He set down his empty glass and came around behind the bar to snatch the vegetable peeler out of my hand.

"Hey!" I wrestled with him only halfheartedly. I knew Dane wanted an excuse to police what was going into the salad. This would be better for both of us—I'd rather give up a few mushrooms than have to withstand Dane's whining and the disgusted flicks of his fork as he cleared unsavory vegetables to the side of his plate.

Of course, we were adults now; the wrestling was only playful. But this hadn't always been the case. Dane and I had some intense tussles—no bite marks or blood, like some of my friends had experienced with their siblings, but certainly moments of uninhibited rage. Moments we lost control. My weapon of choice had been my nails, clawing at his face like a cat. But Dane? Once he'd gotten bigger than me, he could easily pin me, knees pressing my arms to the floor. Then he'd executed "the typewriter": a horrific maneuver in which he had me flat on my back and pounded on my collarbone with his pointer fingers. It brought on a sensation of utter powerlessness.

Eventually, I dropped the peeler.

"Watch and learn," Dane said, applying it to the carrot. Orange streamers fell to the cutting board in a tangle. It was obvious that, of the two of us, Dane worked far more deftly. But of course he did. He had always been better with his hands.

I leaned up against the counter, miffed. To think that particular soreness was just as marked at twenty-six years old as it had been at age ten.

"How's the GF?" I asked him. A devious little edge of me, I suppose, wanted to get a rise out of him and sensed this might do the trick.

Dane lifted one shoulder, looking unaffected. "Good."

"Mom and I were talking after your graduation. She's really pretty."

"Yeah, she is."

The nonchalance with which he said it made my hands fold into fists. I wished I'd opened the white wine before he arrived so I had a glass available. "How's life shacked up with her? God, don't take this the wrong way, bro, but I can't believe you moved in with a girl after knowing her for, what? A month?"

Dane looked down. "Two."

"Okay, yeah." I let out a low whistle, the same way people would do when they asked how long Eric and I had been together in high school. It always drove me up the wall. "My point exactly."

Dane picked up a second carrot to skin.

My brother and I talked about a lot of things. Books. Strangers we saw around the city. Pictures of weird insects he found on Instagram and sent to me. Relationships, however, would always be out of bounds. I knew this. But still, I pressed. Could it be that I was smarting over having the peeler taken away in my own kitchen? No, that wasn't it. Try as I might, I couldn't banish the memory of Maura simpering in front of my parents. *Don't you worry, Mr. and Mrs. Chambers, I'll make sure to whip Dane into shape once he moves in with me. I have a feeling all he needs is a . . . feminine touch.* Who was she to stride into our family, just as its center was giving way? Screw her *feminine touch.* How could she even claim to know what he needed, after two pathetic months of dating? She didn't know Dane. Not like I did.

The truth was, I couldn't stand the thought of Maura being there to take care of Dane—and with such flourish, too.

It highlighted every spectacular way I had failed my own brother.

I tried to sound conspiratorial. "So, spill. What's her most annoying habit? You know, the one thing that just ticks you off?"

Dane used his shoulder to scratch his cheekbone. "I dunno. I can't really think of anything right now."

"What? Come on." He couldn't identify a *single* flaw in her? She couldn't be that perfect; it wasn't fair. "There's got to be something. Does she leave crumpled socks around the house? Snore?"

Dane shrugged again.

I could have let it go, allowed the conversation to float into safer territory. But I picked up on an undercurrent of something in Dane's words—reticence, evasion, maybe even fear. So I stayed silent. I watched Dane peel. I felt my heartbeat in my muscles.

Wait, I told myself.

"Well," he said after a minute or two. "There is this one thing."

"Yeah?"

"Yeah. It's just, sometimes living with her kind of creeps me out."

Of all the things that could have come out of Dane's mouth, I hadn't expected that. "How so?" I asked, inching closer against the cold edge of the countertop.

Dane picked up a third carrot. I didn't think we needed it, but I didn't want to say anything and risk severing the possibility of the moment. *Click, click, click.* The peeler sliced off more coiling strips.

Finally, Dane said, "It's stupid."

"No! Dane, I'm sure it's not stupid. You can tell me." Could he hear the desperation in my voice? The possibility of getting dirt on Maura had me salivating.

For the first time since we'd begun discussing his girlfriend, Dane looked up at my face. His pretty, mismatched eyes were wide and eerie. "I asked her for help. And now I think there's something growing inside me."

My anticipation collapsed into a rubble of panic.

Oh, no.

"Something growing inside you," I repeated, turning away from my brother.

I couldn't be hearing this. Not now, when we were finally about to sit down and share such a delightful meal.

Dad had warned me Dane was experiencing delusions—at least, that's what his psychiatrist had called them. But I'd been provided none of the details, and I didn't want them. I'd reasoned that if I didn't acknowledge this part of Dane, it wouldn't exist.

How did people handle this, watching a loved one deteriorate in real time? I swiped a finger over the countertop. It was sticky; fine crumbs came away onto my skin. I jammed a smile on my face and looked back up at Dane in a last-ditch attempt at humor. "Is this your way of telling me I'm going to be an aunt?"

But Dane didn't smile back. "No, it's not like that."

"Well, what is it like, then?" Dane's psychiatrist had warned us against delving into—and thereby encouraging—any of Dane's delusions. Instead, he'd advised us to "validate." *That sounds scary. I can only imagine how frightening that must feel.*

But I couldn't help myself. "Did you, like, swallow a watermelon seed or something?"

Dane shook his head. "No."

"No? Then what are we talking about here? What's growing inside you?"

Dane wouldn't let me look away. "All I know is it's something . . . bad."

My skin went cold. What the hell was I supposed to do with this? I touched my phone on the countertop, my fingertips shaking. Did I call Mom and Dad so they could contact his psychiatrist? Did Dane need his meds adjusted? Did he need to be *hospitalized*?

"Dane, have you mentioned this to your psychiatrist?"

My brother's eyes hardened. "No."

"Well, maybe you should."

"You don't believe me." Dane's hand tightened on the rubber grip of the peeler.

"I didn't say that."

"No, but it was implied."

I heaved a ragged breath. "Listen, Dane, how do you expect me to react when you tell me there's something *growing inside you?*"

"I don't know. With some support? At least some follow-up questions?"

Looking back on the conversation, I can see this was the juncture I missed. Dane gave me every opportunity to course-correct. But I bulldozed straight through, so driven by my own disturbance.

I took a step closer to Dane, laid a hand on his shoulder. "You need to bring this up with your psychiatrist. I'm seriously worried about you."

"And what good will that do?" Dane spoke so sharply that spittle flew from his mouth. "My psychiatrist is a quack. The license on his wall is a fake. I don't even take my meds most days—it just makes everything worse."

I gasped. "Dane! You need to take your medication," I said, my hand falling away from him. "You need to listen to your doctor."

"Look at you! You're no better than him!" As I reached for Dane's shoulder again, my brother brought his hand up to block me, catching the tender flesh of my inner arm with the peeler. I watched in horror as a ribbon of my skin pulled away. Looking down at the white channel in my arm, I was unable to recognize it as part of my own anatomy. Then blood welled and gushed, spilling over my wrist onto the kitchen tiles.

The floor tilted away from me. For a couple nauseating beats, all I could do was stare down at my own blood dripping onto the white squares below. Then my body leapt to action. I dove for the dispenser on the wall and ripped off clods of paper towels, pressing them to my arm. But my blood was insatiable, devouring the pockmarked paper.

"Oh my God, oh my God." My voice sounded far away. Like it belonged to someone else.

My brother muttered something almost inaudible. He was still stooped over the cutting board, gripping the bloody peeler.

"Wow, did you hear that?" he said. "*Now* she's worried about me."

I'd turned those words over in my mind ad nauseam since Dane's death. Still, they had the power to rip the air from my lungs, pointing like neon arrows to all my sisterly failures. The way I'd recoiled from him when he'd needed me the most. My obsession with his girlfriend. The way I'd refused to believe Dane, just like everybody else, when it mattered most.

Now, months too late, I was finally ready to listen. But the only remaining pieces of him—his illustrations—weren't telling me anything.

I rushed back to Maura's townhouse through the darkened Savannah streets. Bobbing gas-lamp flames twisted by, making shadows squirm across the bricks. The up-lit spire of the cathedral stabbed the sky. I had no idea how much longer Maura would spend at the showcase—and therefore, how long I had to myself. I wasn't even sure of my mission once I got back. Investigating the townhouse for the umpteenth time? I knew only that, like his paltry box of belongings, Dane's illustrations on display at the showcase weren't telling me the whole story.

Back at the townhouse, I pounded up the stairs to the second floor. When I'd first moved in, Maura had mentioned she rarely used the upstairs. Had that been her way of discouraging me from poking around up here? Now I tore through the second-floor rooms: nondescript guest rooms; a room with an old-fashioned sewing machine. I sorted through some of the scraps of fabric on the table, a dusty closet with only a Swiffer and a couple cartons of bottled water.

None of Dane's work.

Next, I paced the first floor, dragging my fingertips along the wainscotting on the walls. My hand stopped on a doorframe right beside Maura's bedroom.

Of course. The basement.

The mustiness was the first thing that registered, pressing like damp wool against my face and arms. That distinctive scent of mold and mildew and rot. A crude wooden staircase led down. I yanked a string hanging from the ceiling and a single lightbulb clicked to life.

Even though the basement was unfinished, it was as tidy as the upstairs of the townhouse. For some reason, this chilled me. I shuffled across the concrete floor, feeling coldness seep through the soles of my flats. Copper pipes snaked through the walls. I shone the light on my phone over the neat piles Maura had amassed. A stack of wooden trellises and metal stakes to— ostensibly—guide the growth of her plants. Bags of mulch. A dehumidifier with a transparent tank half full of water. An old wine crate filled with knickknacks: a Barbie with eyes that were nearly worn away, a snow globe, and a satin drawstring pouch.

I pulled the pouch open. Nestled at the bottom were two

teeth, their long roots still intact. On one tooth there even appeared to be bits of dark blood—or was it flesh?—still clinging to the root.

I cinched the bag shut, disgust and fascination washing over me in equal measure. Had Maura actually decided to keep her own wisdom teeth after getting them extracted? It seemed a bit dark to me, and more than a bit self-indulgent for her to have encased them in satin. Still, there was something wildly appealing about the thought of holding something so intimate— something that had once been part of Maura's skeleton—in my own hands.

Impulsively, I stuffed the pouch in my bag.

On the opposite side of the room was another, smaller room. I entered, blood drumming in my neck. But it was only an old wine cellar, woefully under-equipped. I spun a dusty bottle around in the rack. A splintered workbench sat across from the wine rack. I flicked a heavy switch on the wall and four panes of fluorescent light sputtered on above. Orderly rows of hammers, saws, drills, and bits. Did Maura know how to use all these?

I was about to leave the wine cellar when a metal panel near the floor caught my eye. I crouched to take a better look. It looked like a small door, coming up to my hip. I jiggled the metal handle and it swung open easily. Circuit board, probably. But instead of panels of switches, the door opened to deeper darkness. I shone my phone inside. It was some kind of alcove extending down under the townhouse—I couldn't tell how far it went.

My thighs prickled with goosebumps. *Nope.* I slammed the door shut with an ugly clang.

The impact ran through the walls. Something nearby made

a sound like the clacking of hockey sticks. My head whipped to the left, toward a rectangular mound covered with a white drop-cloth. I ripped away the sheet. And there, buried in the belly of Maura's basement, sat a stack of six or seven canvases. I knew before even looking that they were Dane's.

I drew the first canvas toward me with shaking fingers. Another photo-realistic illustration, but this one of a person's naked back, its spine unzipped to reveal slick red muscle beneath. A tremor ran through me. What could have possibly compelled Dane to create something so grotesque?

Next: pink human ribs stripped of flesh, stark against a black background. Lovely as an antique birdcage and splintered down the middle.

There's something growing inside me.

I swallowed down a pocket of tangy air. The next several canvases showcased frantic, neon slashes and scribbles of paint, unintelligible messes of color. And then—my skin went cold—red-brown gouge marks that could only have come from Dane's own bloodied fingers.

I stepped away from the canvases, my heart hammering. No wonder these hadn't been included in Dane's showcase—they clearly depicted my brother at his most unhinged. I could *feel* his panic radiating from the paint, from the ragged canvas, and it drove a spike of fear through me. What the hell had been *wrong* with him? And why had Maura hidden these illustrations in her basement? Had she merely been trying to protect her fiancé's reputation? Or was there another reason she sought to hide Dane's psychotic break from the public eye—and from me?

I forced myself to return to the stack of canvases to observe the last one. Here, Dane had drawn the silhouette of a human body in marker, its back arched, utterly racked. Something that looked like a collection of blackened daggers burst from the person's mouth. Those daggers—whatever they were—looked almost like they were turning the figure inside out. Devouring him from within.

I drew closer, inspecting the daggers. Electricity coursed down my spine.

Roses. They were dark roses.

CHAPTER 15

F or a while I could only stare, frozen, at the illustration of the tormented figure. I traced a finger along the side of the canvas, willing an explanation to float to the surface. Then, slowly, I turned it over. Dane's scrawl stared back at me, in soft pencil.

H.C.:
5/12/18 12:02 pm

That seemed odd. Did he always include the date and time when he'd finished an illustration? Could that be what 5/12 meant?

A floor above, I heard the unmistakable groan of the front door opening. Maura was home. I snapped a quick picture of both sides of the last canvas before throwing the drop-cloth over the stack of illustrations and racing back up the stairs. Somehow, I made it to my bedroom without running into

Maura in the hallway. I shut the door and sat on my bed, drawing my knees up to my chin.

What the hell had I just seen? I pulled up the photo on my phone and zoomed in on the strange, dagger-like shapes. Could they be simply black knives bursting out of the silhouette? Or were they really roses? I thought of the black roses in Maura's greenhouse and unease laced through me. But maybe that was a leap too far. I threw my phone down on my bed. After all, I'd had several glasses of wine at the showcase and had left feeling woozy. In all likelihood, this was just my subconscious going into overdrive, scrambling to make connections that would only crumble in the daylight.

I snatched up my phone again and stared at the picture of Dane's note.

H.C.:
5/12/18 12:02 pm

Obviously, it wasn't an autograph—H.C. were *my* initials. Was it possible that he had intended that . . . for me? And what was the significance of May 12? It was three months before Dane's death. As far as I could recall, nothing of merit had happened on that day—not this past year, not ever. I pulled up my own calendar on my phone just to make sure. Aside from a dentist appointment on May 12 a year ago, nothing.

I opened the web browser on my phone and typed in the date. Stupid stuff came back: the wedding of an *American Idol* winner, the birthday of an Instagram-famous pug. Dane definitely hadn't meant to denote anything like that.

Dane, Dane, Dane. Frustration clawed at me. My brother

would do this sometimes—indicate that he was smarter than me, that he'd realized something I hadn't. He'd been the only one in the family to predict the end of *The Da Vinci Code*. He'd always say it in the same mild way: *oh, you didn't see that?* He knew I didn't, that nobody else had. It had driven me wild as a kid. Dane, my little brother, should've been the one racing to keep up with *me*. But it would always be the other way around.

Already, I felt winded.

I succeeded in avoiding Maura for almost the entire next day. Our rendezvous at SCAD had been completely overwhelming—not to mention the fact that I was still trying to wrap my head around what I'd found in the basement. So I locked myself in the guest room for much of the day. Between the SCAD website and social media, I zeroed in on Dane's friend Lauren. I studied her profile picture. She had white-blond hair and an elfin face; she seemed to sneer at the camera. She didn't look very friendly, and I had a hard time imagining her appreciating my brother. I agonized over my message to her:

Hi Lauren—this is Holly Chambers, Dane's sister. My dad mentioned you and Dane were pretty close back at SCAD. Is there any chance you'd be willing to chat with me sometime?

I debated whether to mention her illness, but decided against it—I didn't want to scare her off by purporting to know too much about her. I read the message over for the millionth time and finally, wincing, clicked "Send."

It wasn't until the evening that Maura found me in the kitchen, taking inventory of my sorry food supply.

"Hi, stranger," she said, leaning up against the island. "What're you up to?"

What was the appropriate way to address the fiancée of your dead brother with whom you'd spent the night and then fled? I took a moment to arrange my face accordingly, but when Maura raised a brow at me, I realized I had probably made matters worse by doing so.

"I need to go grocery shopping," I said, letting my hands fall to my sides in defeat.

Maura grinned. "Great. So do I."

We walked to the market making small talk, without touching. I had already decided I wouldn't be the one to initiate physical contact, especially after what Maura had told me in the darkened SCAD classroom, but the lack of touch still felt like a minor rebuff. I couldn't stop thinking about the canvases hidden in the basement. Bits of those illustrations had crept into my dreams last night. Bloody gouge marks. A human spine unzipping into wet-red. Something told me not to bring them up with Maura, though—she'd obviously hidden them for a reason, just as she'd hidden her engagement to my brother.

Once we arrived at the store, Maura decided we should share a cart. She led the way around the perimeter of the store, filling the cart with exotic fare: quinoa, wasabi-brushed seaweed snacks, a tin of Himalayan pink salt. Quickly, I tossed in my own English muffins and Cracklin' Oat Bran, hoping she wouldn't notice.

She did. "Seriously? And to think you gave Dane such flak for his chicken nugget habit."

"Hey." I lifted up a box of Annie's mac and cheese. "I resisted the urge to get the bunny-shaped noodles. If that isn't the mark of a refined palate, I don't know what is."

"Speaking of a refined palate." Maura started pushing the cart again. "I have a call with the caterers tomorrow. Did I tell you I'm throwing a party for my clients in a few weeks? I'm still waffling about the appetizers. What do you think—stuffed mushrooms or mini quiches? Wait." She narrowed her eyes at me. "Maybe you're not the right person to ask about that."

"Party?" This sounded like the perfect opportunity to get the last bit of dirt about Maura that had eluded me. Maybe I hadn't been too successful plugging Matias and Odette for information weeks earlier, but I could do better this time around. I *had* to do better.

"Holly Elizabeth Chambers. I do declare." A male voice boomed, the last three words leaning into an exaggerated Southern drawl. My head snapped from Maura and her grocery cart, the fluorescent market lights making me blink hard.

His chest had grown broader since high school, outlines of muscles showing through the fabric of his polo. For a couple seconds, my eyes snagged in the salmon-colored material. Then I looked up. Had he always been this much taller than me? The shape of his face—stippled now with masculine shadow—was a punch of recognition.

"Eric."

He grinned, shoving one hand into his pocket. In his other, he held a shopping basket with a six-pack of beer and a single lime inside.

"My mother mentioned you were back in town," I said. "I just hadn't been expecting—this is such a shock."

Beside me, Maura stiffened.

Eric shrugged. "I guess I could've called before coming back, but there's something fun about that element of surprise, don't you think?"

I looked down at the scuffed floor. "Oh, sure. Wow."

Eric chuckled.

"When did you even get here?"

"A couple weeks ago. I'm renting a place near the river with Mitch. Howard. Remember him?"

"Mitch Howard. Right." The name transported me back to high school. "And my mom told me—you're working for your dad now?"

His smile turned almost contrite. "Yeah, it's come to that. But I'm trying to see the good in it. I missed Savannah." He paused and the smile faltered. "Holly, I heard about your brother . . ."

Oh, no. Not this. Not now. I looked back down at the floor. The wheel of a grocery cart had ground a black streak into the linoleum. "Oh. Yeah."

"I'm so sorry." He sounded it, too, which didn't help. "When my folks told me what happened, I couldn't believe it."

"Thanks, yeah. Me neither."

"Maybe . . . we could get together to catch up?"

"Okay." I forced a smile. "I still have the same number, believe it or not." Suddenly, I was acutely aware of Maura beside me. I still hadn't introduced her. What was she thinking, watching all this?

"Wow. To think that I could have texted you, all this time."

"You could have, I guess." I thought of unfolding Eric's note on my bed. *Remember eating raspberries in the cemetery?* Heat surged through me. It had to be painfully obvious to anyone watching that Eric and I had a history. Maura had to realize it, too. The thought made me squirm.

Eric shifted his shopping basket. "It was great running into you, Holly," he said.

Avoiding Maura's eyes, I watched Eric's Top-Siders disappear into the next aisle.

Maura didn't speak as we loaded our groceries at the checkout. Maybe there was a chance she hadn't noticed anything—what a relief that would be. I'd wondered how we were going to handle payment, as we'd been mixing our food in the cart, but now she took the lead placing her items on the conveyor belt.

"That's it," she told the cashier, after she'd set down the tin of Himalayan salt.

The silence had grown unbearable. "Sorry about that," I said, as Maura swiped her card. "That was a friend from high school. I'd heard he was back in Savannah but—"

"I know who he is." Maura didn't look up from the payment terminal.

"You do?"

"Yes. Dane told me that you and Eric were together nearly all of high school."

A dull headache blossomed at the back of my brain. *Shit.* Dane had not liked my ex. What had he called Eric? A "puffed-up rooster" in a charitable moment, an "arrogant asshat" in another. I could see how Eric's half smiles and passing-time swagger might rub a protective brother the wrong way. Especially when said brother was a scrawny nerd four years his junior.

"What else did he tell you?" I ventured.

Maura wouldn't even look at me. "You don't want to know," she said.

It was my turn to pay for my groceries now. I opened my purse, and my shaking fingers brushed satin: the drawstring pouch I'd found in the basement, holding Maura's teeth like an embrace.

It was a silent walk back to the townhouse. A light mist fell as we crossed the park. Every few steps, I snuck a glimpse of Maura's profile. Her shoulders were erect with her characteristic poise, jaw tight. These mood swings were becoming more disorienting by the day. And frankly, they were starting to piss me off.

I followed Maura into the kitchen to put away groceries. She kept her back to me, rearranging pantry items to make room. I watched the perfect dark waves of hair across her back. Had I really run my fingers through those locks? It felt like a small eternity ago.

When Maura moved on to the produce, I couldn't help myself. My voice came out more snappish than I'd intended. "What's your deal?"

She spun as if she was going to address me, and the side of her hip caught the carton of eggs, sending them over the counter and splattering onto the tile. "*Shit!*"

I ripped a handful of paper towels off the wall and approached Maura, but she rounded on me like a wild animal. "Just go," she snarled, pushing the paper towels away.

I left my groceries in their bags. On my way out of the kitchen, Maura said in a modulated voice, "I just need some space for a minute, okay?" But I was so far out of the room, it was as if she wasn't even talking to me.

I closed myself in my bedroom. Outside, the mist had changed to rain and tapped insistently on the windows. I shut off all the lights except the lamp on my bedside table and curled up against the mound of decorative pillows. Fragments of Dane's hidden paintings spun in my mind's eye like windmills. To distract myself, I pulled the satin pouch from my purse and yanked it open. I dug one tooth out and studied the surface. It was dark and gouged in places, as if showing the beginning of a cavity. Maybe Maura hadn't been able to reach all the way back into her mouth to brush it properly.

How would she feel if she knew I was seeing this rotten part of her? Had Dane even seen this? A thrill turned over inside me. For some reason this discovery made her seem even more beautiful to me, more human.

I heard the front door slam, sending a shudder through the doorframe to my own room. Maura was gone. The downpour started in earnest then, slashing at the windows.

My room suddenly felt very cold.

I grabbed a sweatshirt from my dresser and sat back down on the bed. Then I picked up the second wisdom tooth. This one was smooth, not as pocked with decay.

Good job, Maura.

I'd been stung by Maura's iciness in the grocery store, but turning these teeth over in my hands was starting to make me feel better. Connected to her again. It was almost as intoxicating as kissing her. The only difference? This time I hadn't been invited into Maura's secret world—I'd stolen inside. The realization left me with shame that felt like a hangover.

I put the teeth away, closed the pouch, and drew my knees into my chest as the pelting of the rain intensified. My stooped reflection looked back at me in the cheval mirror on the other side of the room, and I glanced away quickly. I hated being alone in this place, I realized. Hated the creaks and the echoes that spread from one room to another through the townhouse's brittle skeleton, the pulsing presence of Maura's en suite bathroom. I thought, for the millionth time, of my brother's paintings in the basement. For a moment, a freeze-frame flashed: Dane, lunging at me with the vegetable peeler.

It felt like I wasn't alone in that room.

Eventually, I eased myself under the covers. I wished the cheval mirror weren't facing my bed—I kept expecting to see something in it. I considered turning it toward the wall, but to actually get back up and adjust the furniture would be an admission of my fear. Instead I lay on my side, my breath loud in my ears, gripping the drawstring bag loosely like a child holding a stuffed animal.

It felt like forever before I finally succumbed to sleep.

CHAPTER 16

It was one of those sticky, quicksand sleeps that hinted at bad dreams to come. Several times, I tried to resurface—to wake up—but I was only pulled deeper under.

Fragments of dreams followed. Esther scooting a croissant over the circulation desk toward me. Rachel stroking the back of Henry's neck with a single sharp red nail.

All at once, I was sitting across from my brother at the bistro table. The basket of fries with its checkered wax paper lining sat between us. Dane ignored it, picking at his bloody fingers.

"Jesus," I said, "don't keep messing with them!" My voice was so shrill. I could feel my thighs sticking against the vinyl seat as I squirmed.

Dane looked up at me slowly—horribly—and both his eyes went black. I wished I could snatch my words away, but they hung in the air between us, taunting me.

Hastily, I backpedaled. "I mean . . ."

Dane kept staring at me as I fumbled for the right words.

Then he vaulted to his feet in the booth and flung himself over the table at me, hands reaching for my throat.

My eyes snapped open to the dark ceiling over my bed. I couldn't breathe; I couldn't move. Something was pinning my arms, crushing them against the mattress.

I gasped for breath, trying to scrape together a cry. If I couldn't activate my voice, how would I ever get help? My terror built as I flailed against the unseen force. Who—or what—was doing this to me?

I was absolutely powerless.

Amidst the panic, I thought I heard the thread of a whisper—something rhythmic, a snatch of a chant. Then a harsh staccato rained down on my collarbone, thundering through my skeleton.

Finally, I managed a scream.

Maura flung the door of my room open.

"What's going on?"

The merciless pressure vanished, and I flew upright. I sucked down air as if I'd never have the chance again. What the hell had just happened? I'd *never* experienced a sensation like that before. Never felt so completely and utterly . . . helpless. I pressed my fists to my eyes until I saw red. My thighs were still shuddering under the sheets.

When I'd finally caught my breath, I addressed Maura. The back of my mouth felt like Velcro, like I'd just run my first mile since high school gym class. "I don't know. I don't know what just happened. I woke up and I couldn't move, I couldn't breathe . . ."

Maura's eyes closed as if in recognition. She came and sat next to me on the bed, smoothing some of my hair away from my face. "Sleep paralysis," she said. "It's always terrifying the first time it happens to you."

I rushed to hide the teeth under the covers. I'd experienced sleep paralysis before and it *was* terrifying, but this hadn't been it. I pulled away from Maura's touch. "No, it wasn't that. I woke up and it felt like there was actually something *sitting* on me. Pinning me down."

"Sounds pretty textbook to me." Maura's lips flattened with sympathy. "Want me to get you a glass of water?"

"No." I shook my head. "I'm fine."

I couldn't even fathom telling her about the pounding on my collarbone. Speaking it aloud would make it too real.

Maura left me shaking, listening to the drizzle against the windowpanes. I'd never be able to fall back asleep. Not after that. I huddled under the covers, pushing the satin pouch to the opposite side of the bed. It was almost as if something had been reacting to those teeth, as if it didn't want me to have them.

I stared at the red-black behind my eyelids for a long time before sleep returned.

The residue from the night before still clung to me that morning, as I struggled to surface from sleep. I had a foul taste in my mouth and I could feel that I'd tangled my hair into a bird's nest snarl at the nape of my neck. My eyes darted around my lightening room. A bit of color flashed at me in the corner mirror: a small bouquet of yellow flowers. They were shaped like miniature trees. *What?* I blinked and the flowers seemed to falter; sleep swept back in like a tide and pulled me under.

I woke again an hour later and sat up, picking apart the knot of hair with my fingers. My dresser was bare. I must have dreamed the yellow flowers, just as I'd dreamed the Lenten roses before gardening with Mom. I got out of bed and dressed slowly, dreading coming face-to-face with Maura after yesterday's explosion. Even though she'd come to comfort me in the middle of the night, she was probably still pissed. Clearly she'd resented that I hadn't introduced her to Eric in the grocery store. Had she been—was it even possible?—*jealous* of him? I ripped my brush through the snarl in my hair until tears stung my eyes.

When I entered the kitchen, Maura was watering herbs on the window ledge with an antique watering can. She whirled to face me. "How are you feeling?" she asked. "I hope it's okay I put your groceries away."

Funny, how I'd started studying her tone of voice for traces of anger. This glorious morning, I didn't hear any. My relief felt like aloe vera on a sunburn. "Fine, thanks."

There was a pocket of silence. I knew Maura was struggling to apologize for freaking out. In earlier days, I might have closed the distance, making it easier for her. But today, I was too tired.

"Did you ever end up getting back to sleep?" Maura asked.

"Not really."

"I'm sorry. The creaks and groans of an old home take some getting used to, don't they?"

I put my face in my hands, fighting back a rising tide of anxiety. "There's a lot I'm still getting used to around here."

"Listen, Holly." Maura placed the watering can on the breakfast bar with a light *thunk*. "I'm really sorry I overreacted after dropping those eggs. You were only trying to help. I shouldn't have lashed out at you like that."

Maura's half apology didn't touch on her iciness in the grocery store after our run-in with Eric. Or throughout our interminable walk home.

"I think the other night, and especially at Dane's showcase, there were a lot of emotions running high," Maura went on. "A lot happened over the past few days, and I think it's probably best that we . . . take a step back. Let things mellow. Don't you agree?"

My anxiety seesawed into panic. "Take a step back?"

Was it just my imagination, or did Maura's lips twitch with a faint smile? "Well, yes. I think we both got overwhelmed talking and thinking about Dane. I just really miss him and . . . I might have gotten a bit confused. I'm sorry."

Fury pounded in my chest. I knew it would have been the right thing to nod, to go along with what Maura was saying. After all, wasn't I afraid of her? Hadn't I been hiding from her? Maura's words should have been a relief, but my mouth started moving of its own accord.

"Huh?" I heard myself say. "I don't get it. What about what you said to me back in the classroom at SCAD? That without me—"

Maura waved her hand. "I told you. That was an intense emotional experience for me, being back on campus, seeing Dane's work. I just . . . think we need to ease up. Chill out a bit."

My shoulders retracted into my body, blood chugging up past my sternum. How dare she? I hadn't even agreed to any kind of relationship with Maura, and yet here she was, jockeying for control by ripping away the very possibility. *Maura* was the one who'd lain in bed with those tresses spread out like black ribbons against my skin, planning our day together. *She* was the one who'd grabbed my wrists at my brother's showcase, pulled me into a dark classroom, and kissed me against the wall.

"Yes," I said, trembling as I bent over the table. "I think that's for the best."

"Good." Maura picked up the watering can. "Dinner tonight? I can cook us another yummy dish."

She didn't wait for me to answer. After she left the kitchen, I anchored my elbows to the table. For the first time in weeks, I was feeling that heaving sensation inside me again.

Get a grip, Holly. You didn't want this. You never *wanted this.*

My thoughts were becoming soupy. I tried to remember why I had proposed rooming with Maura in the first place. It took a few desperate, wheeling seconds to land on the memory of my father in front of his golf game. *Believe me when I say I'd do anything . . . to understand what happened to my son.*

I chanted the line to myself silently. Twice. Three times.

How many times before I started believing it?

CHAPTER 17

Two days later, while I was reshelving returns at work, a text came in from Eric. At first, seeing his name on my screen made my stomach flutter. But then I felt the crush of obligation. He wanted to get together. When was I free? Where should we meet? I couldn't help it; all the stacked-up questions exhausted me. I stalled until that night to respond.

I had to wait for the weekend to roll around before I had another chance to resume investigating the townhouse. Finally, on Saturday, Maura announced she was attending a client lunch. This time, I lounged on one of the velvet sofas, watching as Maura exited the townhouse, readjusted her beaded purse over one shoulder, and rounded onto the sidewalk toward the park. Once her figure had disappeared from view, I returned to her bedroom.

I stood for a moment in the doorway, bracing myself and smelling Maura's jasmine shampoo. No matter how many times I set foot in Maura's bedroom, it always ratcheted my anxiety into overdrive. Nowhere in the townhouse was Maura's presence so concentrated. Palpable. It plunged me into memories of touching and kissing her. It made me think of the closed en suite bathroom mere steps away, with its revolting tub drain and the flash of blood I'd glimpsed clawed over the porcelain.

I sucked down a breath and strode inside the bedroom.

This time, I went straight to Maura's walk-in closet. Behind her extensive dress collection and rows of shoes, I found a shoe-box full of items from her childhood. Small pastel notebooks crowded with bubbly middle-school-girl handwriting. Glass bottles of perfume—the old-fashioned kind with fabric bulbs to puff the fragrance. Even a glossy Polaroid featuring little Maura and, I guessed, her mother. I studied the image, shocked by her ordinariness. Maura's mom was doughy, with dark crescents under her eyes. How had a woman like that given birth to someone so electrifying? Little Maura had clearly fashioned the picture frame by hand with glued-together Popsicle sticks, topping her creation with dollops of paint that looked like storm clouds.

Along one side of the box lay a silver stick pin with a tiny seated bird on the end. I turned it over in my hands, gripped by a sudden, fierce possessiveness.

I stuck the pin in my pocket.

Diving back into the shoebox, my hand brushed against a smooth cream envelope lying on the bottom. I opened it. Inside was a piece of stationery, thick with pulp and bits of flower petals. The handwriting was whimsical and menacing all at once.

D,
Let's surrender to bliss . . .
N 32.0048° W 81.0910°
Yours,
M

My heart pounded. *D. Dane.* But what did the string of letters and numbers mean? It looked reminiscent of Dane's geocaching clues, not that I'd paid that much attention. I had no idea how he found the coordinates in real life. Was there some rule book out there? Some geocaching almanac? Or could it be as easy as . . . googling them?

It was worth a try. Shaking, I tapped them into my phone's search bar. It brought me straight to a map of Savannah, zooming in on a green trapezoid. The botanical gardens.

I rolled back onto my heels, letting the paper fall to the floor. What the hell did that mean, *Let's surrender to bliss?* Had Dane and Maura . . . been doing drugs together? I thought back to the SCAD students I'd seen at the showcase with their tasteful tattoos peeking out from necklines and sleeves, art-chic thick-rimmed glasses, and asymmetrical bangs. It didn't seem beyond the realm of possibility. But what did all of this have to do with the botanical gardens? A cutesy scavenger hunt date seemed benign enough, but something about the language made my scalp tingle. Could this be the game Dane had referenced in his text? I looked back down at the looping script on the beautiful invitation, then snapped a picture and shoved the invitation back into the bottom of the shoebox.

Minutes later, I was in my car, headed to the botanical gardens. I felt a sharp urgency to follow through on this particular clue—it was the most substantial one I'd gathered yet. As I drove, theories swirled. Maybe Maura had tempted Dane to do some kind of hallucinogen with her in the botanical gardens that had ultimately sparked his psychosis. I'd heard of drugs doing that. Could that be why Maura had been so secretive

about the night of Dane's death? Maybe she'd even manufac-
tured the drug herself from her plants. It would explain why
she'd hidden Dane's paintings in her basement, as if to erase all
signs of the mental breakdown she'd accidentally triggered. It
was a plausible theory and I felt my conviction gathering.

Now I just needed some kind of confirmation.

Once I parked at the gardens, my phone led me into the
rose garden, an explosion of pink-orange blooms ringing a
tiered fountain. A brick walkway encircled it all. I walked slowly
around it. Nothing looked suspicious or out of place. What had
I even expected? The scavenger hunt idea was kind of corny,
but it made sense: my brother loved geocaching and Maura
loved flowers. Why *wouldn't* they have come here? But the language on the invitation kept tripping me up.

Let's surrender to bliss . . .

A couple sat on a nearby bench, their fingers interlaced. Is
that what Dane and Maura had done? It unnerved me to imagine them sharing such a tender moment. What had *really* been
going on beneath the cutesy veneer of that scavenger hunt date?
I stared into the mass of flowers until my eyes lost focus. If
Maura had planted a clue for Dane here, there was no way it'd
still be around for me to find—right?

I glanced around. The couple was wholly absorbed with
each other; no one else was watching me. I stuck my hand inside
the fountain, feeling along the slick blue interior for another
clue.

Nothing, except a shock of cold water.

I shivered and wiped my hand on my shorts. Maura must
have had something planned for Dane once they arrived at the
gardens that night. But what? I returned to the orange flowers,
studying them for any anomaly. They all looked healthy, with

the exception of one close to the bricks. I reached out to touch it. Its petals felt just as velvety as the others. Why, then, was this rose so much darker, as if it had shirked all sunlight or water?

Crunching gravel made me spin. A groundskeeper in khakis and a straw hat approached the wall of roses with a pair of shears. Remembering the shears in Maura's greenhouse, I felt an edge of danger.

"Excuse me?" I called.

The groundskeeper looked at me. His eyes were dark.

I motioned toward the roses. "Do you know what type of flowers these are?"

"Hybrid tea roses," he said.

The name sounded so benign. I pointed to the singular darkened rose I'd found. "And do you know why this one—"

But before I could finish, the groundskeeper swept in and cut the blossom from the stem with a decisive *zing* of the shears.

"Whoa." I leapt back.

He shrugged, closing the clippers. "It's dead."

I didn't look at the groundskeeper. Instead, I knelt and picked the darkened bud off the ground before walking away briskly. The metallic *whisk* of his clipping shears started up again. Only once the sound had faded into the background did I stop to study the flower in my palm. All the while, I kept walking slowly, as if in a trance. I imagined a meditative Dane and Maura circling this same brick walkway, a rose garden transformed into a labyrinth.

Why did you take my brother here, Maura?

I was so absorbed in my thoughts that my toe caught on the lip of an uneven brick. The motion startled a bird crouching on the pathway. It reared into flight, leaving something slimy and tattered-looking below.

I came closer to study it. Revulsion brushed over my skin. The bird had left behind some rodent it'd been feasting on—a mouse or a rat. Its pink entrails blossomed with odd, textured dark polyps.

"Oh my God." I staggered backwards, dropping the rose in the grass. The words were hardly out of my mouth when I saw one pink foot twitch: the rodent wasn't quite dead.

Dane's voice rang in my ears: *Look at it. You owe it that much before it dies.*

But I couldn't look another second. I broke into a power walk, out of the rose garden and toward the parking lot. As blood crashed in my ears, the rodent's torn-open body swam against my eyelids. Something about those dark polyps looked familiar, but that was absurd—I'd never seen a torn-open rodent before. Still, they itched at me with their disturbing prettiness, like layers of black tissue paper folding gently away.

CHAPTER 18

That afternoon, I stood in front of the mirror in the guest room, tossing clothes onto the ground. My get-together with Eric had come at a terrible time. I wanted badly to cancel, but we'd gone back and forth for days trying to pin down a date that worked for both of us. I would have to buck up and push all unnerving memories from earlier that day to the back of my mind.

This was easier said than done. Since returning home from the gardens, my neurons didn't seem to be firing correctly; nothing I tried on felt acceptable. I'd already cycled through a nude high-waisted skirt (too matronly), a black scoop-neck dress (trying too hard), and a pair of cutoffs with a striped top (too childish). Eventually, I settled on the shorts, pairing them with platform sandals I was already regretting. Then I darted down the hall and across the living room to the front door. Maura had returned from her client lunch, and I didn't want her to see what I was wearing.

The cobblestones down to the river were perilous under

said platforms. Down the steep slope to the water, past the Rev-olutionary War cannons on display by City Hall. I clomped over the trolley tracks cutting through the center of the river walk and claimed a bench at our high school meetup spot. There I sat, dangling my legs and looking out at the gray water and the looming container ships. The low hum of a boat cut the briny evening air. I was sure it had been a tongue-in-cheek suggestion to meet here—Eric had always griped about the tourists clogging the waterfront, swarming River Street Sweets—but we'd still escaped to this spot more than a couple times.

"Finals week. Junior year." Eric slid in next to me on the bench. He'd had this freaky way of reading my mind from time to time, and it jarred me to see that this was still the case ten years later. "Wasn't that the last time we were here? Taking a study break?"

I looked sidelong at him. "Brings you right back, doesn't it?"

"Indeed." Eric followed my sightline to the sheet of water. I glanced at his leg next to mine on the bench. He'd worn jeans, the round of his thigh muscle straining against the fabric in places. When was the last time my body had been this close to a man's? Barring my father. It was embarrassing to contemplate.

"I have a confession," Eric said, turning toward me.

I jerked my eyes up from his lap to his face. "What?"

"I hated those Shirley Temples your mom served while we were studying. They were vile, way too sweet. I just kept forc-ing them down, hoping she would finally leave us alone."

I laughed, feeling relieved. There were only so many hours we could study in my room with the door open, Mom passing by again and again with the pretense of snacks and drinks.

What had I been expecting him to confess? "No such luck, my friend. Mom has always been a true Southern lady, hell-bent on guarding her daughter's purity." Too late, I wished I hadn't said that last part.

Eric didn't miss the way my voice wobbled at the end. He arched an eyebrow as he looked back over at the water. "Still?"

"Fortunately, I don't live at home anymore."

"Hallelujah."

"Tell me about your place."

"Holly Elizabeth Chambers, I will most assuredly tell you about my apartment. Plus everything else that you've missed." Eric stood and offered his hand. "But let's walk."

As we walked, he talked about his life over the past decade. None of it surprised me. Eric had carved out a place for himself at Tufts and gone straight on to law school at Boston College. "Short of being systematically abused by the 2L's, nothing of merit happened there," he told me with a shrug. I distinctly remembered a beautiful brown-skinned girl appearing in his Facebook pictures around that time, but I didn't bring this up. I wondered if he'd kept tabs on me like I had on him.

"What made you decide to come back to work for your dad?"

Another shrug. "It was time."

"You make it sound like it was part of your plan all along."

"I guess it was." That startled me. It didn't seem fair that Eric's return to Savannah had been a resolution, like the ends of a circle closing, while mine had felt like such a monumental personal failure.

We slowed to watch a knot of kids chasing one another around a giant sculpture of a globe. The continents shone in faded bronze. On the river, a boat piled high with wooden crates split a path through the water.

"How about you?" Eric said.

My face went hot. "What about me?"

"You know, your story. What've I missed?"

My discomfort surprised me. Dane had always faulted Eric for hogging airtime: *He's just one of those douchebags who loves the sound of his own voice.* Had there been a shade of truth to Dane's remark? Maybe. Like accidentally wearing a shirt inside out all day, the dynamic hadn't bothered me until someone else noticed. Now here Eric was, deliberately carving out space for me to share. And I wasn't sure I wanted it.

"Nothing really." I played with my split ends. "I had a hostessing job in Atlanta, but it sucked, so I ended up moving back in with my parents. Then my college roommate moved here with her fiancé, so I lived with them for a while. But now they're looking to buy, so I had to find somewhere else to live."

"Oh yeah? Where did you end up?"

"Right across from Forsyth Park. You can't miss us. We're the townhouse with the gargoyles."

Eric's eyes narrowed. "Gargoyles, huh? How's that working out?"

I paused. "I'm not sure yet. My new roommate is kind of . . . unstable."

"Uh-oh." Eric looked more delighted than concerned.

I laughed, feeling it was the only appropriate response. "Yeah. She has these freaky mood swings where she's super sweet one minute and jumping down my throat the next. I dared to touch one of her projects and she almost throttled me. In my defense, though, the rent is cheap. Oh, and I'm pretty sure the townhouse is haunted."

That made Eric burst out laughing. "Holly," he said at last, "that sounds like an absolute dumpster fire."

I bit my lip, half my mouth twisting into a smile. I hadn't been trying to make a joke, but even I had to admit my words sounded utterly ludicrous. "I guess I'd never heard myself say it out loud."

I was suddenly relieved to be here with Eric. His self-assurance edged into cockiness at times, yes, and clearly he was still tickled by my discomfort, as he had been back in high school, but I knew what to expect from him. Little had changed in ten years. He would be straightforward with me. He'd call my life a dumpster fire when it was merited. He was even-keeled, always hugging close to that emotional baseline.

There was something to be said for consistency.

Just as I felt my mood lifting, Eric sobered. "I'm sorry," he said. "With everything that happened to you this year, I shouldn't be laughing."

"No!" I swatted at him. "Please. Laugh away." I didn't want him to bring up Dane.

"I know I told you I was sorry back at the grocery store, but . . . holy hell. Your poor brother. I heard about what happened—how they found him—and all I can say is, he must have been very sick to have done that to himself. The guy I remember from high school would've never—" To my surprise, Eric's voice broke.

I looked away, feeling a chill come off the river. I'd grown somewhat inured to consolations, especially after Dane's funeral, but Eric was the first to lean so heavily into the grotesque details of his suicide.

Cleaved open, that was the terminology they'd used. Mom and Dad had begged me not to look at the pictures—I'm not sure I would've been able to even if I had wanted—but the absence of visuals only made my imagination run rampant.

As if he'd been trying to split himself in half.

"Yes," I said, because I felt I had to say something. I swallowed. "He was very sick."

Eric motioned to a bench by the side of the path. "Let's sit."

I did, even though I didn't want to.

"I know I only just came back to town," Eric said. "But I want you to know that I'm here for you."

The more I dealt with well-wishers after Dane's death, the more I came to understand that so much of what they said to me was for their own sake. Nothing against them—everyone needs to do what they must to process death. But sometimes it was exhausting, standing in as the grieving sister so that everyone else could unload their obligations and walk away lighter.

I forced a smile. "That's very sweet."

Eric sighed. "I don't know. Maybe it's more selfish." He ran a knuckle along the bench slat for a beat. When he looked back up, my stomach folded in half. Usually his irises were uniform, but in some moments, the rims turned diffuse and golden. I'd forgotten about this effect until just now. Back in high school, Eric had the power to obliterate my irritation with a single look or touch. It seemed little had changed there, too. Eric's first two fingers curled under my clasped hands. "Maybe it was a mistake for me to leave Savannah in the first place."

My heartbeat vibrated in my lips. Eric was so close I could have angled my face toward him and collapsed the space between us. Would my body remember his? *Remember eating raspberries in the cemetery?* It certainly wanted to.

A toddler cried out for his mother behind us.

I tugged my hands away from Eric's with an apologetic smile.

"It's getting late," I said.

. . .

Back at the townhouse, I took a scalding shower, leaning into the punishing spray. I thought about the cloying Shirley Temples back in high school and the golden rim around Eric's irises, and then I was thinking again of the weird black polyps flowering on that poor mouse's organs. Where had I seen them before? They were delicate and cone-shaped and had reminded me of tissue paper. Of cauliflower florets.

Of miniature roses.

Surely it wasn't possible. Could whatever I'd seen in the botanical gardens be linked to the black roses I'd stumbled upon in Maura's greenhouse? I still hadn't managed to figure out what those flowers even *were*. But maybe I hadn't tried hard enough.

Hastily, I rinsed the conditioner out of my hair, cut the shower, and toweled off. After dressing, I closed myself in Maura's library. I went first to Maura's immaculate desk, beside Dane's, and rummaged through the drawers. If Maura was manufacturing drugs as part of her mysterious side hustle, there had to be some evidence—receipts, POs, *something*. But there wasn't so much as a scrap of paper. Just three ballpoint pens in a pencil cup and a lime-green stress ball. I raked through my wet hair. Maura was too smart to leave evidence out in the open like that. If anything, it'd be on her computer, which she never left unattended.

I went over to the bookshelves and sat cross-legged in front of the botanical section. A wave of purpose washed over me. Even if I couldn't find evidence of her making drugs from her plants, I needed to figure out what those flowers were. I pulled out every book I hadn't already skimmed and searched the indices for "black rose." Each time, my frustration mounted. There was nothing.

How was this possible? I'd seen *multiple* instances of these black roses—once in Maura's bedroom under a bell jar, once in her greenhouse, and maybe even today at the botanical gardens, inside the dying rodent. And yet, according to Maura's extensive collection of botanical tomes, the varietal didn't exist.

My finger stopped on a spine in the bookcase. The letters were cursive, edged in foil. *Floriography,* it read. I hadn't noticed this one before. I slid the book out and turned to a page in the middle. There were illustrations of flowers, stunning and lifelike as Dane's diagrams.

I flipped to the first page.

For thousands of years, flowers have been utilized as a language of their own. This form of cryptological communication has appeared in ancient civilizations throughout the world, and took England by storm during the nineteenth century. At this time, floral arrangements became a powerful tool: a way for individuals to compose and send coded messages that bucked the constraints of Victorian propriety. It was not uncommon for Victorians to own "floral dictionaries" to decode the bouquets they received from others.

I paged through the exquisite illustrations. Something about this book was resonating with me. It called to mind the way Mom had taught me the names of the plants in her garden when I was little, the way she'd intoned them, giving each weight. Even as a little girl, I'd picked up on the hint of ritual. It meant something that Mom had chosen to share this language with me.

I stopped short on an illustration of familiar, treelike yellow blossoms. Where had I seen these before? Not Mom's garden—somewhere more immediate. I strained in my memory until it snapped into place. *My dream.* The one that had lingered, making it appear as if there was actually a vase of these blooms on my dresser. What were they called?

Goldenrods (*Solidago*): An exhortation to take caution.

Well, that didn't sound good. Remembering the goldenrods made my Lenten rose dream leap to mind, the one I'd had on the morning I'd prepared to garden with Mom. I flipped to the index. Lenten roses were on page 112.

Lenten rose (*Helleborus orientalis*): An indication of danger.

I felt the skin lift on the back of my neck. What was with these flower dreams? It had to be Maura's townhouse, filled to the brim with tumbling vines and trees and overflowing flowerpots. I couldn't escape them, even in sleep.

Finally, I found an entry for "black rose" in the index. I fumbled at the thick pages. Beside a blossom with red-black petals, a single line of text sat starkly on the page. After reading it, I felt even worse than I had walking into Maura's library.

Black rose (*Rosa 'Black Jade'*): Long associated with death and dark magic.

CHAPTER 19

I woke Sunday morning to gray daylight skewering through the narrow gap between the blinds and the windowsill. I could tell without looking it was one of those iron-colored days outside, the ones whose weight you can feel. I rolled over on my side, unready to be awake. I hadn't slept well. In fact, the longer I spent at Maura's, the sludgier my sleep was becoming—less like anything restful and more like a moody rumination on everything plaguing me. Maura's iciness. The violent presence in my room. Weird black polyps on the entrails of a dismembered rodent. Each day, it seemed more ridiculous that *I* had been the one who'd proposed moving in here.

To comfort myself, I reached for my phone to scroll through my text message chain with Dane. Ironic that this had become such an ingrained self-soothing mechanism, as our correspondence had such potential to disturb me. Case in point: in June, two months before his death, Dane had invited me to his friend's exhibit, whose work he compared to my favorite childhood book, *Where the Wild Things Are.* I'd pictured the monsters—gnashing teeth, bugging yellow eyes—and convinced myself they would lay the perfect groundwork for Dane's delusions. What if he had a freak-out at the exhibit? Started seeing the creatures lunging off the canvases?

Sorry, I'd lied, *got a girls' night with Rachel. Some other time?*

Dane had replied with a gif of a giant, shaggy monster-head crumpling in sadness. I'd forgotten about this, only to stumble upon the gif during one of my scrolling sessions. When I saw that deflating monster, it felt like my heart had been ripped out through my mouth.

Despite the land mines buried in our chain of text messages, it was my last remaining tether to my brother. And so, that morning, I began to meander through our old texts again, pausing on the lines and phrases that felt like an especially potent infusion of Dane.

One of the time stamps brought me to a stop.

Wait.

I flipped to my photos on my phone, the one I'd snapped of the back of Dane's exploding-figure illustration.

H.C.:
5/12/18 12:02 pm

Fingers shaking, I navigated back to our text message chain and scrolled—fast. Up, up, up to May, speeding past gray and blue bubbles.

I stopped. Dane *had* sent me a text on May 12. At 12:02 P.M. It was a single emoji: the sun. The text had gone unanswered; I didn't even recall receiving it.

How had this happened? Even if I had seen it, I wouldn't

have known how to reply. What did a single sun emoji mean, anyway, with no context or explanation? Could it have been a typo? Or was this Dane's psychosis starting to show? Uneasiness sizzled along my spine. There had been a certain comfort in knowing—in thinking—I'd been insulated from that.

How had I missed a message from Dane? I'd been going over and over our text chain daily—though, admittedly, I had been focusing more on the texts sent during the last week or so before his suicide. Maybe I'd glossed over it, dismissing the sun as a regular yellow smiley face. But it definitely wasn't. I stared at the sun emoji, its dagger-shaped rays stark against the screen. It reminded me of a medieval illustration that might appear on a tarot card. Something about its vacant eyes and smirk made my stomach tangle.

I stared at the mysterious emoji for a long time as the light in the room shifted around me and my stomach turned into a fist, until my hunger was, finally, impossible to ignore.

I ran into Maura in the kitchen. She had her hair swept up into a messy topknot, just like the day I'd first met her at the townhouse. With her face scrubbed of mascara, she looked more childlike.

I was unprepared for her glare. "Where did you go yesterday?"

"To my parents'. Why?"

"You're lying." Maura bit down on her index nail, a habit I was beginning to find off-putting. It made a hard clicking sound. "You were with *him*, weren't you? Your ex."

"What if I was?" I opened a cabinet in search of a cereal bowl with a little too much vigor. The door thwacked against the next cabinet with a sound that almost guaranteed chipped paint.

Maura didn't seem to notice. "Then I would tell you to cut it out. He isn't good for you."

"You know what?" I spun to face Maura. The heaving feeling was back, driving my blood against my wrists and temples. "I don't know what Dane told you about Eric, but it doesn't really matter. I'm twenty-six years old. I didn't sign up to live with a chaperone."

The comment flew out of my mouth unchecked; I feared, too late, that it would only fan Maura's anger. It seemed to do the opposite. Maura looked winded before dropping her gaze to the kitchen floor. She said something I couldn't make out.

"What?"

"I said, I don't like the way he looks at you."

"What's that supposed to mean?"

"He looks at you like you're a piece of meat. It's disgusting. It's like he's looking at you . . . without seeing you."

Where did Maura get these lines? I rolled my eyes, turning away from her.

"Dane told me about the way Eric treated you in high school," Maura went on. "I heard he went to a party and got wasted the night y'all had already decided to put down your dachshund. Mitzie, right? I mean, what kind of boyfriend does that?"

I felt a lash of sadness. It'd been years since I'd contemplated that terrible night. But then my grief shifted to spidery discomfort. I didn't like Maura saying the name of my childhood dog. What other personal tidbits had Dane shared with her about our family? About me?

Disoriented, I sat down at the table with my cereal and

bowl. When my eyes had refocused, I caught Maura studying my face with evident concern.

"Hey," she said. "Don't you need some milk? And maybe some berries for your cereal? Sit tight." She flitted to the fridge to pull the items she'd suggested. I was too distracted to fixate on the rapid shift in the room, the thawing of Maura's cold front.

"There you go," Maura said brightly, setting a carton of raspberries and milk in front of me. She poured the milk into my bowl and even dotted a generous number of berries on top of the cereal with my spoon. As if that weren't enough, she turned away to pour me a cup of coffee; when she presented it to me, I noticed she'd added exactly the amount of cream I liked. When had she picked up on that?

She is *really good at taking care of people,* I thought, reaching for my spoon. I had to hand it to her. I moved the oat frames around in my bowl, letting the milk soften them. Maura had come running when I'd woken from my "sleep paralysis." That eerie, chant-like whisper threaded through my head now. I'd been trying to force the memory from my mind, but every so often, when my guard was down, it leapt at me. I thought again of being pinned to the mattress, my collarbone assaulted. There was absolutely no explanation for that. *Except . . .*

I put my spoon down, feeling sick. "Maura? Can I ask you something?"

"Sure."

"Do you believe in ghosts?"

"Of course I do." Maura pulled out a chair and sat opposite me at the table. "We live in one of the most haunted cities in the country. I think the real question is, why *wouldn't* I?"

"Fair point."

"Do you?"

I chewed, calibrating my response. It felt alarmist to admit I suspected literal ghosts in Maura's home, so I'd have to keep things vague. "I don't know. This is going to sound weird, but it's almost like there are certain . . . situations that make my hackles stand up. Like, have you ever tried to flip on a light switch, but you don't quite hit it right, and the filament does this weird crackling thing that makes the room kind of light up, but not really? It's like this half second of in-between-ness . . ."

Maura closed her eyes and nodded. "What you're describing is the interstitial, and it's a real thing."

"The what?"

"Interstitial." She looked over her shoulder at the stove. "Do you have time for a cup of tea? I know I just made you some coffee, but . . . humor me. I'll explain."

Maura opened the same tea cabinet that stored the purple rosebuds she'd steeped the first day I'd visited. Now her hands closed over a different flat tin, with gold filigree around the lid.

"What's that?" I asked as she took pinches of wispy herbs and pressed them into two bulb-shaped metal infusers.

"Vervain. Think of her as the warden of those in-between spaces. Like doorways—halfway between one place and another. And dusk, midway between day and night. The Druids would only pick vervain when the sky was empty of the sun and moon. They believed there was something mystical about these kinds of transitional spaces."

Once she'd poured hot water over the infusers and let them steep, Maura handed me a cup.

I let it sit in front of me to cool. "You said 'think of *her*,'" I said, stalling. "You talk about plants like they're real people." If

I could get Maura to talk more about all her bizarre flowers, maybe I could steer her to explain the black roses.

"Yes, I guess that's how I think about the herbs and plants I work with, like characters, each with their own personalities and capabilities. Some of them are quite powerful, really. They certainly deserve respect."

"Like, which ones?"

Maura stared at me.

"Which are the most powerful, I mean," I amended, sheepish.

She gave me a judgmental look. "What do you want, some ranked list? Come on, Holly, that's ridiculous. All of my plants are powerful in their own right."

I looked down at the tabletop. *Okay, so that didn't work.*

Maura motioned at my tea. "Try it." She sipped her own, as if to demonstrate it was safe.

I took the smallest sip possible. It was far stronger than I'd expected.

I must have recoiled because Maura said, "Easy. I didn't pour us much, but you probably shouldn't even drink the whole thing. Vervain is all about coaxing out those parts of the mind and the world just outside our view. A few sips can be illuminating; a whole cup might have you spinning out."

"That's the very last thing I need," I muttered, pushing the cup away.

Maura laughed gently, nudging the teacup back toward me. "Come now. Who doesn't want a peek into those unseen worlds, every now and then? Why do you think kids spend so much time playing make-believe? You told me yourself you and Dane would spend hours wrapped up in your little stories."

"We did." At my brother's name, I thought again of the pounding on my collarbone.

"Those liminal spaces are just easier to access when we're children," Maura continued. "We tend to lose the ability once we grow up. Maybe it's because we grow self-conscious."

"Or maybe we just become afraid."

Maura's eyes flicked at me like a pair of cast dice. "That too."

I ran my finger over the gold plating on the teacup handle. Although I was sure Maura's anger from earlier had dissipated, the air felt prickly now for a different reason.

"You talk about these in-between spaces and junctures between worlds," I started slowly. "Would that include a link between our world and"—I couldn't believe I was going to say it out loud—"the spirit world?"

"Absolutely. That's what made me think to brew us the tea in the first place."

The hand that had been on my teacup handle jumped into my lap. For a minute or two, Maura and I sat in silence. I listened to her delicate sips and the ticking of the pipes in the wall as the townhouse next door turned on its water. How on earth was I supposed to ask her if my "sleep paralysis" had really been a run-in with a ghost?

"Maura," I said, "do you think there's any possibility that this place is haunted?"

Maura sat back in her chair. "You know about Old Candler Hospital, right?" She got up from the table, and for a minute, I thought she might be leaving the room. Instead, she rummaged around in the pantry and came back with a tin of cookies. She started to pry the top off.

I shifted in my chair at her mention of the hospital just south of Ridgewood Park. "What about it?"

Maura had succeeded in opening the tin. She stuck the edge of a cookie in her mouth and used her other hand to push the tin toward me. "During the yellow fever outbreak of 1876, they were completely overwhelmed. They didn't want to alarm the city by carting out stacks of corpses. So they did what any respectable hospital would do: they dug a secret tunnel underground to house the dead."

I felt a knock in the depth of my belly.

Maura turned to look out the kitchen window, with its cheery butter-colored valance, as if she were admiring a pretty bird at the feeder. Then she added, in a casual tone, "The tunnel runs from Candler Hospital underneath Forsyth Park. Right under this house, in fact."

I thought, with a start, of the small door I'd found in Maura's basement. The crawl space within. Surely . . . no. It wasn't possible. I hadn't been able to really see inside—it was probably just a dead end. I didn't want to indulge her by asking, but the question shot past my lips. "So . . . you're saying your place *is* haunted, then?"

Maura clinked her teacup down on her saucer and laughed, throwing back her head so her topknot keeled to one side. "Oh, Holly," she said, once she'd recovered. "I tell you these things in the symbolic, theoretical sense. You understand that, right?" Then she reached across the table and bopped me on the nose with her rolled-up napkin.

Was she messing with me again? That seemed needlessly cruel. And the presence in my bedroom? Maybe it *had* been sleep paralysis all along, just as Maura had claimed.

I was overreacting. Shame engulfed me.

Maura crinkled her nose at me as she smiled. "You really are adorable, aren't you?"

. . .

I wore Maura's bird pin with me to work that week, which was both a thrill and a crushing responsibility. I hadn't made up my mind yet whether I'd be returning it.

On one level, I felt ashamed for stealing Maura's things and wearing them out in public. It was creeper behavior to be sure, worse even than ogling Maura's ass in line at CVS. But the deep satisfaction I got wearing that pin superseded any shame. I wore the bird threaded through the side panel of my bra. Sometimes when I reached across the circulation desk for a pen or a piece of paper, the sharp end of the pin dragged against my ribcage. Later, in the bathroom, I pulled up my shirt to find three dotted lines of blood. *That* satisfied me. Maura had been haunting my mind for months—finally, I had a few physical marks to match.

I kept thinking about our talk over the vervain tea. Now it made me bubble with rage. How had Maura managed to make me feel so small and scared, when she herself was several years younger than me? I often forgot she was Dane's age—something to do with those whirlpool eyes, I'm sure, coupled with her exquisite posture. But back in Maura's kitchen, after being bopped on the nose and called adorable, I'd slunk from the table feeling both ashamed and—strangely—titillated.

I hated how she had that effect on me.

CHAPTER 20

Friday night, I was alone, reading a book in the living room. I was getting less and less comfortable using the common spaces in the townhouse when Maura was around. This was limiting. It meant having to wait until she left to lounge on the couches or cook meals that required more than just the microwave. Things with Maura had gotten so . . . tense. It felt easier just to avoid her, but that also meant that my habitable world was shrinking by the day.

A knock on the door made me jump. I tossed my book on the coffee table and went to answer it.

Eric stood on the front steps, looking up at the façade of the townhouse.

"Eric! What are you doing here?"

His eyes skipped to me and he smirked. "I was in the neighborhood."

"What do you mean? I never even told you where I lived." I shook my head. "Creeper."

"Sure you did. Townhouse across from Forsyth Park. With

the gargoyles. It wasn't hard to find. And honestly, with every-thing you've been telling me, my interest's been piqued." Eric looked past me into the foyer. "Aren't you going to invite me inside the haunted house for a tour?"

Oh, great. I tried to scrape up an excuse, but before I could, Eric had swept past me and into the house.

Good thing Maura was out.

Eric stood in the foyer, taking in the stained glass and exposed beams. "Damn," he said in a low voice.

"I know." Maura's home looked even more impressive now that she had added her elegant Halloween décor. White pump-kins marched up the porch stairs; candelabras with black taper candles sat on the mantelpiece, over a drape of black lace. Maura had brought in tall vases filled with twisting, gnarled branches that groped in the corner of every room. She'd even set a skull as a centerpiece on the coffee table, exploding with dark blossoms.

Eric turned back to me. "How much are you paying for your room here?"

I told him.

"That's it?" He let out a whistle. "Okay, it's official, your roommate is crazy."

I smiled for his sake, though bristled internally. "Crazy" was one of those words that took on a new meaning after Dane's death. I used to throw the term around, too. Back in high school, a couple girlfriends and I had gotten into TLC's *My Strange Addiction*, hungering to see those twisted psyches teased out in invasive interviews. A woman who ate insulation out of her attic walls! A guy sexually attracted to his pool toys! The more unhinged the individual, the more we delighted in it. We even made a mix CD to honor our Thursday night viewing parties, a clever riff on the theme. "Crazy" by Britney Spears. "She Drives Me Crazy" by Fine Young Cannibals. I listened to the CD nonstop that summer.

After Dane's death, though, the term wasn't fun anymore. It grew serrated edges.

Eric gestured impatiently. "Well? Aren't you going to show me around?"

I groaned. "Really, Eric? I'm not sure there's much to see." Hastily, I was making mental calculations. When had I noticed that Maura wasn't in the townhouse? How much longer did I have before she returned? I did not relish the idea of her coming face-to-face with he of the eyes who *looked at me but didn't see.*

"Seriously? I'm only in the entryway and already this place is blowing my mind. Screw the ghosts, I just want to see the rest of the goods." He was already headed for the living room.

I skipped forward to keep up with him. "You know, there's this really cute coffee shop around the corner—"

"Holy shit." He'd found the living room, overflowing with potted trees and hanging plants. "Is that—?" He pointed past the sofas to the sheet-covered glass doors.

"Yes, it's a greenhouse." Impatience made my voice snappish. This was typical Eric—homing in on my discomfort and capitalizing on it because he got such a kick out of watching me sweat. It was a character trait I hadn't loved back in high school, and it was infuriating now. "My roommate's a florist, but she's made it very clear she doesn't want anyone in her space. That's where I went when she . . . well. When she freaked out at me."

"Oh my God. Did she seriously hang a *sheet* over the door to keep you from seeing in?" Eric went right up to the door to study it.

"Eric! Don't." Maura had looked murderous the day she'd caught me in her greenhouse. If she saw *Eric* there?

She might just kill us both.

Eric gave me a devilish look over his shoulder. "Why not? What'll happen if I go inside? Is this where she keeps the ghosts?"

Before I could formulate a response, he'd twisted the handle on the door. Then he drew back, frowning. "Locked."

Relief surged inside me. "Told you." But at the same time, I felt a stab of worry. Hadn't the sheet on the glass been enough? Why *was* Maura so adamant about hiding her plants from me? She'd never locked the greenhouse before she'd caught me messing with her black roses. But maybe there was a viable explanation for this. Maura seemed to make a lot of money from her business, which made sense if she really was some kind of herbal drug-dealer. Could it be that she worried I'd soiled her flowers in some way by touching them?

"Come on." I motioned to him. "Let me show you the library. I think you'll like it."

"*Library?*" Eric let out a whoop that reverberated through the hallway. "Man, this just keeps getting better and better."

He quieted, though, once we entered the space. Clearly Eric was awestricken, just like I'd been the first time I'd set foot into the magic hush of Maura's library. "Shit," he said at last.

As Eric began to explore the rows of books and the scrolling ladder, I turned away with a secret smile. It felt good to see someone else enchanted by the space. I trailed my fingers along the wall of books, thinking back to the information I'd uncovered in the *Floriography* book. I imagined Maura behind the glass doors of her greenhouse, cooking up the illicit concoction that had sparked my brother's psychosis. Dark magic, indeed.

"Remember our library?" Eric's voice shattered my thoughts.

I fixed an innocent look on my face. "What about it?"

"Come on, Holls." Eric took a couple steps toward me. "Don't be coy. You've never been very good at that."

I flushed. Just like eating raspberries in the cemetery, those trysts in our high school library were ingrained in my memory. Most days it had been out of the question—too many groups of students studying at nearby tables and the roving librarian, looking for mischief-makers. I remembered the late-afternoon sunlight slanting in through tall windows, the smell of yellowed paper and dust. Book spines digging into my own as Eric pressed me up against the shelves . . .

I shrugged one shoulder, looking up at him. "Okay. Maybe it's coming back to me now."

"Yeah?" A wry smile.

"I think so."

We were very close now, my back to the wall of books. When had Eric's shoulders gotten so wide? His gaze jumped from my eyes to my lips, and back again.

Hungry.

Suddenly, I needed to feel the crush of his body again. I reached out, hooking a finger through one of his belt loops.

It was all the invitation Eric needed. He took my face in his hands and I went molten at his touch. Something unfurled inside me, feeling the softness of the inside of his mouth, the familiar bite of the bookshelves in my spine. God, why had I resisted this?

After a minute, I pulled away, heart galloping against my ribs.

"Well," Eric said, stuffing his hands in his pockets.

I looked down at the ground. In a quiet voice, I asked him, "Should we finish the tour down the hall?"

Eric's eyes went round with understanding.

I took his hand. On our way out of the library, we passed by Maura's desk.

"The fuck?" Eric said under his breath, pulling his hand away.

This book hadn't been here the last time I'd investigated the library. It was an old volume with curled pages, cramped text, and black-and-white illustrations. The opened page bore the title: *The Ancient Practice of Leeching.* Figure 45A showed the underside of a leech, its gaping maw ringed with needlelike teeth. There was a picture below it of a person's forearm suctioned over with the glistening, alien-like creatures.

"Jesus," Eric said, shaking out his shoulders. "That is some creepy shit right there."

That was an understatement. What was Maura doing, reading about *leeches*? Something cold filtered into my veins. The image of the fanged leech itched at me, raising a fragment of a memory. Something I couldn't quite place.

I rushed Eric out into the hall, toward my room. It would be a welcome distraction for us both.

There was something intoxicating about living out the adult version of our relationship, a version that had been off-limits in high school. Back then, I'd cobbled together scenes from romantic-comedy montages to inform my fantasy: I'd wear a sheet like a strapless dress and have rumpled sex-hair; the sunlight would shift over our entwined bodies, marking the passage of time. But by nine that evening, my window showed a square of night sky and I'd long since given up on the sheet pretense. I lifted a hand to my head. At least I had the sex-hair down.

I grabbed the mason jar of tiny, folded notes and placed it on the comforter in front of Eric. I waited to gauge his reaction, wearing a mischievous expression of my own.

Recognition flashed across his face and then he covered his eyes. "Oh, God. I can't believe you still have that. I'd been hoping you threw it out."

"Throw it out? How could I?" I opened the lid and ran my fingers through the little sandwiches of paper.

"Stop it, stop it." Eric snatched the jar from me.

"Why are you so *embarrassed*!" Now it was my turn to enjoy his discomfort.

Eric reached inside and plucked out a slip of paper. His eyes were intense as he unfolded it. "Whew, okay, this one isn't that bad." He barked out a laugh. "Oh my God. Remember this?" He flashed his pointy high school writing at me, bracketed by scrawled-in music notes:

There's a big white stretch mark right outside, and no one there to share your ride

It was an allusion to my butchering of the Nine Days song. Eric had heard me singing along in his car and actually had to pull over he was laughing so hard.

"Big white stretch *parked*," he'd said, gasping. "As in, a stretch limo. Oh my God."

Self-conscious of my own singular stretch mark that had appeared on my butt around seventh grade, I'd been positive the song was about a woman rendered undesirable by one of those pesky white gashes. I'd looked down at my lap in Eric's car, hot with shame. Though Eric and I had been a fairly functional couple—at least when Eric was paying attention to me—there'd been something irresistible about cracking each other open like Easter eggs to find genuine abashment inside. If it weren't for this dynamic, I doubt we would've gotten together in the first place. Eric and I had moved in different circles in high school. A group project on nuclear fission had sparked hours of delicious banter. Later, Eric admitted to me he'd been pleasantly shocked by the way I—unlike many others in his orbit—dared to poke holes in his ego.

"I can't read any more of these," Eric said, closing the mason jar. "It's too cringey. God, I was such an idiot."

"Were not." I snatched the jar away from him, cradling it to my chest. "It's one of the sweetest things anyone's ever done for me."

Eric's eyes were far away. "Ugh. The things I'd do back then." He looked down at his fist and I knew what he was seeing: a tiny white scar on his second knuckle. He'd gotten it punching a locker outside our homeroom. Onlookers had probably thought swaggering Eric Monroe had gotten back a less-than-stellar grade on his midterm or butted heads with his lacrosse co-captain after a scrimmage. Only I knew the truth—that my boyfriend had just stumbled upon Facebook pictures of his blond half brothers he hadn't known existed. Eric's mother, beauty queen and star of an Activia commercial filmed in Atlanta, had left Eric and his father when Eric was four. The portrait of her "replacement family"—all overlapping front teeth and patchy sunburns from the Santa Monica pier—hadn't landed well.

Now, I ran a finger over Eric's knuckle. I felt like I was supposed to say something, but each time I started knitting together the words, claustrophobia squeezed up my throat. Instead, I tugged at Eric's arm. "Come on," I said. "Let's order takeout. Or take a walk."

Eric buried his head in my pillow. "Too tired," he mumbled. Then he reached for me, pulling my head into the groove in the middle of his chest. "You fit here so well," he said, running a finger down the part in my hair. His touch made me shiver. "You're cool with me staying the night, right?"

I hesitated. I still hadn't heard Maura return to the house. But what if she did and found Eric here? Then I felt a burst of righteousness. *Screw her.* She didn't have the right to tell me who I was allowed to see, to bar people she didn't like from visiting me. She was not my mother. Besides, Maura had been the one wanting to "take a step back."

"Yes," I told him, trying my best to sound definitive.

"Good. Because I've been having nightmares." Now his voice was flirtatious.

"Poor baby. You're in good hands." I paused, glancing at the cheval mirror across the room. I'd kept looking over at it for the past couple hours, especially as the light outside waned. "What are the nightmares about?"

Eric's body shifted beneath me. "Actually, I don't remember. I just don't like them."

"That's generally how nightmares work."

"Tell me about yours."

"My what?"

"Your deepest nightmares." Eric gave an evil laugh, his grip shifting to my hips under the sheets.

I clamped my legs together tight. "I'd rather not."

"No?"

I twisted a piece of hair in my fingers. Why was he pushing this? "Well. I've been dreaming a lot about Dane, actually."

Eric must have sensed my disquiet, because he started rubbing my back. Up and down, rougher and less refined than the little circles Maura had traced on that same skin. Immediately, I felt a jab of frustration for making the comparison.

"Holly," Eric said after a bit, "your housing situation probably isn't helping. You really should consider looking for a new place. One where your roommate isn't a leech-obsessed psycho."

Irritation stung me. "I know," I said, "I know. I'm just not ready yet."

"Not ready yet? What are you waiting for?"

I thought for the millionth time of the information I'd been steadily amassing. The invitation in Maura's shoebox. Dane's unnerving artwork in the basement and the sun emoji it had led me to. The black roses under Maura's bell jar and inside the tattered mouse carcass. These strange, thrumming flowers had to be involved in the drug Maura was making in her greenhouse. I *had* to stay, especially when I was so close to breaking new ground. "I'm not sure. It just . . . doesn't feel right to leave at the moment. It's hard to explain."

Eric's silence was heavy with judgment. I squirmed against the urge to defend myself. Back in high school, I probably would have.

A few minutes passed. I whispered, "I'm hungry. Should we make scrambled eggs or something?"

Eric lay immobile beside me, his lips parted in sleep. It seemed I'd be on my own scrounging for food. I slid out from under the covers and reached for my crumpled clothes on the floor.

I took wide steps to cover the hallway as quickly as possible, the floor icy against the balls of my feet. Maura's bedroom door was closed—she must have returned from wherever she'd been. Once in the kitchen, I rooted in the fridge for butter and a carton of eggs, then scrambled the eggs with a spatula straight in the frying pan. When finished, I stood with my back to the heating pan, watching the dark expanse of the living room and thinking about Eric.

Being with him had felt like returning to a warm bed. He was different enough from high school—those cutting calluses, the new broadness of his chest and shoulders—to provide glimmers of excitement. But even in the moment, I'd surprised myself by cataloging sensations and comparing them to my night with Maura. I missed the give of her lips and butt, the startling smoothness of her inner thigh and the way she'd sighed against me. With Eric, we'd raced to the finish; with Maura, the pleasure had been so exquisite and protracted it was almost painful.

Exquisite and painful: that was the Maura aesthetic for you. I thought of Maura drinking her pastel coffee she drowned with cream. Wearing her filmy dresses, ballet flats, and little braids in her hair at the temples. It was all clever sleight of hand to trick you into thinking you were dealing with something soft. And when you finally felt the teeth underneath the silk—yeah, you'd recoil at first.

But eventually you'd be back for more.

It didn't seem fair. After experiencing Maura, I was sure everyone else would pale in comparison. If it weren't for her insistence that we take a step back, would I have even entertained sleeping with Eric?

Unlikely. The truth? I'd rather be entangled with Maura in her bed right now.

I pressed my eyes shut. Why was I doing this to myself? There was no reason to think of Maura in this way. It was infuriating to see she'd had the power to sully my night with Eric when she wasn't even there.

I forced down the scrambled eggs while seated at the kitchen table, still staring into the dark living room. The streetlights backlit a vase of groping branches, casting clawed shadows against the wall. A knot of anxiety tightened in my chest. I wondered when Maura had come home, if she'd heard Eric and me at all. But I was torturing myself, thinking of her and sitting alone in this eerie space. The refrigerator shuddered into a robotic drone behind me. I cleared my plate in a few more bites, set it in the sink, and hurried back to bed.

That night, I dreamed again of Dane. As his mouth widened, the pressure bearing down on my own body intensified. I struggled away in my dream. But I was forced to watch. I always had to watch.

Eric shook me awake. "There's something here," he said.

Was I still dreaming?

"We need to leave," Eric said. I could see the whites all the way around his irises.

"What are you talking about? What's here?"

"I don't know. We need to get out of here."

"What? Eric, come on. It's the middle of the night. Go back to sleep."

"No way in hell. I'm getting out of here. You can stay if you want."

My body was raked by cold needles. He was serious. Had he experienced an encounter like I had? Woken to something bearing down on him, squeezing the breath from his lungs? I was too afraid to ask. "Fine, I'll go with you. You're driving, though."

Still dulled by sleep, I staggered out of bed. My left arm prickled like the dead weight of a sandbag. I shook it violently in an attempt to force blood and sensation back in. Eric already had his sweatshirt on. He kept glancing over his shoulder at the dark mirror.

"There's something here," he said again.

I wished he'd stop saying that. It made me forget how to breathe properly. "I'm just throwing on some clothes, okay?"

Eric said nothing.

I scrabbled at the handles on my bureau and the drawer came tipping out. Sleep was sloughing off me now; my hands trembled with adrenaline. I avoided my own face in the mirror, but out of the corner of my eye I glimpsed the muscles in my neck, stark against the hollows. It looked like the neck of an old lady.

"Holly?" Eric said. There was an edge of desperation in his voice.

We left my room and moved through the hallway to the front door. "It's okay," I said, turning to him. "We're out of the room now. You probably just spooked yourself in the mirror after waking up from a nightmare. I do that all the time."

"No," Eric said. He sounded hoarse, and I realized his pupils were huge. Impossibly huge. "I think it's following us. I just felt it touch me."

Iciness seeped through me. "Let's just get to the car, okay?"

The hallway appeared longer than the rules of physics should allow, as if we were looking at it through a fish-eye lens.

"It's like I can't see right," Eric said.

I took his hand. "I know, it's dark." I led him forward, past the darkened library, farther and farther from Maura's closed bedroom door.

We were in the living room now. Through the French doors, I could see the black heads of oak trees shivering, their scarves of Spanish moss stirring in the night.

Eric was wringing the sensation from my arm, turning it back into a deadened, sand-filled limb. I squirmed out of his grip and shook my hand out, wincing. "Sorry."

He reached for the front door. "Where the hell are the locks?" he whispered, feeling the wood.

"Chill, I got it." I stepped in front of him, feeling in the dark for the dead bolt. Eric watched me, shifting from one foot to the other.

"I don't feel so hot," he said.

"I know. We'll get you home soon."

Finally, I found the dead bolt and flipped it free. The last lock was on the doorknob itself. Every other front door I'd experienced unlocked automatically when you turned the handle. But for some reason, Maura's didn't. It added one more step, made it that much more difficult to escape in a moment of panic.

Beside me, Eric made a sound like a gurgle. Then his body crumpled against the doorframe before sliding to rest on the hardwood.

"Eric! Oh my God!" My voice was a whisper-hiss. I knelt by his body, feeling his face. Sure enough, his forehead was blazing. "Eric, wake up. You're really sick. We need to get you back into bed."

Eric's eyes rolled under half-mast lids, as if he were dreaming. Horror lanced through me—what if he didn't wake up?

But a beat later his eyes flipped open. He stared at the ceiling, dazed.

"God, you scared me. We need to get you back into bed, okay? Get some fluids in you, make sure you get some rest."

Eric gripped my hand, hard. "I don't want to go back in that room."

What had he seen in the guest room? Did *I* want to go back? I ran my tongue over dry lips. No—Eric was clearly febrile. He was imagining things, just as I had. "Come on. You'll feel better in the morning. I promise."

This time, Eric didn't fight me. Taking my hand, he let me pull him to his feet. I flipped the dead bolt on the door and guided Eric back toward the guest room, despite an uneasy seed in the pit of my stomach telling me we were headed the wrong way.

CHAPTER 21

E ric fell asleep almost instantly, leaving me to stare at the ceiling and listen to his husky breathing. I placed a hand on his forehead, the way my mother would when I was a kid, and was relieved to find that much of the heat had dissipated. About an hour later, he started thrashing about, ripping the covers from my body, soaked with sweat. His fever—whatever it was—had broken. Finally, at five-thirty, I gave up on sleep and went to make myself a cup of tea.

The trip to the kitchen was exhausting—more dark rooms and hallways to traverse as I tensed for flight. My eyes jumped away from every reflective surface: the stainless-steel fridge, a peek of mirror from the hallway bathroom. Would I ever sleep through these haunting hours again?

I stopped short in the entrance to the living room. A hunched figure sat on one of the settees.

"Maura! What are you doing up?"

She turned to me. The skin below her eyes strained. "I know he's here."

"Who?"

She lurched off the couch. "Don't screw with me. You know who. Your ex. He's in your bedroom."

I backed a couple steps away from Maura. As I spoke, I tried to press the tremor out of my voice. "He has a name, Maura."

"I don't give a fuck what his name is."

I felt myself recoil from her expletive. But then my resolve strengthened. That was it. This couldn't go on anymore. "What the hell is your problem? You are my roommate, okay? Not my mother. Not my chaperone. I'm allowed to have my own life. You really need to chill out."

Maura was silent for a terrible, suspended minute. She laughed, low and hollow. "I need to chill out," she repeated.

"Yes. I think you do."

Then she was approaching me in the dark, her center of gravity low like a stalking cat. Before I could bolt, Maura caught my wrists in both hands. She gripped them, nails burrowing into the tender flesh, until tears burned in my eyes. I turned away from her, wincing; a flare of her hot breath caught on the edge of my face.

"This is my home, Holly. Lest you forget, *I* was the one who so graciously invited you inside. And I am telling you now: your ex is not welcome."

I was mortified to feel a sob rip from my mouth. Maura dropped my wrists and I clasped them to my chest, massaging the searing skin.

"Oh," Maura said, her voice sloping into genuine concern so quickly I felt whiplash. "Please. Please don't cry."

My entire core quivered; I was going to fall apart. But to do so in front of Maura would be humiliating. I dredged strength from somewhere subterranean. "Eric isn't feeling well, but he's finally asleep and I'm not waking him up. I'll tell him to leave in the morning."

Maura looked at me. I braced myself for a challenge, but it didn't come. In that instant, I felt a second burst of courage. Keeping my growing unease to myself was getting to be too much. "To be honest," I said, "you're really starting to freak me out."

Maura gave me a dangerous smile. "What makes you say that?"

My mind brimmed with all the unnerving clues I'd been gathering. I didn't even know where to start. "Those . . . those black roses I saw in your greenhouse. The flower you put behind my ear the night of Odette's party. It left *bite marks* on me, did you know that?" My teeth clamped my lower lip as the pieces slotted together in my mind. "There's something weird about the plants in this house, Maura. Really weird."

Maura shook her head, the side of her mouth lifted. Her eyes rose to meet mine like two black buoys. "Oh, Holly," she said. "Sometimes I really wonder what's going on in that haunted little head of yours. It must be a scary place, with all those skeins of make-believe and fantasy tangling you up. Just like your brother." Then, before I could prepare myself, she took my chin in her hand and drew my face to hers. Her lips were a sour thrill—one I'd spent too much time telling myself I'd never feel again.

Maura pulled away. "Just like your brother," she said again, touching her tongue to the edge of her mouth. "Except, you know what?" She studied me in the dark. "I have more hope for you."

Maura left me trembling in the living room, turning her

words over in my mind, touching fingertips to my wrists, to my lips, and back again.

Eric woke around eight. Beside me, he shielded his face with a hand.

"How are you feeling?" I asked him.

He pressed his eyes shut. "Ugh. My eyes hurt. Is it just me, or is it super bright in here?"

I went to the window, closing the drapes more tightly. "You probably have a migraine. You had a rough night last night. I'll drive you home. You should plan to spend all day in bed, okay?"

Eric rolled over, groaning. "I feel like shit. Much as I don't want to stay here . . . can I just hang out for an hour or two? Sleep this off?"

I bit my lip. "Normally, I'd say no problem. But we've got a bit of an issue. My roommate . . ." I hoped that would be enough, but Eric looked at me expectantly. "She doesn't want you here," I finished. "I'm sorry. I told you she's weird like that."

"What? That's messed up." Eric sat up against the head-board. "She can't bar me from staying over."

With Eric directly facing me now, I noticed something I hadn't before. "Eric," I said, elbowing the fear from my voice. "Let me see your eye for a sec?" I jumped onto the bed, taking his chin in my hands. My breath hitched.

Eric's pupils had consumed his irises, turning his eyes completely black.

"What?" Eric demanded, pushing me away. His voice was cross, but I knew he'd heard my sharp intake of breath. He was headed for the mirror in the corner of the room, and I felt an urgent need to warn him what he was about to see.

"Eric—"

With his index finger, he pulled his bottom lid down to study his bared eye. Terror flashed in his face. "Jesus," he said, under his breath.

"Did . . . did you sleep with your contacts in or something?"

"Fuck, no I didn't, Holly!"

"Okay." Someone had to be the calm one in this situation. I sucked in a shaky breath. "Get your stuff. I'm taking you to Urgent Care. Now."

"Ugh." Eric turned away from the mirror. "You know I can't stand hospitals."

I motioned back to the mirror. "Did you see what I just saw? Your eye is completely *black*, Eric. I'm taking you. No questions."

For the second time in the span of mere hours, I was startled that Eric didn't fight me.

After a couple hours, they finally took Eric in at Urgent Care. I sat alone in the waiting room, jiggling my foot and ripping at my cuticles, trying to decide what to do next. Maura had crossed a line last night. Most people would have taken that as an indication to move out, and part of me was tempted to do just that. But I couldn't give up; I was far too close to figuring out what had happened to Dane. I decided to stop by Mom and Dad's after dropping Eric off at his apartment—maybe there I'd be able to think more clearly. Plus, if I gave Maura a day or two to cool down, maybe everything would be stabilized by the time I returned.

Eventually, Eric slunk back into the waiting room clutching a prescription for eye drops and a referral for an ophthalmologist. He seemed relieved to have the medication; taking my cues from him, my muscles uncoiled a degree or two. Still, we drove in relative silence back to Eric's apartment.

Mom and Dad were still eating a late brunch when I arrived at the house that afternoon. Mom placed half a grapefruit on a plate, drizzled it with honey, and set it in front of me. As I sawed at the pink flesh with the serrated spoon, I felt my parents' eyes on me. I never showed up unannounced.

"So, I'm thinking about looking for another apartment," I said, after my third bite of the fruit. I tried to shape the words to sound as casual as possible.

"Why would you do that?" Mom said. "You've only been at your new place . . . what, a month and a half?"

I squirmed. "I know, and I haven't made any decisions yet. But I don't know . . . I might want my own place. A one-bedroom, if I can swing it."

Mom frowned. "Can you even afford that?"

"I'm not sure."

"Whatever you need to do, Holls," Dad said.

"Thanks, Dad. Would it be a problem . . ." The words stuck in my throat.

"Hmm?"

"If I do decide to move out—which I haven't yet—would it be okay if I stayed with y'all for a little while? I'm not sure I have enough for a security deposit right now—"

"Holly. Of course." Dad cut me off with a wave. "You know you don't have to ask. This is your home." Across the table, Mom fiddled with her napkin, giving it a sharp twist in the middle before draping it over her grapefruit carcass.

"Thanks." It was nice to know I had a contingency plan if needed, but any way I cut it, leaving Maura's before I was truly ready would still signify a failure. A lump rose in my throat and I pushed my grapefruit away. Suddenly, it was all too much—my night with Eric, him collapsing in a feverish heap by the door, my charged encounter with Maura. A headache pounded at the base of my skull. How many hours of sleep had I even managed last night? Three? Four?

"I think I'm going to take a walk around the neighborhood. To clear my head." I stood to put my plate in the dishwasher.

"Stop in the yard on your way back," Mom said. She gave me a frail smile. "You'll want to see the colors of the hydrangea petals before the temperature drops and kills them all."

I found a quilted vest in my closet upstairs and layered it over a flannel. Then I slipped out the front door and tipped my head up. The sky was a white sheet, sterile and infinite. As I walked, I found myself stroking the bruises on my wrists. Maura had contorted into some unrecognizable creature last night; it still made my skin prickle remembering it. She'd lunged at me. *Hurt* me. I couldn't stop replaying the hot flare of her breath against my face. And then her urgent lips on mine.

I wasn't sure I could muster the courage to return.

I glanced down at my phone, checking for any texts from Eric. He'd been really pushing me to move out. But the more I thought about this, the angrier I felt. I contemplated the patchy grass between the sidewalk and the street, dragging a toe through it. Frizzled, with dirt showing through like bits of scalp, it looked diseased. Why should Eric be able to sweep back into my life and tell me where to live? Yes, some of his concerns had proven to be legitimate, but I had decided to room with Maura for a reason. And I still didn't have closure about Dane.

Dane. It was impossible to escape his presence here at Mom and Dad's house. When I was ten or eleven and banished to my room for yelling back at Mom, Dane had taken it upon himself to free me with a "get out of time-out" potion. He'd filled a recycled ketchup bottle with tap water and added "magical" odds and ends scavenged around the house: a rusted screw, a broken matchstick, a pinch of glitter. He'd passed by my closed door every so often to update me on his progress, promising me it would be ready to drink soon. Luckily, I was freed from captivity before the potion was complete.

Something inside me squeezed at the memory. It gutted me to think that fifteen or so years later, that earnest, dark-haired boy would be a not-quite man, racked by inexplicable illness and ripping a steak knife through his own abdomen.

I needed answers.

On the way back from my walk, I stopped in the yard as Mom had suggested. I walked over to the hydrangeas. Their petals were the colors of a bruise; when I took one between my fingers, it felt mossy and alive.

Mom had clearly spent a great deal of time in the garden this summer. The beds overflowed with velvety lamb's ears, black-eyed Susans, hosta, and balloon flower—amazing how the names swam back to me from my childhood. Mom would mulch and weed as Dane and I played in the grass. By the back-door was a bush dotted with the berries we used to pick and bury like treasures. What were they called? I could still feel them between my fingers, squishy and red, with a mean dark pit. The sundial lay nestled in the lawn, partially obscured by a spray of ornamental grass. It depressed me to think that within a few weeks' time, all of this vibrancy would be brown and curled to the ground.

I approached the sundial, contemplating its face. Twelve-fifteen on the dot. My eyes extended the line of the shadow off the sundial and into the yard. If Dane and I had been playing our game now, we'd be rushing to bury the red berries in the corresponding mint plant. It was wild how familiar the sundial face seemed, even though I hadn't really looked at it since I was a kid.

Something jolted in me. I ripped my phone from my pocket and scrolled up to Dane's mysterious text sent on May 12. I held the sun icon next to the stone disc. The emoji was almost an exact replica of the sundial, with the same heavy-lidded eyes and jagged rays that pointed into the perimeter of the garden. Then I dropped to my knees in the grass, clearing debris away from the dial's face to find 12:02: the time Dane had indicated on the back of his illustration.

With a shaking finger, I traced a line out from the 12:02 mark, through the grass, and into the flower bed. I squatted, just as Dane and I would have done playing in the garden as kids. The imaginary line intersected a stubby bush. I ripped off a leaf to smell it. Thyme. I made a few moves to peer between the leaves and then stopped, feeling ridiculous. What was I even looking for? A message in a bottle? A scroll? Then I rolled back onto my heels, bracing my hands on my thighs. No, if Dane had really intended to leave me a message, he wouldn't have placed it in the open, where anyone could find it.

I looked around the garden. Mom had left out a wheelbarrow. In the compartments by the handle sat a pair of rumpled gardening gloves and a spade. I grabbed the small shovel and cleaved up dirt around the edges of the thyme plant.

Dane, Dane, Dane. What are you trying to tell me?

I dug until I'd passed the last wispy ends of the thyme plant's root system. There was nothing in the soil except for a round, translucent pebble and a couple earthworms. I cradled the stone in my palm for a moment, rocking it back and forth. Then I thrust it back into the earth and pushed the soil into place.

I redrew the imaginary line from the sundial into the herb garden. Had it been pointing instead to the nearby lavender? I glanced back at the spade. The prospect of uprooting yet another of my mother's plants felt exhausting and pointless. This wasn't right. This wasn't what Dane had meant.

I returned to the sundial and traced another line out from 12:02. This time, I passed the lavender and strode deeper into the planting bed. Behind the lavender, behind a couple other unidentifiable herbs, was a birdhouse sitting atop a stake in the soil. Mom had bought it at a craft fair years ago. It was pale and weathered by now, with two sets of faux shutters glued to the front. A bit kitschy, if I was being honest. I placed my fingers on the shingles—bits of spiderweb clung to the rough wood—and jiggled the box gently.

A rasp sounded from within.

I plunged a finger inside and felt something dry and papery. Too late, I imagined I might have jabbed right into the heart of a wasp's nest, but no stings came. The papery thing shifted around inside the birdhouse and lodged into a corner. I tried again, using my index finger to scrape the object up and off the bottom of the wood. Then, gingerly, I pulled it through the tiny circular hole.

It was a slip of paper with an address penciled on it in the same scrawl that had adorned the back of Dane's illustration:

512 Webb Dr., Springfield, GA

I n my car a few minutes later, I typed the mysterious address into my phone. Finally, it felt like I was gaining some traction, catching up to whatever road map Dane had drawn for me. I was certain that whatever I found at this address would shed light on Dane's decline and death, and maybe even Maura's involvement in it all. My brother was communicating with me from the grave. Okay, yes—maybe I hadn't been the most understanding when he'd tried to tell me what was going on with Maura directly, but I could make up for that now. Dane was giving me a second chance through his clues.

As I drove, I made plans for the rest of my day. I'd go to the address, gather all the information I could, and then hit Eric's place on the way home—he still wasn't answering my texts. Likely he was resting, just as I'd instructed him, but it wouldn't hurt to check in.

It took me close to an hour to get to Springfield. As I exited the highway, I felt the same way I often did pulling up to my parents' house—startled by the flatness and sparseness of sub-urbia. No sidewalks here. Lawns and driveways bled right into the road. The lack of people milling about felt eerie.

The address took me to a cream-colored ranch with a red pickup parked outside and an American flag anchored to the mailbox. A small concrete patio held two wicker chairs and a potted plant with scaly leaves. I parked two houses away so as not to arouse suspicion.

A worn welcome mat sat against the door of the house. *God bless our happy home* in cursive lettering. I rang the doorbell. In all likelihood, no one would answer and then I'd be back to square one. But even if someone did answer? I wasn't sure I was ready to hear whatever they had to say.

A plump woman with thin blond hair curled at the ends opened the door. "Can I help you?"

"Maybe." I took a breath, my eyes zeroing in on the striped cat pin at her neckline. Its tail curled into the shape of a question mark. "I'm Dane Chambers's sister, Holly. Dane died two months ago and left me your address—he seemed to think it was important. Did anyone here know Dane?"

The woman's mouth shrank. "Yes. My daughter went to school with him."

"Oh." The metronome of my heart cranked faster. "And . . . is she in?"

"She is. However, I'm afraid she hasn't been feeling well. For a while now, actually." The woman glanced behind her into the house, either anxious or annoyed I was still standing there.

I took a step closer. "I'm sorry to hear that. Is there any chance at all I could talk to her for five minutes? I drove all the way here from Savannah. I'm trying to connect with people who were important to my brother . . . anyway, it would mean a great deal to me."

The woman propped the door open. She looked into the house again—a cat that was the exact replica of her pin slunk behind her—then back at me. "Lauren told me what happened. God rest your poor brother's soul," she said. Then she nodded once. "It will have to be a very short visit."

Realization slammed into me. *I'm at Lauren's house.* Good—she'd never returned my message, anyway.

Lauren's mother led me into a cheery yellow kitchen with butcher-block countertops. Without asking, she poured me a glass of sweet tea from a blue pitcher. "Lauren was in Dane's illustration program at SCAD," she said, as the liquid glugged out. "She had big plans to stay in Savannah for a job, but unfortunately she fell ill shortly after graduation. I'm telling you now because you won't get a peep out of her on that front. She doesn't like to talk about it."

This must have been what Dane's professor had alluded to. "May I . . ." I swallowed. It was wildly inappropriate, but suddenly I *needed* to know. Was Lauren experiencing anything like Dane had? "May I ask what she's dealing with?"

Lauren's mom looked up from the pitcher sharply. I could tell from her eyes I'd crossed a line. "You may. And the answer is, we don't know. Doctors tell us it's some kind of neurological disorder, but there's a psychological component to it as well. It's been very distressing for us all. The symptoms were more severe at the beginning of the summer. They've evened out, somewhat, but nowadays she's . . . different. My daughter used to be so bubbly, so full of life. It's as if she's become a husk of her former self."

Neurological disorder with a psychological component. I

couldn't have summed up Dane's condition better myself. Just as my skin began to creep, the woman pushed the glass at me and said, "You'll see."

She took me around the corner, through a living room with garish flowered curtains, and down a hallway. At every turn I was certain the glass would slide out of my sweaty hands. A narrow grandfather clock loomed against the wall. Something about its face looked mean. We padded forward on the carpet to a cracked bedroom door. The woman knocked gently.

"Lauren, honey," she said through the opening. "You have a visitor. Dane's sister. I told her she could stay for a couple minutes, if you're feeling up to it."

Silence on the other side of the door.

The woman looked back at me as if to say, *See?* Then she pushed the door open.

The person in the room was not apparent, not at first. My eyes were pulled to everything else: an enormous fuchsia pouf in the corner. A full-size easel and sheaves upon sheaves of dreamy watercolors. Terrariums hanging from the ceiling like jewels. All the trappings of a family trying to soften the blow of their daughter's imprisonment in a dysfunctional body.

"Lauren," the woman said, with a note of scorn in her voice. There was a slight figure buried under the plush comforter. I wondered, with a shock of fear, if Lauren had always been this wisp of a person, with white-blond hair, colorless eyes, and a crease of a mouth.

"Both of your eyes are the same color," she told me. Her voice was bereft of emotion.

I touched a finger to the hollow under one of my eyes. "Oh, yeah. Not like Dane, I know. He was always the more interesting sibling."

Lauren's mother gave me a tight smile and disappeared behind the cracked door. Terror bloomed inside me. I was almost positive I'd remembered to put on deodorant that morning, but I smelled the tang of fear seeping out from my own body. Why had Dane sent me here? How was I supposed to extract any kind of useful information from this girl? The more I looked at Lauren, the less human she appeared.

Lauren's knuckles crested the dark comforter. Maybe it would be easier looking into her face if she had more than a trace of eyebrows to bracket those transparent eyes. She stared back at me.

"Um." I cleared my throat, toeing a clover-shaped stain on the carpet. "I know it's kind of weird, me just showing up here. So let me try to explain. Dane left me a note with your address on it. I'm trying to figure out more information about his mental state prior to his death. I actually messaged you a while back. Not sure if you saw it."

Lauren's face didn't indicate I'd even spoken, but her eyes locked on mine like burrs.

A squirmy feeling started in the pit of my stomach. "Were you . . . talking to Dane at all? Toward the end?"

Still, that impassive expression.

I glanced back at the door to the hallway, frantic. Was Lauren even capable of conversation? Did I need her mother here as a translator? I ran sweaty palms down my thighs. My eyes lit on the pouf in the corner of the room. "Mind if I sit?"

Nothing.

I lowered myself into the pouf, legs trembling. The way the cushion sucked my body in made me feel defenseless. "So," I said, after a few uncomfortable beats of silence. "When was the last time you talked to Dane?"

Lauren flicked her eyes from me to the ceiling. Finally—movement. "Dane and I were friends since freshman orientation. We only stopped talking after he moved in with Maura," she said in that monotone of hers.

"Oh."

She studied the daisy print on her comforter. "He tried to disembowel himself, didn't he."

It wasn't even a question. My stomach buckled at her bluntness. Fleetingly, I fantasized about descending on her bed and wringing her neck. Instead, I swiped for the glass of sweet tea I'd placed on the desk and wet my parchment tongue.

Finally, I composed myself. "Did you know Maura?" I asked, changing tack.

"I met Maura a year after I met Dane. We were roommates for two years. It's thanks to me the two of them even got together."

"Oh?"

Lauren said nothing, her eyes roving the ceiling over her bed.

"What was your relationship like with Maura?"

"Great." Her voice was still flat.

My frustration mounted. For Lauren to have said such a crass thing about my brother's suicide was unforgivable. And now she was evading my questions? "Do you mind elaborating?" I couldn't hide the edge in my voice.

"We were close. Still are." Lauren looked straight at me with her blank eyes. It felt almost like she was challenging me.

I stood my ground.

Finally, Lauren looked away.

"Tell me more about Maura," I said.

Lauren's mouth gaped slightly, revealing the slimy inside of her bottom lip. "We met sophomore year."

"And?"

"That year was hard. I had personal shit going on. I was so depressed I stopped going to class; I even stopped eating for some time. Maura was there for me."

"Go on."

Lauren sighed, as if I were exhausting her. The gesture made her frail body slump forward. "At first we were inseparable."

"And then?"

"And then, what?"

"You said 'at first.' Were you not inseparable after that?" Why was Lauren making this so goddamn difficult?

"No."

"Well, how come?"

She turned her attention to her nails then, picking at them violently. My mind flashed to sitting in the bistro, watching Dane pick his bloodied fingers under the table. What was going *on*?

"She disappeared," Lauren said.

"Wait, what?" I struggled to stand up. "What do you mean, she disappeared? She left SCAD?"

"No, she just wasn't around for, like, a year."

"Well, what was she doing?"

One shoulder came up to her jaw in a kind of half shrug. It looked like a tic; I didn't like it. "I don't know. Working on her thesis."

"Did . . . did she ever come back?"

Lauren's eyes went even deader than they'd been before, and

I scrambled to assess what she might be looking at. Her paint-ings? The window? None of the sightlines matched up. She seemed to be looking *through* the various items in her room. "Of course she did. End of senior year. Then she made up for lost time."

For some reason, that made my heart speed up. "What does that mean?"

A gentle smile spread over Lauren's face. It was unnerving, like watching the unnatural animation of a doll's eyelids click-ing open. "She made me better."

I eyed Lauren warily, the sunken face and crease of a mouth. Was she actually claiming to . . . be healthy? She didn't look it.

"Was that"—I cleared my throat—"before or after your neurological symptoms started?"

Her face hardened, the first hint of emotion I'd seen. "Who told you about that?"

I swallowed. "Your mom might have mentioned it. I only ask because Dane started having seizures shortly after his grad-uation. And before that, he started having some mental health struggles, too." The symmetry was just too perfect. I ached for Lauren to shed some light on this.

Her eyes returned to mine. "I don't like talking about that."

"Okay, that's okay." I realized I was standing six inches from Lauren's bed now. I backpedaled into the center of the room, my palms raised.

Easy.

Lauren dissolved into a coughing fit. I watched her, grow-ing more and more unsettled. This cough was violent, guttural, audibly dislodging stuff in her throat. It racked her body, play-ing with it like a mannequin. Finally, I turned away, unable to take in another second.

Lauren groped for a glass of water on her bedside table. After she'd calmed, she said, "I'm feeling faint."

The tangy, human-body scent of my fear had invaded Lauren's room—maybe that's why she had looked nauseated—but I wasn't done. "Lauren," I said. "This is very important. Is there anything you can tell me about my brother? What he might have been going through?"

"I told you. I hardly talked to Dane once he moved in with Maura."

"Yes. You did say that." My lips were so dry they stuck to my teeth. I took a breath. "Hey. I might be grasping at straws here, but is there any chance you heard about . . . a game? That Maura was playing with my brother?"

Lauren cocked her head to one side. It looked robotic, like an insect. "The night he died, right?"

My heart lurched. "Yes!"

Lauren paused, gazing around at the corners of the room. I stopped myself from throwing myself at her, grabbing her, shaking her until her teeth rattled in her skull. *Answer me!*

"He texted me," Lauren said at last.

Guilt drilled into me. Was it possible that, when I hadn't answered my phone, he'd texted Lauren instead? What a spectacular sister fail. Me, taking shots and dancing with my friends as my brother begged for help on the night of his death.

I was just starting to spin out from the guilt when the anger rushed in. All this time we'd been talking, Lauren had a text from my brother and she had waited until *now* to bring it up?

I stuffed my fists in my pockets, fairly vibrating with fury. "Can I . . . can I see it?"

Lauren sighed again, as if I'd made an unreasonable request. She took an excruciating minute to lift herself off her pillow, shift onto her side, and reach for her phone charging on the bedside table. As she scrolled through her messages, I dug my nails into my thighs through the fabric of my pockets.

Wait, I commanded myself. *Just give her a minute.*

At last, Lauren lifted her phone to me. I snatched it away from her to read the text chain. On August 17:

Dane
So Maura wants to play this weird-ass game
with me and I figured I'd let you know in case
anything happened
(I told my sister but wanted to tell you too just in
case)

Lauren
Yeah that doesn't sound sketch at all

Dane
Never mind, just a scavenger hunt at the
botanical gardens. Plz disregard.

Lauren
Consider yourself disregarded

And then the last text in the thread, at 11:01 P.M.:

Dane
Lauren. She just took me to see a human
corpse.

I dropped Lauren's phone next to her on the bed, stumbling away. A *corpse*? What the hell had Maura done to my brother? I flashed back to the beautiful invitation I'd found in Maura's shoebox.

Let's surrender to bliss . . .

"Lauren," I choked out. I felt a trickle of sweat snake between my shoulder blades. "I'm not even going to ask you why I'm just now seeing these or if you went to the police. Just answer me: did you hear anything else from Dane after these texts? Please tell me you *called him?*"

Lauren took a breath. Then her body went rigid on her bed, her water-colored eyes rolled back into her skull as one claw-shaped hand began thumping the mattress rhythmically.

CHAPTER 23

Lauren's mother rushed in, maneuvering her daughter onto her side. "That's a girl, that's a girl," she murmured, until Lauren stopped jerking.

Lauren lay back against her pillow, looking dazed. A rope of saliva hung from the edge of her mouth.

"You're okay," her mother said, dabbing at Lauren's face with a scrunched tissue pulled from her pocket. Then she turned to me. "We went past the five-minute mark. My fault. I'll show you out." She turned on her heel and exited Lauren's room.

I followed, my tongue rammed against the back of my teeth.

Back in my car, I stared out the windshield at the gravel on the side of the road until my eyeballs went numb. I couldn't banish Lauren's racked figure from my head. Is that what it had been like for Dane, when he'd had his seizures? Had he understood what was happening to him? Recognized his own jerking limbs? I couldn't decide which was worse—having your mind blanked by a sudden animal terror, or being a powerless spectator in the hijacking of your own body.

Lauren's seizure had come at the worst possible time, too. What had she been about to tell me? I thought I'd scrolled to the end of the text message chain, but what if Dane had said something more? What if they'd spoken over the phone? My desperation to know pulled at me, a sucking undertow. There was no going back right now, but maybe I could return tomorrow or the day after. It would have to do.

I tightened my ponytail until I winced. I needed to turn off my brain for the time being so I could check on Eric. After that— after ensuring he was okay—I'd take stock of everything else.

I parked in the first spot I could find, two blocks from Eric's apartment. Then I pulled the cords of my hoodie tight and started briskly along the sidewalk. Driving in, I hadn't noticed the crowd of people at the corner of the street. Impatient, I brushed past a woman in a fleece with a stroller. I must have passed too close.

"Pardon me," she said, even though she hadn't moved an inch.

"What's going on here?" My question was motivated more by irritation than genuine curiosity.

She turned to me and I saw that she was more of a girl than a woman, the apples of her cheeks fat with youth. Her movement also revealed the source of everyone's attention: a black SUV, its hood crumpled against the wheel well of a Sysco semitruck. "Some kid died. He was driving out of this complex and collided with that truck. The paramedics just pulled him out; they had the whole street blocked off until recently."

A tide pool of dread gathered in my stomach. "Some kid? What do you mean? How old was he?"

She shrugged and I saw her for who she was—a housewife tethered too young, salivating for a dollop of horror to flavor the monotony of her day-to-day.

"I don't know. Midtwenties?"

Black spots swam behind my eyes. I staggered away from the young mother, swallowed in a sea of bystanders. Clustered around the ruined SUV were three cop cars and an ambulance. A middle-aged officer in a windbreaker stood writing something on a clipboard. Every now and then she squeezed a radio at her shoulder, emitting squawks and bursts of static.

"Excuse me," I said, pushing my way through the last of the throng.

The policewoman looked up at me, lips parted as if I'd caught her mid-thought.

"Someone told me there was—someone who died in this wreck?" My voice shook; I didn't recognize it as my own. "Can you tell me who it was? My friend lives in this building and—"

She shook her head decisively. "Ma'am, I can't release that information."

"*Please.* He was having vision problems and I'm really worried—"

"Ma'am," she said again, laying into the grating term. "Please go home. Now."

Instead, I ran toward the ambulance and a knot of paramedics. I struggled to see past their backs, the gaps between their shoulders and arms. For too long, there was nothing. Then, I saw it: a black, body-shaped bag being zipped closed over Eric's enviable natural highlights.

My vision went dark and my knees jellied. When I righted myself, my eye snagged on a familiar sweatshirt-clad figure standing next to a different policeman, evidently being questioned. Even though his face had turned bloated from years of college partying, it was undeniably Mitch Howard from high school. Eric's roommate.

Mitch looked at me. His eyes were smeary and red.

I turned and fled back to my car.

I sat there in shock for a while, my knees knocking against the dashboard. Eventually, I cracked the door and heaved against the curb.

This couldn't be happening.

Not again.

The symmetry of Eric's and Dane's deaths felt both terrible and inevitable. Almost like the way my nightmares of Dane always closed the same, despite my ineffectual writhing in bed. I knew the feeling of those dreams narrowing to the finale as that chanting built to a crescendo around me.

Had there been a part of me that'd known this would happen all along?

I laid my forehead against the top of the steering wheel, fighting the roiling of my stomach. How the hell had this happened? Why had Eric tried to drive himself with his eye condition? I'd *told* him to stay home, to stay in bed.

I shouldn't have left him. I shouldn't have gone to Lauren's.

Lauren. In the tumult of the last few minutes, I'd completely forgotten about my unsettling visit to Springfield and what I'd learned about Maura. Suddenly, as I trembled in the front seat of my car, she was all I could think of. Maura hated Eric. Hated that I was seeing him, hated that he was in her home. I thought about the way Maura had grabbed my wrists and left bruises. The fact that she had—for whatever reason—taken my brother to see a corpse on the night of his death.

Goosebumps studded my skin. I turned the key in the ignition and peeled away from the curb.

I needed to get my things out of that townhouse.

I sat on the street beside Forsyth Park, working up the nerve to go inside. If all went according to plan, I'd dart in, grab my computer, throw my clothes in my suitcase, and be out before Maura even noticed. As far as I was concerned, we could handle the messiness of my leaving—and any financial implications—via text.

I stared at the digital clock on the dashboard. How long could it take to empty a bureau into a suitcase? Five, ten minutes, max. In ten minutes, I would be back in this seat, heading away from Maura's townhouse forever. I gripped the steering wheel once, hard, before cutting the engine and getting out of the car.

Maura was in the greenhouse when I walked in. I could hear her music seeping out from under the door, that languid synth-pop. Hopefully, it would be enough to mask my presence.

Ten minutes. I only needed ten minutes.

In my room, I ripped my suitcase out from under my bed and flung open the drawers to my dresser. In went the clothes, rumpled heaps of them—everything could wait until later to be folded. I caught a glimpse of my jagged movements in the cheval mirror. It seemed to be mocking me. I did, in fact, look ridiculous. Deranged.

Less than ten minutes now.

The flaw in my plan emerged when I tried to close the suit-case. Unfolded, the clothes bulged, preventing the zipper track from closing. I remembered, now, painstakingly folding my clothes the night before move-in. I swore and pulled a handful of clothes from the top to begin rolling them.

The bathroom—I still had things in the bathroom. *To hell with them.* I could replace everything once I was out of there. I pressed my elbows onto my overflowing suitcase. I just had to get it to depress about an inch . . .

"Going somewhere?"

Maura's figure cut into my doorway.

My stomach tilted. I kept my eyes fastened on my heap of clothes and fought to keep my voice level. "Yes, Maura. I'm moving out. My parents need me, so I'll be with them. I'm sorry."

"Really?" I could tell, without even looking, that her fin-gernail was in her mouth.

"Yes. I'll pay you the full month's rent to make up for the hassle."

Maura remained standing in the same position, her body halfway in the hall. Then, slowly, she entered my room, and dread constricted my chest. "Are you sure you need to leave?"

"Yes."

Her mouth twisted to one side. "I *really* wish you wouldn't."

"I'm sorry."

Maura paused, looked down at the floor. "Do me a favor," she said. "Have dinner with me tonight. One last time. I'll make us something nice."

"Thanks, but I don't think that's going to work."

"Fine. Not dinner. Just a drink—right now. For old times' sake."

I looked longingly at my bursting suitcase. "Maura, I really have to go."

"Holly." She was approaching me now; my body went stiff as she reached for my hand. Maura stroked the sensitive inside of my wrist, which sent a jangled mess of sensations through me. Fear. Desire. Pain: her dark nails skipping over the bruises she'd imprinted in my flesh. "Remember what you promised me at Dane's showcase?" she whispered.

"I know. I—" I turned away from her.

"Hey." She caught my chin with her fingers, forced me to look at her. Her jasmine shampoo was making me dizzy. "One drink," she said, with an encouraging smile.

I scrunched my lips together, rooted around in my mouth for my voice. Even if I'd wanted to leave, in this moment, I doubted my legs' ability to carry me.

"One drink," I squeaked.

"Good." Maura released me and then limped out of the room.

I watched her go, my heart thudding. Reflexively, my thumbs navigated to those crescent-shaped indentations on my wrists.

They had started to turn purple.

Fifteen minutes later, my suitcase sat next to the front door, ready to go. Except I wasn't. For some reason, I was sitting across the table from Maura.

She smiled at me. "You look nice."

That was a lie—all I'd done was splash water on my face in the bathroom and now my eyeliner was smudged. A cold sweat broke out under my polyester top.

Maura reached toward a cluster of bottles at the end of the table. "Red or white?"

"Red, please."

Maura sliced the seal on a bottle and extracted the cork. I bit the inside of my mouth, watching as a ribbon of wine wound into my glass. I lifted it to my lips almost immediately.

"So," Maura said, pouring herself a glass. "What are your plans now?"

I took a breath to formulate an answer, but before I could, Maura added, "Actually, don't answer that. I don't really care."

"Wow. Tell me how you really feel."

"You know what? I will. That's exactly what I love about you. The fact that I can tell you anything—*anything!*—and you'll sit by me and listen without judgment."

I stared at my napkin, trying not to cling to the word she'd used. *Love.*

"No," Maura said, and it took me a minute to track that she was contradicting herself, rather than my illicit thoughts. "That's not quite it. Yes, having an empathetic listener is one thing, it's wonderful. But you make me feel *seen* in a way no one has before. Not even your brother."

I put my wine down, feeling a flash of danger. "I'm sure that's not true."

"The thing is, you can't be sure, because you weren't a part of our household back then. You weren't privy to . . . everything. The expression 'behind closed doors' exists for a reason, you know."

My body quivered. "What don't I know? Tell me."

"Ohhh." Maura drew out the word and then laughed into her wineglass. "I don't know, Holly. I'm not liquored up enough yet for that."

I snuck a glance at my suitcase by the door. *One drink,* Maura had promised, but this was turning into more than that. My desire to bolt out the door, into my car, and escape to the safety of the suburbs was visceral. But then Maura had dangled information about my brother. I was acutely aware of the way she was yanking my puppet strings, but I couldn't turn away.

I picked up my glass.

After Maura had poured us both more wine, she left the table and returned with two shot glasses and her maroon case of dominoes. "We never got to play," she pouted, emptying the tiles. They clacked against one another noisily as she spread them about. Then the sound turned soothing, ivory washing against the tablecloth. "Pick seven," she said. As I did, she poured me a shot of vodka and scooted it toward me.

My fingertips touched the beveled glass. I thought about protesting, but decided against it. Fine, so I wouldn't be driving home tonight. I could still call an Uber or walk to Rachel's place. I had options.

As I threw back the shot, Maura said, "Good girl."

The bird stick pin in my side pricked me as I set the shot glass down. Somehow I'd grown addicted to lacing it through my bra every day.

Maura showed me how to match up dots on the dominoes by number. Tile by tile, we constructed a path that snaked along the tabletop, pivoting at points like elbows and knees. At first, it seemed almost elementary, but when Maura trapped me—by forcing me to search for a number I didn't have in my hand—I realized there was some strategy to the game after all.

"Ha-ha!" she cried out, delighted. "That means you have to pick another tile. And another, and another, until you get a three. Pick, pick, pick! It could keep going forever!"

As I picked tiles off the table to add to my hand, she poured me another shot. I must have taken it, because shortly thereafter, the dots on the dominoes started to swim.

"Hey," I said, picking up a domino. One dot on one side, seven on the other. "The seventeenth. Dane's anniversary."

Maura didn't look up from her hand. "We never did anything for his one- or two-month anniversary."

"I know." My heart clenched.

She looked up suddenly, with a smile. "Want to do something next month? Eat some bland, bell-pepper-less dish in his honor?"

I thought I'd wanted this, but as soon as Maura made the offer, a ball of tears wedged in my throat. If I felt this way at the mere mention of it, I wasn't going to be able to hold myself together during an actual commemorative meal. My voice scraped. "I don't know if I can."

"Okay." Maura shrugged, setting down another tile. We resumed playing, the clacking of dominoes the only sound in the room. The silence made it easier to focus on smoothing down the back of my throat.

"Why did you go to Lauren's house?" Maura said suddenly.

The room swerved to one side.

Oh, shit.

I should've guessed that might happen. Lauren had mentioned that she and Maura were still friends. Had Lauren relayed all the questions I'd asked about Maura's character? How was I ever going to cover for this?

"What?" My voice shook.

Maura was rearranging her tiles into a pattern on the table like little tombstones. "She texted me. Told me you'd been over there to talk to her."

My eyes buoyed to the seam between the ceiling and the wall. There, the crown molding disconnected from the ceiling and twisted like a swirled lollipop. Panic speared my chest. "Maura," I said, pushing away from the table, "did—did you put something in my drink?"

Finally, Maura looked up from her tiles, her wine-darkened lips puffed out. Her serious eyes scared me. Then she rolled them. "Do you really think I'd have to stoop to roofying you? Come on. I've gotten you into bed with a lot less."

That felt like a low blow. Had my mind been functioning properly, I might have said something about it. Instead, I slumped in my chair, staring at the painted grooves in the dominoes that had come to life, rising off the tiles like beetles in flight. They were holes, I realized. Lots of them.

The room went black.

I was in the guest room bed. I recognized the slippery feeling of the pillowcase against my skin. I tried to raise my body, but it wouldn't comply. Were my clothes still on? Somehow, I couldn't tell.

Maura's face floated above me. Her long hair dangled down, brushing my collarbone. "Hi," she said.

My body—traitorously—strained upward to meet hers. She laughed before taking my bottom lip between her own. That deep ache I often felt looking at her redoubled inside me, amplified like a shot of light in a hallway of mirrors.

"How did I get here?"

Maura pulled something slender out from behind her back.

"What is that?"

"So many questions," she scolded, brushing damp hair

away from my temples. "You know," she went on, "you told me you felt like Belle when you first walked into my house. But I think you might have gotten your fairy tales mixed up."

Terror crowded in me, despite the fact that—or maybe because—I couldn't make sense of her words. What language was she speaking? How had I gotten here?

Something humid and alive fluttered against my skin.

Black petals.

"I have one last botanical story for you," Maura said, as my head lolled against the pillow. "I know you're getting tired of them, so I'll be quick. You're always so good at indulging me, Holly." She drew the black rose between us, stroking a petal. "You might be surprised to learn that this is a varietal of a sweet briar, or Eglantine rose. Get this: they're actually known as the Devil's roses."

My eyes rolled, of their own accord, to the ceiling and stayed there. "Maura," I said thickly, as it dawned on me how little control I had over my own body. "Please stop this. Help me stand up."

Maura went on softly. "As the story goes, when the Devil was cast out of Heaven, he amassed a bunch of these roses to build a ladder and climb right back up. But the roses failed him—they wouldn't grow tall enough—so he cursed them with thorns for the rest of time."

"Seriously, Maura." An edge of terror had crept into my voice. "I'm done with this."

Maura ran a finger tenderly over the back of my hand. "Shhh, it's okay. When I first encountered these roses at SCAD, I was definitely turned off by the name. But eventually I came around, as I'm sure you will. Too often people see things in black-and-white terms. They hear 'Devil' and they dismiss something as pure evil. I don't think that's fair. There's nearly always more to the story."

Maura drew close to me. So close I could feel her lips against my earlobe.

I flinched. "I want to go home."

"You *are* home, Sleeping Beauty," Maura whispered.

Then, in a blaze of pain, she clamped my fist around the rose's thorny stem.

CHAPTER 24

Sunlight poured onto my bed. What time was it? I grappled for my phone on the bedside table—the alarm should have woken me up. But I didn't feel anything there.

I was definitely going to be late for work.

Maura breezed in through the door, singing an unfamiliar tune and holding a square-shaped item in one hand. She had a beautiful voice, even if the melody sounded eerie. That's when the horror from the night before came crashing over me: struggling—and failing—to raise myself off the bed as Maura leaned over me. She'd been holding . . . something. Not the folded washcloth she gripped now.

"What time is it?" I demanded.

Maura consulted her own phone. "Eleven-fifteen."

"Shit." I tried to sit up. But when I activated my legs, nothing happened. "Oh my God." My vision dimmed; static filled my ears. "I can't feel my legs."

"You're okay, you're okay. You drank too much last night

and this morning you came down with a fever. I checked your temperature while you were sleeping—101.2. Don't worry, I'm not going anywhere until you're feeling better." Maura took the washcloth and applied it to my brow. A rivulet of cold water dribbled down the side of my face.

She had checked my temperature *while I was asleep*? I imagined Maura accessing my useless, flopping body for any information she wanted and my throat tunneled closed with panic.

Since when did having a fever mean losing sensation in my legs?

I groped in my memory for clues from the night before but came up empty. We had been playing dominoes . . . then what?

"What the fuck is going on, Maura? I need to go to the hospital. Now." I slapped her hand away.

That forced the edge of the washcloth into my eye. There was something more than water on the washcloth—some essential oil maybe—that burned the moment it made contact. I gasped, clutching at my face as the liquid dripped down my cheek.

"Holly!" Maura dropped the washcloth and pressed the corner of her sleeve to my eye to soak up the offending substance. Then she pulled away, her mouth stern. "Stop this. You're overreacting and making everything that much worse for yourself. You need to calm down."

"Overreacting? I told you, I can't feel my legs!"

"And *I* told you, you're sick. I'm taking care of you. And you aren't going to get better if you keep resisting." Her sleeve had, admittedly, soaked up whatever had irritated my eye, but the truth was sinking in now: I was helpless. Numb, paralyzed, and completely dependent upon Maura's care.

"Where's my phone?"

Maura acted like she hadn't heard me. "Get some rest. I'll be back to check on you."

"*Maura!*"

She shut the door gently behind her.

I stared at the doorknob, commanding my legs to swing over the edge of the bed.

Go, go, go. Move, *goddammit!*

But it was as if they had been disconnected from my brain. Eventually, exhausted from the exertion, I collapsed against my pillow, sinking my teeth into my fist. What was going on with my body? What the hell had happened last night? And why wasn't Maura answering my questions?

Was I going to die here?

The world went black again.

It was nighttime. It didn't feel right to be this awake when the curtains were shadowed. How many hours had passed?

Days?

Something was rising in me. Not a backed-up garbage disposal of emotion but the real, urgent rebellion of my insides. I leaned over the side of the bed and retched.

Your floors are safe, I'd joked to Maura on move-in day. I wanted to go back in time and scrub the levity from my words. How had I looked at anything inside these walls and *laughed*? More important, I wanted to herd myself out of the townhouse to save myself from my current horror. What had I been thinking?

Maura entered the room, saw the vomit on the floor, and rushed to me. "Oh, *darling*." Leaning over me, she positioned her hands under my arms.

I flinched away from her reflexively.

"Hey," she said with a laugh, as if I were a misbehaving dog that had nipped her in its overexcitement. "That's not very nice. We need to get you to the bathroom."

Maura helped me place the soles of my feet on the ground. Then, supporting my weight, she drew me to standing. My naked legs wobbled beneath me. They looked pale and foreign, like they belonged to a puppet or a cartoon character. I still couldn't feel them.

"We can do this," Maura said, and it took all of my strength not to dissolve into tears at her encouraging tone.

We shuffled to the bathroom in the hallway. It was an ordeal for us both. Several times, one of my legs buckled, and Maura had to shunt forward to catch me before I fell. I saw Maura's biceps shaking under the strain of my body.

In the bathroom, Maura took a hand towel from the wall, wadded it up, and placed it against the base of the toilet so I could kneel more comfortably. Then she guided my body down onto it. As soon as my head slotted into place above the lip of the seat, my body turned inside out again.

Maura rubbed my back as I heaved into the bowl. "That's it," she told me.

When I was spent, she handed me a moistened piece of toilet paper to wipe my mouth. Then she filled a plastic cup with tap water and gave it to me. After rinsing and spitting, I drank greedily, driving each gulp of water against the gnawing thirst at my core. I handed the empty cup to Maura, hoping she'd refill it. Instead, she set it down by the sink. Then she slid her hands back under my arms. "Come on," she said, hefting me to my feet. "Your bladder is probably about to burst."

It wasn't until she'd said anything that I realized the intense pressure in my pelvis. Maura guided me onto the toilet seat and I gasped with relief.

"That's better, isn't it?" Maura held up a folded piece of toilet paper. Was she suggesting she'd *wipe* for me, too?

I barely succeeding in fighting down a sob of humiliation. "What the hell, Maura." For a second time, I pushed her hand away, ripping my own piece of tissue off the wall.

This seemed to upset her. "Fine," she snapped, throwing hers in the trash. "I'm only trying to help."

But I needed her again to help me return to standing. At the sink, she tested the water temperature with two fingers before guiding my own hands into the basin.

Looking for myself in the mirror over the sink, I realized that Maura had covered it with a sheet. It matched the one hung over the greenhouse windows.

"It's for your own good," she said, noticing my stare. "You're a beautiful girl, Holly, but I must admit, you've looked better. Please don't worry, though. This will pass. It always does."

A ringing started up in my ear. "What's wrong with me?" My mind kept returning to dead-eyed Lauren, staring like a corpse at the ceiling over her bed. Was I going to end up like her? Like my brother?

I pushed the thought away. *No.*

"Nothing. Nothing! I'm taking care of you, okay?" She buffed my wet hands with a towel the same way my mother used to dry my hands when I was little. Then Maura assumed my full weight again, preparing to strike back out into the hallway. "Let's get you back to bed."

There I curled onto my side, facing away from Maura.

When I was sure she'd left the room, I turned over. Something nicked me in the tender flesh of my ribcage. I slid a hand down into the side of my bra: the bird stick pin was still there. Thank God Maura hadn't found it.

It was the closest thing to a weapon I had.

CHAPTER 25

I dreamed of trailing Maura through the labyrinthine rose garden. Clotted tatters of clouds pressed low in the sky. The manicured hedges lining the brick path were so immaculate they looked artificial. She was moving too quickly; I stumbled to keep up. All I could see of Maura was the dark cascade of her hair down her back. I had the sensation of winding after her in concentric circles, tangling deeper and deeper into the heart of the garden.

I called after her, but she wouldn't turn around.

The second time I stumbled, I looked down at the path and saw the bricks shifting underfoot. My hand flew to the hedge to steady myself and I noticed something odd about the rows of bushes filling the labyrinth: every flower head had been severed.

Now I was falling. My arms flailed in the direction of the hedge again, but the mass of leaves swallowed my hands, thorns burning up and under my nails.

I woke to a stabbing pain in each of my nailbeds. It felt

deep, as if embedded in the muscle, or maybe the bone beneath. I flicked on the bedside lamp and held a trembling hand in front of my face. My hand looked normal. How had merely dreaming about thorns created such intense pain? Could this really be due to the fever Maura had described? I waited a few minutes for the pain to subside, but it only redoubled in strength, my fear spiking along with it. This wasn't any normal fever, which raised the question: why the hell was I here? Why hadn't Maura taken me to the hospital?

I grimaced, squeezing my nails with each opposite hand, and dredged in my memory for my night playing dominoes with Maura. I remembered drinking red wine, taking a shot from a beveled glass that Maura had poured for me . . .

Lauren. She had asked me why I went to visit Lauren.

Panic unspooled in me. Maura had caught me snooping behind her back again. She must have connected the dots and figured out I was suspicious of her. And now—what was happening? Had she done something to make me bedridden, to ensure I'd stop looking for answers?

A coughing fit gripped me then, racking my body until my windpipe went raw. Each time I thought I'd calmed myself by sucking down a pocket of oxygen, my airway closed again and the convulsions started back up. It felt like there was something lodged in the very back of my mouth, expanding by the second.

I felt a sudden zap of electricity to the brain. My limbs jerked reflexively. Another zap and the lower part of my body danced again on its own, in hiccup-like spasms.

What was *happening* to me?

Then, just as soon as it had started, the cough released me. Shaking, I lowered my head to the pillow. Did I even have control over my own body anymore? Had I just had one of Dane's seizures? I didn't dare move, lest the zapping sensation return.

I stayed awake all night.

Maura came along with the daylight holding a cerulean vase. It was stuffed with lotus seedpods.

"What is that?"

She barely looked at me as she set it on the bedside table. "Some decoration for you. Do you like them?"

All those holes—gumball seeds buried in their circular wells—made the walls of my brain shriek. I'd told Maura about my trypophobia. Google the phobia, and a photo of a lotus seedpod is the first thing to pop up. This decoration was intentional. Maura was screwing with me.

I thought of the stick pin in my bra. Each day, I grew more determined to use it.

"I also brought you some toast." Maura indicated a plate on the bedside table and a tall glass of orange juice. A layer of pulp floated on the top. "How are you feeling?" I flinched as she reached out to brush some hair away from my face. Then she wrinkled her nose. "One of these days, we *are* going to have to get you in the bath, you know."

One of these days. I tried to tamp down on my anger, but it betrayed me, making my voice shake. "How long have I been in here?"

Maura went back to adjusting the seedpods. They scritched against the porcelain of the vase. "I don't think that's going to help you feel any better."

"You ignored me the last time I asked about my phone, but I know you have it. Please give it back."

"That isn't a good idea, either. The blue light is bad for you and you need to focus on recovery."

"This is bullshit." Rage lifted my upper body off the pillows. "My legs are unresponsive, I've got some horrible stabbing pain in my hands and the worst cough of my life, and I think I might have even had a seizure last night. I need to see a doctor."

Maura regarded me with a slight smile, her arms crossed over her chest. "Holly, you're being alarmist. You haven't had a seizure. I told you: you're feverish, and I'm taking care of you. I've seen people go through what you're going through. This will pass."

"*Fever?*" She couldn't keep doing this to me, playing off my hysteria as overreaction. Anyone in my situation would be freaking out, just as I was. "What kind of fever makes you lose feeling in your *legs*?"

Maura sighed. Then she perched on the edge of the bed and ran a hand along my shin through the covers.

I couldn't feel it.

"You're still febrile. Trust me, everything you're describing is psychosomatic. All you need to do is remind yourself it's in your head, okay? Your fever is coming down. Give it another day."

I pressed my lips together, hard. "And if I'm not feeling better by then?"

Maura reached over and twisted the vase a few degrees. "Then we'll revisit things."

It seemed Maura wasn't budging. *Okay, then.* I prepared to slap down my trump card, feeling the delicious weight of my threat before speaking it. "You know," I said quietly, "people are going to be worried if they haven't heard from me."

Maura looked down at me sharply, lips parted. Then she straightened her spine, brushing off her thighs. "You don't have to worry about that. I texted everyone from your phone to assure them that you're okay. That you're recovering from a nasty flu and keeping your distance. Mom, Dad. Even your boss—Esther, right?"

"You *what?*"

"I unlocked your phone by scanning your face while you were sleeping. You may want to check your security settings! Anyway, I've taken care of everything. No one's going to bother you."

It was that last sentence that did it for me. Had she really texted Mom and Dad, pretending to be me? Severing my only possibility of escape? I imagined them reading her texts on their own phone screens. Mom, as she marched between the potting shed and the yard. Dad, against the deep body-shaped impressions he'd made in the couch. The thought was unbearable.

"Listen to yourself." I looked up at Maura, hating that I could feel tears crowding. "This is so fucked up."

But she was already at the door. "I need you to get some rest, Holly. Can you do that for me?" Maura blew me a kiss, waggling her fingers like she had the day she'd surprised me at the library. "Happy Halloween," she added. Then, before I could think of what to say next, she'd slipped around the doorframe and into the hall.

Halloween. I stared at the ceiling again, my molars knocking together with residual anger. So I'd been sick for almost a week now. I wasn't imagining my numb legs or the pain in my hand. So why was Maura brushing off my concerns? Why was she messing with me like this?

A horrifying thought emerged: is this what it had felt like for Dane? None of us had taken his concerns seriously. Had he felt this petrified? To think that I had played a part in making someone feel the way I was feeling now—it was unfathomable.

As it turned out, Dane hadn't made it out of Maura's townhouse alive.

Who's to say I'll be any luckier?

I punched my pillow with an ugly grunt. It felt good; I wound up and pummeled it with all the strength I could muster. The pillow sat there, cold and deflated, accepting my abuse. It wouldn't change anything. Eventually, the beating jostled the second pillow to an angle and it toppled over the edge of the bed. Just before it fell, there was a flash of something green-brown sliding from the pillowcase.

What the hell?

Punching my pillow had already left me exhausted, but I had to see what had fallen out of the pillowcase and onto the floor. Gripping the fitted sheet, I dragged my body across the mattress, inch by excruciating inch. Then I peered over the edge. A bell-shaped flower with browning, frilled petals lay bent-necked on the floorboards.

What had a plant been doing in a pillowcase? And why did it look so familiar? I thought first of the satchels of rose petals I'd found in Maura's underwear drawer. But this definitely wasn't potpourri.

I grabbed the other pillows on the bed, sticking my hand inside the cases. Nothing—they were all empty. It didn't make any sense. What *was* this plant? And why had Maura slid it into one random pillow?

The memory sideswiped me, the moment I'd seen this flower for the first time: flipping through that botanical tome in

Maura's library. *If absorbed into the skin or eyes, the alkaloids from angel's trumpet can enlarge the human pupil until it fills the iris, causing vision problems.*

Another memory. Maura, lying next to me in bed the night of Odette's party.

So you're a right-side-of-the-bed sleeper, huh?

Oh, God. Eric's eerie, consumed irises.

What was it Maura had said about him? *He looks at you like you're a piece of meat. It's like he's looking at you . . . without seeing you.*

She'd taken the analogy way too far.

I pulled the covers up over my head to block out the world. I had never failed anyone like I had failed my brother. Until now. Maybe Maura was to blame for his death, but the truth was this: Eric would be unscathed if it weren't for me. If we hadn't run into each other in the grocery store, if Maura hadn't seen our reawakening chemistry . . .

I clamped my teeth down over my lips until I tasted blood.

Maura had killed Eric by blinding him with the angel's trumpet. It no longer seemed a leap too far to assume Maura had been involved in Dane's death as well. There were too many parallels. Dane and Lauren, both suffering from some mysterious ailment. And now me. Here I was, body racked with coughs, legs numbed, and seizing. Maura was the only thing we'd all had in common.

What had she *done* to us?

I raked through my matted hair. Dane had tried to tell me about this illness growing inside him. Who knows? Maybe he'd been imprisoned in this townhouse, too. Had he felt that suicide was his only escape? What options did *I* have? I needed to get out—if not for myself, then for Dane. For Eric.

I rolled onto my side, waiting for night.

. . .

Halloween meant trick-or-treaters. I lay on my back, waiting for the doorbell with a scream ready in my lungs. But it never sounded. Several times another burst of sound—a chime from Maura's laptop, a child's cry outside—made my senses prick with hope. But no one ever came to the door; Maura must have turned off the porch lights, indicating she didn't want visitors. I forced myself back to sleep.

Finally, later, my eyelids flipped open to a dark room. It took a minute or two for the details of my waking nightmare to coalesce around me, like beads of mercury. The darkness was amplified in the holes of the lotus seedpods. I sat up, staring at the shadowed curtains.

Time to go.

I wriggled my toes again under the sheets. Sensation registered and hope lifted inside me. Was it possible? If I had feeling back in my legs, maybe I could move them. All along, I'd assumed I was paralyzed, a prisoner to this bed. But getting mobility back would be a game-changer.

I drew in a breath and slid one foot toward me. To my amazement, my limbs complied. So I mustered my strength and swung both legs over the side of the bed.

My soles landed flat on the hardwood.

Victory coursed through my body. Maybe I stood a chance of getting out of the townhouse, after all.

Next, I had to stand. I knew I was capable, because Maura had been taking me to the bathroom in my gaps between sleep. I just needed to get into a standing position without her help. I gripped the edge of the bedside table. Grimacing and shaking, I levered myself off the mattress in juddering starts.

For the first time, I realized Maura had removed the mirror from the corner of my room. I thought of the covered mirror in the bathroom. Could I make it down the hall to rip off the sheet and see whatever horror was inscribed in my face? I'd patted my features in the dark between nightmares, palpating for something terrible. But I didn't feel any blood. No horns, no extra eyes. Just my normal features—wide-set eyes, column of a nose, full lips—all clammy with sweat.

As I hesitated, my limbs turned wooden with fear. Then I felt a surge of determination. I needed to escape. What was the point of wresting myself to my feet if I didn't at least make an attempt?

I cast around the bedroom for something to help me. A black umbrella hung from a hook on the outside of the closet. I pulled it down and offloaded some of my weight onto it. Took a few experimental steps into the center of the room, using the umbrella as a makeshift cane. Its metal tip striking the ground made my heart stick in my throat each time.

Tap. Tap.

I didn't have a choice. I wasn't making it out of this bedroom without that damn umbrella.

I held my breath and sank my incisors into my bottom lip. The umbrella shook in my grip as I guided it farther and farther from the bed. I lurched shakily after it.

Tap. Tap. Tap.

The pace was agonizing, and my hamstrings burned. I noticed, with a start, that my back foot was dragging slightly across the floor.

I held my breath as I twisted the doorknob. The heavy mechanism groaned in protest, and panic harpooned through me. But then I was staring down the length of dark hallway to the living room and, not too far beyond it, the foyer. The chandelier overhead looked like a brain, made of rivulets of darkness. The other doors off the hall were closed: the bathroom, library, Maura's room. The challenge, of course, would be tapping and scraping my way down the hallway undetected.

I took a shuddering breath and began, wincing as the metal touched down on the floorboards, far harder and louder than I had intended. Pain radiated down my side as I dragged my leg across the wood. There was something my middle school gym teacher used to shout at us as we'd run laps on the track. I could picture him now with the hair he kept long and shaggy to disguise his receding hairline. The paunch that sat like a small animal over the waistband of his gray sweatpants. What had he said? *Pain is just weakness leaving the body.*

That didn't seem quite right. If anything, I felt myself growing weaker with each step. When I'd exited the bedroom, the end of the hallway seemed accessible, leading straight into the living room. But the hallway had expanded like a telescope. I swiped the back of my hand over the cold sweat beading on my forehead.

Another violent cough rose in me. Panicking, I fought it down. I could not—would not—let my body betray me like that. My shoulders shuddered to contain the cough. I swallowed down the substance that had risen in my throat. Whatever it was, there was more this time. It felt rough as it gathered, like gravel. I prayed that horrifying electrical current wouldn't seize my brain again.

I turned to look at Maura's bedroom at the end of the hall. My left knee buckled, and I barely stopped myself from falling. I imagined Maura sleeping inside, and all at once, the door between us seemed thin as paper, pulsing like an organ with her every inhale. What did Maura look like when she slept? I'd never had the opportunity to see for myself—the only time she had fallen asleep with me was after Odette's party. My back had been to her and I'd been too petrified to turn around. Who knows? Seeing Maura in that vulnerable state might have been what it took to break her spell.

My blood kicked into a gallop as I entered the living room. A blur of moonlight streamed in through the French doors. I focused on moving toward the foyer, screwing up my courage.

Suddenly, the throbbing in my fingertips returned with such intensity that I dropped the umbrella and fell to my knees on the hardwood. Never before had it struck me this forcefully. I sucked in lungfuls of air, gripping the ends of my fingers. What was *happening* to me?

I looked down.

Was that—?

It was dark. Too dark to tell.

I staggered to my feet and swept my hands over the wall, searching for a light switch. I didn't care if Maura woke, didn't care if this announced my presence and my attempt at escape. I needed to know. I needed to see.

My palm brushed plastic, and I flicked on the switch, breathing hard. Then I spread out my fingers in front of me, hands shaking, palms facing the ground. A whimper twined in the back of my throat.

Beneath each nail thrust a flushed, pointed claw.

Horrified, I curled my fingers toward my palm to study them as blood pooled in my cuticles. The "claws" were green-brown, the shape of miniature shark's teeth, each with a wicked, needlelike point that had finally burst through my skin. Not claws at all, I realized—

Thorns.

"What are you doing out here?"

Maura was an outline in the mouth of the hallway.

I stared back at her, voiceless with terror. At first Maura said nothing. Then she lunged at me and burrowed her own nails into the tender skin of my inner wrists, tearing at the bruises she'd left before.

Now I really cried out. Taking me by the shoulders, Maura dragged me back down the hallway in the direction of my bedroom.

"*Maura!*" I screamed.

But she was merciless, pushing my limbs against the mattress with astonishing force. I swiped at Maura's face, but the thorns had deserted me. Instead, I reached for the metal bird in my bra. But then Maura wrenched me toward her and I lost purchase. The pin flew out of my hand and skittered onto the floor. I watched in horror as it dashed away from me.

No.

"You've really got to stop this, Holly," Maura said. When I looked back up, she was at the guest room door, pulling something from her pocket.

I began to tremble violently.

"It's a shame I had to resort to this," she said. "Your brother stayed by my side until the very end, even though he was afraid. Do you know why that is?"

Maura closed the door on me. I heard the churn and click of the ancient skeleton key she'd just maneuvered in the lock. Through the door, I thought I heard her say, "It's because he trusted me."

CHAPTER 26

Maura stopped bringing me food. Once each day she unlocked my door, entered the room with her mouth set like a pin, and placed a glass of water next to my bed. I'd gotten proficient at plotting time by now, relying on the level of brightness behind the curtains to chart the rising and setting of the sun. That's how I knew it was three days that I subsisted on water alone.

The hunger really hit in the late afternoon on the first day, making my insides clench.

"Maura," I said, brushing her hand when she came to deliver my water. "Can I have something to eat? I'm starving."

She looked down at me with expressionless eyes.

"I really have to go to the bathroom. Please."

Maura left the room and turned the skeleton key in the lock.

I chugged the entire glass of water. Then I lay down, pressing my stomach against the mattress to quell its grasping. Time wore on, and it became clear I'd have to relieve myself in my own bedroom. I lifted the seedpods out of the vase.

Don't worry, your floors are safe.

Afterward, I went to the windows, flicking the locks along the bottom. I peered outside—the guest room looked out onto an alleyway filled with snarls of bushes. I was only on the first floor; I could probably get away without even spraining an ankle. But when I tried hefting up the windows, it was clear they'd been painted shut. I strained until the veins in my neck bulged, until I was so exhausted I had to lie back down on the bed. Breaking the window—even if I had a suitable implement—was out of the question: it was an old-fashioned twelve-paned affair with intersecting grids that wouldn't accommodate anything wider than my arm.

On the second day, I began loping around the perimeter of the room to build my strength. My drag had turned to a kind of shuffle—not ideal, not anywhere close to normal, but better. I didn't need the umbrella now; I was propelled by a grim determination. I circled the room ten, fifteen, twenty times. Only once did I sit back down on the bed to relieve my screaming thighs. Then I got up and resumed circling.

I tried appealing to Maura again on the third day. The hunger dropped off sometime in the middle of the night, but bludgeoned me full-force when I woke in the morning. This time, when Maura came with my water, I dared to grab her wrist. "Please," I said. "I'm so hungry."

She shook my hand off, looking disgusted. "You're acting like a spoiled child, Holly," she said. Then she was back at the door, churning the ancient metal machinery inside. Once again,

I barely heard her voice in the hallway: "And this is what spoiled children get."

I grew very lightheaded that afternoon. I drank the water to inflate my stomach and tried to sleep the day away. But by evening, the hunger had turned coiling and mean.

I wasn't sure if I was dreaming or hallucinating, but suddenly I was back in the bistro with Dane, staring at that stupid basket of fries. My brother picked and picked at his nails until blood dribbled down the side of his wrist. The cute waitress with the diamond stud in her nose looked on, appalled.

Dane trained empty eyes on me. "I think there's something growing inside me," he said. Then he reached out and grasped my hand with his own bloody one.

I jolted back into the guest room, clutching my throbbing fingers. The scabs that had grown over the thorns were breaking as the little green needles burst back through. I hissed with pain and scrabbled to make a bandage out of the bed sheets. I tried to focus on the task of staunching the blood instead of the ugly truth filtering through my starved brain: whatever had happened to Dane was happening, now, to me. Worse still, I was locked in Maura's guest room—no phone, no food, no bathroom.

And not a single fucking person knew where I was.

On the fourth day, Maura brought my water with a slice of yellow cake. I forced myself to wait until she left the room. Then I broke off the end of the cake with a fork, stuffed it in my mouth, and sank to my knees, groaning. It was soft and delicious, with a delicate flavor. Vanilla?

No. I knew exactly what flavor it was.

Each day, Steel would come to deposit a slice of almond cake and a glass of water at the door.

I dropped the fork with a clatter.

How had the story gone? Anna Powell had betrayed her husband by getting pregnant by another man, and she'd been locked in room 204 as punishment. Was that it? Had I betrayed Maura by trying to escape? Was she indicating I *deserved* this? The dense sweetness hit my empty stomach and I retched onto the floor. I stared at the clods of disintegrated cake. My sobs were tearless—shuddery gasps that shook my body and made the back of my throat raw.

It wasn't fair. Finally, finally, I'd been handed food. And I couldn't even keep it down.

I took a sloppy pull of water and spat it onto the floor. Then I shoved the rest of the cake in my mouth using both hands.

I had no dignity left.

On the fifth afternoon of my confinement, I heard a commotion in the belly of Maura's townhouse. Soon, rich smells of meat and garlic wafted under the door, twisting my gut into writhing vines. Saliva frothed in the sides of my mouth. I pressed my face against the pillow, dampening the case with spit.

I was so lightheaded I was convinced I'd summoned Maura with my desperation. Her key sounded in the lock chamber, and then my door swung open. Maura stood in the hallway wearing an apron printed with cartwheeling sunflowers. "Come on," she beckoned to me. "Time to wash up. My clients are arriving in an hour. I wasn't about to reschedule my party just because of you."

I stared at her, disbelieving. Of course—I'd completely forgotten about Maura's party. When she'd told me about it in the market, I'd seen it as an excuse to wring intel from the likes of Matias and Odette. But now the party represented something far more critical: an opportunity to escape. Woozy with relief, I raced to get out of bed and follow Maura down the hallway.

She'd already drawn a bath for me. Pale rose petals floated in the tub. Maura sang quietly as she dipped the back of my head in the water and massaged my scalp with shampoo. It was the same jasmine shampoo she used, I realized, and I felt a squeeze of relief. But then I remembered: Dane. The thorns under my nails.

"Maura," I said.

"Hmm?"

"What's happening to my hands? My nails?"

"What do you mean?"

I studied my wrinkled fingers in the water. Any traces of thorns had disappeared; even the scabs were healing. "I thought—" I said faintly.

"You've been very sick," Maura said, digging her fingers into my scalp a bit harder. "I'm so glad you're feeling better now."

Could I believe her? I needed to. Every fiber of my being screamed at me to relax into her care, so glorious after four days of torture. I could allow myself this one moment of reprieve. I leaned back against the scalp massage, sighing.

After the fragrant bath, Maura wrapped me in a towel. I shivered with pleasure as the plush fabric enveloped me. Then Maura slung an arm around my shoulders and led me into her bedroom. She left briefly and came back with a tray covered in small ribbed bowls. "You're the first to get a complete sampling of tonight's meal," she said, setting the tray in front of me. "The caterers weren't happy, but oh well. It isn't up to them."

It took all my self-restraint not to scoop out the contents of the bowls with my fingers. I forced myself to pick up the fork on the tray, then shoveled the food into my mouth indiscriminately. Each and every bowl yielded something delectable: pickled purple radish, spicy and sweet at once; tender lamb in smoky brown sauce; spears of crisp white asparagus. I savored the exquisite textures and flavors layering over one another, licked the tines of my fork, using them to excavate the ribbed innards of the bowls. Maura watched me, seeming to draw something from my evident display of pleasure. Then she moved to her dresser and pulled out a blow-dryer from one of her bottom drawers.

"Keep eating," she instructed.

The roar of the blow-dryer in my ears didn't stop me from scraping the flavor from each bowl. Then I let my body slump, my stomach tight and swollen. Maura ran her fingers through my wet hair as the machine droned.

When my hair was dry, Maura plugged in a curling iron and reached for the lacquered black box where I knew she kept her makeup. Wordlessly, she painted my face with foundation soaked into a pink egg-shaped sponge. I flicked my eyes around, politely avoiding her hands as she worked. There might have been a time I would have felt compelled to speak, or wished that Maura would, to fill the silence. But that wasn't necessary anymore. Maura had seen and touched every layer of me. The tenderness with which she was dabbing makeup under my eyes now called up tears.

She noticed, of course. "Sorry, did I poke you?"

"No, you're fine."

Eyeliner and shadow came next, then a velvety pink lip gloss that Maura applied with avid concentration. By then, the curling rod was hot. She took pieces of my hair and wound them around the wand. I couldn't see her face anymore, so I relied on her touch to gauge her mindset. She seemed focused. Fastidious, yet confident. Maura was intense about her work—that I knew. And today I was her project.

Yes, I still needed to escape; I would get to that. But for now, I reveled in Maura's gentle affection. I needed it as intensely as the food that had been withheld from me for days. For now—in this moment—I was Maura's doll. And I wasn't sure I minded.

Guests began to trickle in after nightfall. The women stepped through the door in furs and exchanged kisses with Maura, and then with me. Even though I wasn't sure it ever got cold enough in Savannah for fur, this indicated we were approaching winter. Somehow, during my imprisonment, we'd settled into November.

Maura had zipped me into another one of her dresses, black silk. She'd smoothed the fabric at my hips in front of her closet. "You're so small," she'd told me, pressing her thumbs against my hip bones. They were more pronounced now than I'd ever seen them. "You need to stick to these close cuts, otherwise you'll be swallowed."

I wanted to point out that she and I had pretty much the same body type, and Maura seemed to wear whatever silhouette she damn well pleased. Her closet was full of A-lines, mermaids, and even a handful of full-skirted ball gowns.

Plus, hadn't I already been swallowed?

Maura linked her arm through mine and pulled me into the thick of the party. Clearly, she had every intention of keeping me close. I glanced back toward the door, aching to feel the slash of cold air on my bare shoulders. Part of me wanted to stay close to Maura and continue to bask in her attention and affection; another wanted to fling myself headlong into the night.

Guests converged around us almost immediately. I recognized most of them from Odette's party. Matias and the fox-faced girl showed up together, the girl in a pale blue column dress and Matias with a face creased with judgment. Did I stand a chance of isolating any of Maura's guests and explaining what she'd done to me? Would they even believe me?

I had to try.

"Holly," Matias said, reaching over to kiss my cheek. "A pleasure to see you again."

"Holly is just recovering from a nasty flu," Maura said. Her voice sounded exaggerated, like a kindergarten teacher explaining a concept to her students for the first time. Was that a flicker of recognition I saw pass between Maura and Matias? Or was I starting to imagine things again?

"I'm sorry to hear that," Matias said, turning to me. "I hope your recovery is swift and that you're back to normal in no time."

"Or better than normal," the fox-faced girl said.

Maura made a tiny curtsy. "That is always the hope."

Just as before, the conversations went over my head. It seemed that Maura, Matias, and Odette made up the sun at the center of this group. Those too reticent to join our huddle periodically shot over covert looks. I chased eyes around the circle and smiled until my mouth hurt, then faltered. I felt as if I were standing in an oversaturated photograph. Despite the women's furs, the air was stifling and hot. Voices were too loud and faces too close. When one young man—sweat-beaded hairline, wiry red hairs on his forearms—brought up cryptocurrency, Maura began to caress the inside of my wrist with a finger. Her touch, in front of all of her party guests, shocked me.

The caterers came around with trays of drinks. Maura was not to be outdone by Odette—the martini glasses floating around were topped with colored foam and sprinkled with leaves and flower petals. With her mouth open mid-laugh, Maura grabbed two. She pressed one into my hand. The stem felt like ice.

"No," I said. "I'd better not." Every time I drank with Maura, something seemed to go wrong.

Maura pouted. "Don't be a spoilsport. You're well enough to drink now. Besides, who doesn't like an elderflower-rose martini?" She was letting go of the glass and I had no choice but to take it, lest it shatter against the ground. I held the drink limply. When Maura glanced over a couple minutes later, I pretended to dip my mouth into the foam. She gave me a kind of secret smile before turning back to the group.

I looked over my shoulder. The front door was so tantalizingly close, I felt a pang. There was no way I was getting out of there with Maura attached to me. I stood motionless in the circle for a full minute, feeling my lips thrum. I didn't want to drink the foamy martini, but how could I dispose of it with Maura latched to my body? I waited, scrunching my toes against the bottoms of Maura's sandals. The glass grew heavier in my hand. I didn't stand a chance of making it out the front door—directly within Maura's sightline—but I could ditch my drink and gather my wits. When Maura threw her head back in a hearty laugh, I inched out of the circle, making sure to address everyone.

"Excuse me. I'm just going to the ladies' room."

Maura snapped out of her laugh. "Do you need— Let me help you. I know you're still a bit febrile."

I raised my glass. "Feeling well enough to drink, right? I'll only be a minute."

Victory coursed through me as I power-walked across the living room to the hallway. I'd timed my exit right. Surely Maura wouldn't dare push the issue in front of her guests— would she? What would happen if I just walked out the door? Would Maura actually come after me? I wasn't sure.

I could feel her hard eyes on the back of my neck as I scurried away.

It was my first time alone in the bathroom since my imprisonment. I shut the door and leaned against it, my heart racing. Maura had placed a lit candle on the tank of the toilet that gave off a thick vanilla scent, making me lightheaded. She must have cranked the heat to full blast before the party; the bathroom was no escape from the heavy air in the rest of the townhouse. I wiped sweat off my upper lip, following the finicky candle shadows with my eyes. They bounced against the walls and caught in the reflection of the mirror, jagged bits of darkness like crows crowding at a window.

The mirror.

I tripped over my heels to see my reflection for the first time in days. A mask stared back at me. Maura had layered my features with so much makeup that I no longer resembled myself. I was, in fact, her perfect porcelain doll.

I had hoped that such a finding—no horns, no extra eyes— would be a relief. But the painted perfection of my face felt uncanny in another way. I stretched the skin of my cheeks taut in the mirror, rubbed off a bit of foundation at my temple. I even studied my nails for traces of the thorns. Nothing looked out of the ordinary, except, of course, the expertly applied makeup.

I reached for my martini, emptied it down the sink, and rinsed out the basin with fresh water. Then another coughing fit seized me. I hunched over the sink, gripping the edges as my body shook. Something stuck in my throat and I spit into the drain.

A black rope of saliva slapped against the porcelain.

Did that . . . just come out of me?

I inched back into view of the mirror. Shakily, I opened my mouth, stretching my glossed lips wider and wider in a silent scream.

The back of my throat was black as ink.

My hands tremored where they gripped the sides of the sink. I peered closer. No—there was something else back there, some kind of . . . texture. It wasn't just a flat discoloration. I opened my mouth until my jaw strained, needing to see, and yet dreading it.

It looked almost like bunched tissue paper in the back of my throat. Like layers and layers of fine fabric—taffeta petticoats—climbing my windpipe, gathering beneath my uvula. The petals of Maura's sweet briar rose, bursting forth just as Dane's illustration had promised.

Back in the dining room, my head spun.

There's something growing inside me, Dane had said.

I hadn't believed him, and now it was happening to me. I felt like throwing up. I took a gulp of the ice water at my place setting with a shaky hand; maybe I could smooth down the petals. Drown them. I had thought I was getting better, rebuilding my strength day by day, but what if this thing inside me had just been getting bigger and bigger all the while? Feeding on me, like one of Maura's red-mouthed pitcher plants?

A missing memory snapped into place. All this time I'd been imprisoned, I hadn't been able to recall how my night playing dominoes had ended with me paralyzed in bed. But now I did: with Maura, clamping my palm around one of her black roses. I turned my hands face up at the table now, studying them for traces of wounds or scars. Nothing.

The heaving sensation returned. I grabbed the sprig of lavender that had been tied to my napkin with a piece of twine and held it under my nose. I could not—would not—vomit at Maura's table.

Maura sat at the head and had placed me next to her, Odette and Matias on either side of us. Now, Maura stood, lifting her wineglass in a toast. The table fell silent. It seemed everyone had already been watching her.

"To my lovely clients," Maura said, eyes sweeping around the table. "My inner circle. Without you, I would be nobody."

"Oh, nonsense," Odette interrupted, jumping to her feet. She raised her own glass, making deliberate eye contact around the table. "To Maura," she pronounced. "Our healer."

"To Maura," the table echoed.

Maura gave a sheepish smile. "If you insist." A few guests laughed as she sat back down at the head of the table.

I was too nauseated to enjoy the reprise of the colorful meal I'd sampled in Maura's bedroom. Instead, I pushed the food around on my mirrored plate, listening to Maura laugh beside me. In the spot vacated by the lamb, I could see the reflection of my own hooded eyes peering down at the table. Time seemed to slow around me. I don't know how long I stared, immobilized, at my plate.

A tickle started in my throat. I cleared it; Maura glanced over at me.

Oh God, oh God, oh God. This thing is going to choke me to death.

Another tickle. I coughed, covering my mouth with my napkin. When I lifted it from my face, dark clumps trickled out and into my lap. Foreboding swept through me. I looked around the table to see if anyone had noticed—the guests went on talking, oblivious. Slowly, I pressed a fingertip to one of the clods. It was moist and springy, bringing me back to potting plants with my mother in the garden.

Soil.

At that precise moment, Matias pushed away from the table. He ambled in the direction of the hallway bathroom. I watched his receding back as my panic climbed. This was my only chance at escape; I had to go after him. Abruptly I stood, jostling the edge of my plate. Maura looked up sharply from her meal. I ignored her, staggering after Matias. Thankfully, he hadn't bothered to lock the bathroom door; I threw it open.

Matias spun away from the toilet. He gripped the top button on his fly. "Jesus," he said, those creases of judgment gathering again on his face. "As if I'd let you look for free."

Hurriedly, I shut myself inside the bathroom with him. "Matias," I said, voice pitched low and urgent. "I need your help. I'm sick. Something is really wrong with me, and Maura won't take me to the hospital. She won't let me leave her house. Please help me get out of here. Please."

Matias's hand dropped to his side. He blinked once at me behind his glasses, slowly, and I saw that things were going to be all right. I'd explain everything to him. He'd usher me out of this prison and take me straight to Urgent Care, where the doctors would prescribe some medication to wipe out whatever terrible infection Maura had spawned in me. I'd get to eat dinner with Mom and Dad, be back to Esther in the library the following day. I'd finally get my act together and make plans with Rachel—

But then Matias threw his head back and uttered a single, mirthless laugh. "Oh, sweetheart," he said. "You're not sick."

My palms pricked with sweat. "But I really am. For the longest time, I couldn't feel my legs. Now there's something growing in the back of my throat and I'm coughing up . . ." I couldn't bring myself to say it. *Dirt.*

There was a rap on the door. "Holly?" It was Maura. "Everything all right in there?"

Matias cracked the door with a smile. "All good," he said to Maura, in that same exaggerated whisper they'd used earlier. "Holly and I are just having a little tête-à-tête."

My heart plummeted.

"As I was saying." Matias shut the door, turning back to me. "There's nothing to worry about. Maura is taking good care of you. She's helping you, lovebug."

The petals were rising in my throat. "*Helping* me? Like"— I thought back to Odette's party—"the way you 'helped' your exes? 'God rest their souls'?"

The humor fell away from Matias's face. "All Maura—and the rest of us here tonight—have ever done is help people. I need you to understand that."

His words meant nothing to me. My ears churned with white noise.

"Let me be explicit," Matias said. "Maura creates, and we spread her healing."

But it wasn't explicit at all. Why did he insist on speaking in riddles? I thought, suddenly, of Matias appearing the night I'd slept with Maura. How Maura had come to the door carrying a tray of glass bottles and vials.

"How?" I demanded. "What kinds of remedies is Maura making you?"

But Matias ignored my question. "Let me tell you, there's such joy in watching someone be relieved of their pain, of their internal wounds. My advice? Don't fight it. Your brother did, and that's why he ended up . . ." He gave me an expression somewhere between a smile and a grimace. "Well, you know."

A shudder ran through my body. "What are you saying?"

Matias clapped me jovially on the back. "I'm saying, stop being such a worrywart! Maura's been honing her craft for years. You're in good hands."

Her craft?

Matias took advantage of my confusion to open the door. Then he pushed me out of the bathroom. "Go. Enjoy the party. And for God's sake, at least consider knocking next time."

Once I'd toppled into the hallway, he closed and locked the door behind me.

stared at the sliver of light under the bathroom door, readjusting the damp top of my dress. What the hell had I just heard? The notion of Maura as some venerated healer was unsettling enough, but even more disturbing was the wide-eyed reverence with which Matias invoked her name.

Maura creates, and we spread her healing.

So it wasn't just Maura. She had a small army of evangelists, congregated now in the living room since dinner had ended. The hum of easy conversation filled my ears like fuzz. But how, exactly, was Maura *healing* people? And what could that possibly have to do with the monstrosity unfurling in my throat?

Coffee would be served soon, if it hadn't been already. I was running out of time. When would I ever have Maura distracted like this again? After cornering Matias in the bathroom—before he'd opened his mouth, that is—I'd finally allowed myself to indulge in the possibility of escape. It had all felt within reach: Dad, Mom, Esther, Rachel.

I ached for my old life. I had to get out of that townhouse.

If I made a run for the front door, how soon would Maura catch me? I'd be crossing directly in front of her and all of the guests in the living room. I sank to a crouch in the hallway, feeling dizzy. I didn't even have my car keys, and the very real possibility of being apprehended by Maura—or one of her followers—shriveled me.

First I tried the back door. But of course, Maura had already thought of that. The dead bolt was engaged, locked from the inside with a key.

Windows—yes. Since I'd already tried the windows in the guest room, I rushed to the master. There, the windows were much larger, their panes painted gray. I flicked the locks on the sills and shoved them skyward until my eyes bugged. They wouldn't budge. I doubled over, breathing hard, my elbows sliding against the silk on my knees. With a sinking heart, I realized I'd never seen Maura open a single window in her home. The only fresh air came in through those beautiful French doors, which were, in this moment, inside a room full of guests.

With my back against the wall, I slumped to the ground. I was out of ideas. How much longer before guests started leaving? What if Maura came to check on me? I had to think of something before—

"I spy someone hiding."

I jerked away from the wall. Maura was in the doorway, watching me with a faint smile twisting to one side. Softly, she closed the door behind her.

"I . . . I was just—"

If Maura knew what I had been attempting, she didn't show it. She crossed into the center of the room, dusting her hands off with satisfaction. "Whew, I would say that was one more successful party for the books. Everyone's gone except

Matias, who probably just wants to hang around to keep drinking and gossip about everyone behind their backs."

That was it. I'd blown my very best chance at escape. I'd probably never have an opportunity like that again.

"Holly! What's wrong?" Maura rushed to me. For a fleeting moment, I felt grateful for her concern, longing to be wrapped up in it as I had in the past.

Then reality struck. Maura had made me sick. Locked me in my bedroom and denied me food. Because of her, I had, shaking and whimpering, used a vase as a toilet. Because of her, I had black petals growing in my throat, thorns thrusting through my nailbeds. Some "Devil's" organism devouring my body from the inside.

But the worst part of all? Maura had, without question now, done the same to Dane.

My ribcage expanded as my body prepared itself for battle. I bit into the words: "What did you do to my brother?"

Maura stared back at me, her eyes frigid. She wasn't going to give me anything.

That was it. I lunged for the lamp on Maura's nightstand and shoved it onto the ground, reveling in the cacophony of glass. "*Answer me!*"

Maura reared back against the door. "Holly," she exclaimed. "We've been over this. Your brother was mentally unstable. He killed himself. You *know* this."

"I don't believe you."

"Well, that's your prerogative."

This wouldn't do. Striding deeper into Maura's bedroom, I swept my arm over her dresser, casting her ceramic dish and her photo with Dane onto the floor with a crash. Maura's shoulders jumped to her ears.

"What the hell were those roses in your greenhouse?" I yanked open Maura's dresser, tore out her lacquered makeup box, and slammed it to the ground. Splinters of wood and glass shimmied away from my feet; the gold hinges cracked, sending jars and brushes flying.

"Holly," Maura said. I could tell she was fighting to keep her voice level.

"Oh, no. I'm not nearly done here. It didn't take me long to remember—you pricked me with one of those flowers and now I have something black growing in my throat, some kind of *thorns* coming up from under my nails." I grabbed the spined succulent on her dresser that had—somehow—evaded danger and ripped it out of its pot, exposing its spidery roots. Then I flung it at Maura's head.

She shunted to one side, dodging it. "Holly, please. You're scaring me."

My laugh came out maniacal. "*I'm* scaring *you*? That's rich." I looked down at the framed photo of Dane and Maura. It had fallen face up, a spiderweb of cracks over Maura's face. I wound up and kicked it, sending it smashing against the opposite wall. "You're the reason Eric died in that car crash. And I know you must've gotten Dane with the same kind of rose you used to prick me, because his fingernails were all bloody, just like mine!"

Maura was shielding her face with her forearms. "Okay," she said. "That's it. I'm going to get Matias." But as she reached for the doorknob, I grabbed the bell jar off her bedside table.

She froze. "Holly. *Don't.*"

"Don't what?" I lifted the glass by its smooth knob, exposing the black roses beneath.

"Just—" She took a step toward me, palms out. "Put that down, okay?"

I picked up the flowers and tossed them from one hand to the other, mindful of their thorns, and enjoying the fear spreading across Maura's features. "Okay, Maura. I think it's time for us to have a chat, then."

Slowly, Maura lowered herself onto the edge of the bed. She swallowed, every muscle in her neck visible. "What would you like to talk about?"

A knock on the door made us both jump.

"Everything okay in there, sweet cakes?"

Matias's voice.

Maura pressed her lips together. Then she made eye contact with me, her chest heaving with fury.

I tossed the roses to my other hand.

"Fine and dandy," Maura called back, straining to match Matias's playful tone. "Just give us a minute, please? We'll be right out."

We both listened until Matias's footsteps faded down the hall. Maura's room was in shambles, strewn with shards of glass and wood and soil. Her labored breathing filled the space.

"I'm going to ask you one last time," I said, once I couldn't hear Matias any longer. "What did you do to my brother?"

Maura stared down at the floor for a long stretch. When she looked up at me, her eyes were wet. "I was just trying to help him," she whispered.

My anger faltered. "What do you mean?"

Maura sniffled, wiping the back of her hand across her nose. Coming from her, the crudeness of the gesture shocked me. "He was so sick. Whatever mental illness he had, it was causing him so much suffering. I couldn't stand to watch it unfold. I *know* you can understand that."

I bit the inside of my cheek, remembering the evening I'd

cried against Maura and unloaded my guilt. Told her about the excruciating experience of watching Dane's illness take hold, knowing there was nothing I could do except run away. I could still feel the coolness of Maura's shirt against my eyelids. It was the first time I'd been utterly vulnerable with her.

It had also been the preamble to our night together.

"Your brother asked me for help." Maura sniffed, pushing a strand of hair away from her wet face. "You saw his mental illness—whatever it was—starting to emerge. The withdrawing. The paranoia. He knew I had a way with plants and in a lucid moment he said to me, 'I don't know what's happening to me. I'm not usually a fan of alternative medicine, but I'm desperate here.'"

My head spun. Dane, asking for Maura to hook him up with some holistic remedy? I couldn't imagine it—at least, not coming from the Dane I knew.

But then I remembered my wide-eyed brother. *I asked her for help. And now I think there's something growing inside me.*

"Then what did you do?"

Maura's face transformed. The anguish smoothed away, replaced by something like beneficence. "You're holding the answer in your very own hands."

I looked down at the black roses. There'd been no water under the bell jar—how on earth did these flowers look so vibrant? The leathery leaves along the stems fluttered; I hadn't realized my hand was shaking. I closed my eyes, forcing myself to keep gripping the stems even though my body screamed at me to cast them on the ground.

The Devil's roses, Maura had called them. Revulsion bubbled through me. "What are these things?" I whispered.

Maura tilted her head to one side in that coquettish way

she often did. "What do you know about the practice of leeching?"

I took a step away from her. *The Ancient Practice of Leeching.* The diagram of that gaping, needle-filled maw on Maura's desk.

"Don't look so appalled. Leeches proved effective for treating many infections and illnesses back in the day. There's something so relieving about the idea of having sickness siphoned right out of you, isn't there? Gone, forever."

"These things"—I looked down at my hand holding the roses, now shaking violently—"they feed on people?"

"Well, that's a pretty dramatic way of putting it. Technically, yes, I guess you could categorize these black Eglantine roses as parasitic. But I made them that way intentionally."

I shook my head. "What are you talking about?"

"Don't you remember?" Maura frowned. "I thought you saw the blood when you broke into my greenhouse."

I thought of the warm, slick redness on the ends of the roses, and my stomach turned.

"Okay, Holly, I'll give it to you straight," Maura said. Her chest puffed and it occurred to me she might actually be relishing this moment, the same way she'd relished playing tour guide on our walk through Savannah. "I wasn't afraid to be experimental while working on my thesis back at SCAD. I liked playing around, pushing the limits of horticulture and botany. Somewhere along the line, I discovered that if I raised these lovely Eglantine roses on a steady diet of blood, they would turn black with an abundance of iron." Her voice dropped to an awestricken whisper. "They actually grew *stronger.*"

"What blood?" I took another step back from Maura.

"Doesn't really matter. I started off using some of my own.

When my business took off here in Savannah, I needed to be harvesting greater quantities, so I befriended a butcher in town."

I saw it clearly: little, five-foot Maura, carting home bags of cow's blood over one shoulder.

"That was the key," Maura continued. "Human blood, cow's blood, it didn't matter. Feeding it to the roses gave them a taste for flesh and leechlike properties. *Curative* properties. Would you believe me if I told you these roses absorb human pain? Well, they do! Pain, guilt, grief. Every negative human emotion you can imagine, the roses will absorb it right along with the blood."

Was Maura telling me another botanical story? Or just screwing with me? I thought of Dane and deep vibrations of anger started up in my bones. "I think you're leaving out some important points, Maura," I said through gritted teeth. "Like why I saw black petals growing in the back of my throat. And *thorns* coming out from under my nails." As I said the words, that deep stabbing sensation started up again in my fingers. I shook out my free hand, blinking hard.

"Well." Maura gave me a tiny shrug. "Every species is pro-grammed to survive and reproduce. We can't fault them for that, now can we?"

I felt like gagging. So Dane was right. He *did* have some-thing growing in him. And now, so did I. Eventually, I'd be like Lauren, little more than a corpse staring with vacant eyes at the ceiling above her bed.

It's as if she's become a husk of her former self, her mother had said.

"Wait a second. If these roses leech away all negative human emotion"—I swallowed—"how can the person that's left . . . even be considered human?"

Maura sighed. "I'm not here to quibble about semantics, Holly. But you have a point. Once the negative emotions are consumed, the roses move on to the rest of them. Eventually, yes, the host is left without feeling. But what they do get, in return? *Relief.* And that's powerful."

I stared at her, uncomprehending.

"The process is about transformation," Maura went on, "but it's about enrichment, too. Hosts—like you and your brother—have the invaluable opportunity to surrender themselves to something greater."

That chilled my skin. "You say that like it's a good thing."

"Of course it is." Maura looked at me like I was dense. "Imagine ceding your damaged mind . . . to fill it with something beautiful. Can you think of a more noble purpose than that?"

My brain limped forward, trying to process Maura's words. "You're using people. Stripping away their humanity and turning them into . . . glorified incubators. Into *greenhouses.*" No wonder my brother had killed himself. Dane must have known what was next, what he'd become. "He must have been so afraid."

"He was." Maura toed the ground. "Even though Dane enlisted my help, he fought the process every step of the way. I kept working with him, trying to encourage him to let go. But he just couldn't do it."

All the times I'd tried to imagine my brother's animal panic—the force that pushed him to turn that knife on himself—I'd been at a loss. Until now.

"I just wish he'd given it a chance," Maura went on mournfully. "But after he cut into himself, it was over. Corpses have a strange way of absorbing these roses in death, as if to ensure the roses die along with them. Dust to dust, and all that."

So that's why nothing turned up from Dane's autopsy. My body crumpled. This was it. Whatever monstrosity was growing inside me was only going to keep growing until it consumed what made me human. Siphoning my emotion, claiming my body and mind until I became a husk that withered of old age. Would I register when I lost my ability to relate to the world? What would even be left of me by then?

"I know," Maura said quietly. "It's a lot to take in. But soon, everything—all the guilt, all the grief—will dissipate. You'll thank me. And guess what?" She smiled through her tears. "We'll always have each other."

My body went hot, then cold. "Right," I snarled. "So I can be Dane's replacement. Since things didn't go according to plan with him."

"Holly." Maura was approaching me now, her voice gentle and chiding. "Come on, that's not what this is about. You must understand: the kind of pain that you both were harboring—Dane's mental illness, your guilt and grief—it isn't the kind of pain that goes away. It lingers. *Festers.* Forever. I was only helping. You get that, right?"

I brandished the roses in front of me, warding her off. "No. No. I didn't ask for your help."

"Not in so many words, but from the moment I saw you at Dane's funeral, I could see the suffering written all over your face."

I remembered making eye contact with Maura as she'd read her *Charlotte's Web* excerpt. Feeling so . . . exposed.

"And then that night after our chowder, when you started telling me how your guilt was practically eating you alive, I just knew . . ." Maura trailed off.

I sank to my knees. The room looked like it was capsizing, folding in at the edges.

"I did this for you and Dane. I love both of you so dearly."

"What are you even talking about?" I pressed a fist to my eye. "You *love* Dane?"

"Of course I love him. That's why I did what I did. Why I made sure we got married before . . . well, before Dane surrendered himself."

Maura and my brother had been *married*? Despite my horror, it all made sense. The pear-shaped diamond and the rushed nuptials, all initiated by Maura. Dane would've never chosen to do it that way. No wonder she'd hidden the ring from my family at the funeral and the showcase.

I lurched to my feet. "You 'love,' him," I said again, "as in, present tense? I've got news for you. Dane is *dead*."

Maura looked meaningfully at the roses in my hand. "Is he?"

Nausea corkscrewed up from my gut.

Maura lifted her chin at the flowers. "Those flowers *are* Dane. Part of him, anyway—whatever the roses siphoned off before Dane killed himself. That's all we've got left of him. See now why we must protect them?"

Oh, God.

Suddenly, I remembered Maura, looking over at the bell jar on her bedside table the morning after we'd slept together.

If it helps, think of last night as bringing us both closer to Dane.

The realization slammed the wind from my lungs: my brother was here, trapped forever in this townhouse. Was it possible that my sleep paralysis had been Dane "typing" on my collarbone? What about my dreams of Lenten roses and goldenrods? Had that been Dane's way of warning me?

I staggered backwards a few more steps. There was something else I needed to ask, but I wasn't sure I could handle the answer. I gritted my teeth. "What game were you playing with Dane? The one in the botanical gardens?"

Maura looked shocked. "How did you find out about the gardens?"

"Just answer me!"

She grimaced. "Okay, okay. Hear me out, all right? I was trying to get your brother to relax into the process. I was doing everything I could to make things easier for him. I knew how much he loved geocaching, so I thought, why not make it into a game? If nothing else, it would give him a sense of control. For the last time."

For the last time. I fought past the tidal wave of anger. "What was the game? What did you do?"

"I . . . well." Maura laughed, sounding a bit embarrassed. "I set up this cute scavenger hunt. It took us first to the botanical gardens so I could explain the process to him. So we could appreciate the flowers, both outside Dane and within. I even brought a vial of blood with me to show him how, if fed to the roses there, they'd begin to darken almost immediately."

I barely repressed a shudder. I thought of the single, darkened rose I'd found in the botanical gardens. Maura must have created her own crop of black roses that night—the same ones I'd seen coating the innards of that dying rodent months later.

But that wasn't the whole story. I thought of the text Dane had sent to Lauren that night. "And then what? You brought him to see a corpse?"

Maura gaped at me. "What? Absolutely not!"

"Well, what did you do, then?"

"I wrote Dane's next clue to lead us to Odette's place. To see Odette's mother."

I shook my head. "What does Odette's mother have to do with this?"

"She was one of the first people I treated here in Savannah. Most of my clients you've met have utilized my black roses in some capacity—often for an ailing friend or relative. I wanted Dane to see firsthand how relieving it would be once all his pain was gone."

I stared at her. "Odette actually let you do this to her *mother*?"

"Of course she did." Maura's mouth went small with hurt. "Poor woman was suffering from dementia and God knows what else. And she's in such a better place now. I wish she'd come down to Odette's party so you could have seen her yourself."

"Did she have a *say* in being 'treated'?"

Maura looked confused. "Holly, the poor woman couldn't even remember her own name."

That would be a no.

So after taking Dane through the gardens, Maura had led my brother to one of her victims—a blank-eyed husk even worse off than Lauren. The "corpse" from Dane's text. I tried to imagine my brother taking in the scene, standing in a doorway at Odette's mansion, with that sheaf of dark hair over his face. What thoughts had been hurtling through his mind in that moment? Had he connected the dots, realized he was seeing his own future?

"Actually, I thought about taking him to see Lauren since they were friends," Maura continued, "but her condition isn't quite as advanced as I would have liked."

Lauren. I remembered her seizing on her mattress with her hand frozen in the shape of a claw. "You pricked her with one of your black roses, too, didn't you? Why would you do that to her?"

Maura looked affronted. "Because she asked me for help, just like your brother did. If only you could've seen it, Holly— Lauren was going through some very intense mental health struggles. Introducing her to the roses was the least I could do."

"But I saw her," I blurted. "Even after you'd 'treated' her, Lauren was *not* doing well. She was having seizures and—"

"—and a cough, and that tic. I know." Maura grimaced. "It's only in the first few months that the roses are more . . . aggressive. They're battling the body and mind, but once they win out, it's smooth sailing. This stage will pass for Lauren, just as it will for you."

Something jolted deep in my core as I remembered: we were talking about the horror gathering inside my own body. My throat tightened as I pictured a mass of midnight-colored petals gathering there like tumors. "How . . ." My voice caught. When I spoke again, I hated the mewling tone that emerged. It sounded nothing like me. "How do I get rid of this thing inside me?"

"Oh." Maura took a step closer. "I'm very sorry, but that's not possible. This is bigger than just you, Holly. Those roses were nurtured with my blood. You see, we're all interconnected, in such a beautiful way."

I couldn't take in everything she was saying. I remembered Dane's illustration of black roses bursting from a racked silhouette. *They're battling the body and mind, but once they win out . . .*

I froze, looking down at the three black flower heads bobbing in my grip. "I thought . . . I thought you said the roses are absorbed once their host dies."

"I did say that, didn't I?"

Maura and I stared at each other.

I felt something awful—even more awful—coming. Every one of my reflexes commanded me to drop the roses on the ground. But that would mean relinquishing the power I had over Maura in this moment. I forced myself to grip the stems, my eyes watering. "Maura," I said, slowly. "Please tell me where the hell you got these roses."

She had a strange, tight smile on her face. "Don't judge me, Holly, okay? The police didn't show up right away that night, and I knew that if I didn't act fast—if I couldn't recover the roses before they died along with Dane's body—"

I fought down the contents of my stomach. "Please tell me you're not saying what I think you're saying. That after my brother *cleaved open his abdomen,* you went"—I lost my voice momentarily—"digging through his body? To rip out a handful of flowers that had been growing inside him?"

Maura's bottom lip trembled. Then her face hardened with resolve. "I had to. Since these roses were salvaged from a human body, they're the most extraordinary of blossoms. Dane will be with us forever."

"Jesus Christ." Bile was flooding my mouth. "This is so fucked up."

Maura watched me with a soft expression. She laid a cool palm on my arm. "It's going to be all right. You're overwhelmed right now. But rest assured that the ugliness will pass and peace will close over you soon enough. Just imagine it: freedom from your pain, from your guilt."

I snatched my arm away from her. "I don't need your help with my guilt."

Maura looked wounded. "Don't you?" Then her lips curved back into that beatific smile. "I hate to remind you, Holly, but you failed your brother. You said so yourself—you weren't there for him. I hope I've served as a nice little diversion while I could, but it's time to face the truth. This one is on you."

My vision constricted. This went beyond all the horror Maura had just revealed to me. I'd been so vulnerable with her over the past two and a half months. I'd let her strip away my walls, layer by layer, to reveal the festering guilt at my core. I'd never shown that to *anyone.* Maura's desire to relieve me of it was one thing. But to take my guilt and flip it around on me like a weapon? That was unthinkable. Finally, the heaving thing inside of me drew up, slopping over my defenses.

I was on the bed in an instant, forcing Maura's back against the mattress, grabbing at her chin.

Her scream was muffled against my hands. "Let go! *Let go of me!*"

I scrabbled at her lips—those gorgeous, poisonous lips that had just been smirking at me. She struggled and cried, her tears wetting my hands.

"No, Maura." In a rather detached way, I marveled that my voice wasn't shaking anymore. "You think you have the right to decide for people that they should *surrender themselves* to a noble cause? Don't you think that's a little presumptuous?"

The muscles in Maura's neck strained against my fingers. It only made me grip her harder.

"Some of us have our own causes, you know. They might involve pain and heartbreak and guilt, but they're no less noble." I paused. "Maybe it's time for you to feel what it's like, having someone else make that call for you."

Maura let out a whimper.

I looked down at her with mock concern. "Why are you struggling, Maura? I'm only trying to help." I pulled one black rose from the bouquet of three that I'd let fall to the bedspread. Then, with as much force as I could muster, I rammed it deep into her mouth.

Maura's body jerked against me as warm blood dribbled down her chin. Watching her undulating on the bed, I thought of Dane, of Eric, and of Lauren—the way they'd all been betrayed by their own bodies. Finally, it was happening to Maura.

Gasping, Maura tore the rose from her mouth. Her hands clasped her face. She turned them over, examining her slick red palms as if entranced.

The next second, Maura's body slumped against the side of the bed, crumpling into a heap on the floor. I looked down at her, stunned. Touched a couple fingers to the side of her neck. Nothing.

I went numb.

Matias. He was still inside the house, and if he saw what I'd done . . .

The mangled, blood-drenched rose sat on Maura's ruined bedspread. I snatched up the remaining two black roses— ostensibly still holding Dane's essence—and fled Maura's bedroom.

CHAPTER 28

On my way down the hall, I pulled the lit candle from the powder room. There wasn't much time—I was certain Matias would find me soon. I rattled the handle to the greenhouse door. Locked, just as Eric had announced to me the day he'd visited. I looked around the living room, littered with cast-offs from the party: used coffee mugs and crumb-strewn dessert plates. Then I grabbed the fire poker from the hearth and rammed the heavy iron handle into the greenhouse door again and again. Finally it gave way, shards of glass spilling onto the concrete floor, so I could reach inside to undo the lock.

I stood in the center of the room, staring at the rows of flowers and feeling the heat of the candlelight on my hands. After setting the candle down, I snatched up a burlap drawstring bag from Maura's workbench and emptied it of iridescent glass pebbles. Then I tucked Dane's roses into the bag, cut a length of ribbon from a spool anchored to the wall, and knotted the pouch around my waist. Maura's words echoed in my head. *Those roses were nurtured with my blood. You see, we're all interconnected, in such a beautiful way.* I crouched and dragged the canister of black roses out from under the worktable.

My hands shook as I picked up the candle and held it out, coaxing the flame up against the white shroud. The fire took far quicker than I'd expected, tearing along the fabric with an audible rush. Then it settled, crackling, into the flower heads below. I was mesmerized by the hungry orange tongues. I forced myself to exhale. Would this do the trick? It would have to.

"Maura? What the Devil is going on?"

Goddammit—Matias. I didn't stand a chance mimicking Maura's voice convincingly, so I pressed my lips together. I had to wait until he left. Then I'd burst out of the greenhouse, through the living room, and out the front door.

Except Matias wasn't going anywhere. His figure darkened the entrance to the greenhouse and I started, my foot snagging on the end of the metal canister. The flaming roses spilled out, colliding with bags of soil and fertilizer stowed under the workbench. I leapt back as one of the bags exploded ablaze. A violent popping sound started up, the stretches between little explosions growing shorter and shorter.

Shit.

I broke into a run, but Matias intercepted me before I could escape into the living room, grabbing me by the arm.

"Where is Maura?" His breath, hot on my cheeks, smelled like the lamb from tonight's meal. "What did you do to her?"

I struggled against him. "Let me go!"

I was fighting a losing battle. Matias had a small frame, but he was still stronger than me. His eyes, amplified behind his horn-rimmed glasses, had turned to slits.

We both turned at a tearing sound and a burst of renewed

heat. The fire had spread now to the filmy curtains on either side of the French doors. We watched, transfixed, as the flames gobbled the fabric, leaping to the first of Maura's overflowing terra-cotta flowerpots. I'd never noticed how many plants she'd packed into her sitting room, but I counted them now as each flower, fern, and tree went up in flames—nine, ten, eleven. Within seconds, my escape route to the front door was blocked.

Matias's grip slackened as he took in the carnage. Red light reflected in his lenses. I took advantage of the moment to lunge for the fire poker on the ground.

"Don't you dare," Matias growled, snatching for my arm again.

But my hand had already closed over the poker, and I brought the butt swiftly up to his temple. Matias's eyes veered to one side, as if he were suspicious or about to ask me a question, before his body keeled over.

Chest heaving, I took in the burning living room. Though the front door was blocked by flames, I still had the fire poker to shatter the windows farther down the hall—in the kitchen, or even the library, if needed. I took off down the hallway, shielding my face from the smoke and the heat. Perhaps another home would've smelled more synthetic, of melting carpets and polyester. But Maura's blazing townhouse reeked of burning leaves.

When I arrived at the kitchen, it was completely swathed in flames. I'd have to go farther to outrun the fire. I bolted to the library. Fortunately, the windows here were wide, one big pane instead of multiple smaller squares within. I lifted the poker, gathering my strength.

Something grasped my waist from behind and I screamed, the poker clanging to the floor.

"Holly. Wait." Maura's eyes were wild, her lips bloodied and torn. She pressed her head into my shoulder and I felt the outline of her teeth through her ferocious embrace.

"Get away! Get off of me!" I was shrieking, ripping her arms from my body. How was she still *alive*?

This only made her grip me tighter. "You can't do this to me. I won't let you." Maura knocked me to the floor, pinning my shoulders beneath her.

It was one of those moments in which I felt, acutely, the crushing power Maura had always possessed over me, ever since that day at CVS. I struggled against her.

"Stop fighting me!" Maura's screech tore at my eardrums, inches from her mouth. "*Stop* it!"

Frantic, I ripped at her long hair. Something—anything—to make the nightmare end.

Maura cried out. "Why are you hurting me like this? I just want to help you get better."

I took the opportunity to leap to my feet, but Maura was close behind, grasping for me. I fled from the library, rounded the corner into the hall, and stopped short at the destruction that had claimed the front of Maura's townhouse in the span of only a few minutes. Dark, acrid smoke burned in my throat and nostrils, clogging the space. I couldn't see more than a foot in front of me.

"Holly, *stop*." Maura reached for me through the haze; I tore away, down the hallway in the direction of the bedrooms. The fire was spreading to this wing of the house now, popping and creaking through the walls. A lightbulb shattered overhead.

I put my hands out in front of me to feel along the sides of the hallway. Maura's bedroom was my only remaining option for escape. Since I'd lost the poker in the fray, I'd have to find something else in the room heavy enough to shatter her window—

Maura snatched my arm and I yelped. Blindly, I reached for the door to her bedroom. But amidst the smoke and my own panic, I'd opened the basement door instead. Maura's body slammed into me; together, we tumbled down the wooden staircase.

The damp stillness in the basement was a respite from the blaze a floor above. But I didn't have even a second to take a breath before Maura rushed at me, forcing me to the concrete. She knelt on my chest, lowering her face to mine. "Okay, then," she said, in a level tone. "Are you going to stop running from me now?"

Even as I clawed at her face, Maura seemed unaffected. Her hands were around my throat now, tightening, until my vision turned grainy and began to trickle away like sand. I gasped for air, but she was crushing my windpipe closed.

This was it, then: my sleep paralysis nightmare come to life.

Distantly, I was aware of something touching my mouth. Maura's fingers, brushing the contours of my lips.

"Why would you do this to me?" she whispered. Something wet touched down on my cheek. Maura's tears.

I bit her finger. Maura recoiled, and I noticed there was something more than teardrops—something thicker—falling to my face from hers. Fresh blood. I glanced down at my hands. Sure enough, the thorns were back, little knifepoints under my nails.

I slashed at Maura's white throat.

Her eyes went wide. A second later, Maura sagged to the floor as dark blood blossomed beneath her. The way she fell—on her side, with her legs tucked up neatly—looked like a little kid pantomiming sleep.

Panting, I scrambled to my feet. Our scuffle had ripped the burlap pouch from my body—I snatched it off the ground and reknotted it around my waist. Then I thundered back up the basement stairs and flung open the door. The thick black smoke surging in confirmed my fear: the blaze had claimed the hallway, cordoning off Maura's bedroom and trapping me below-ground.

I slammed the door and paced the perimeter of the basement, feeling nauseated. Even if I worked up the courage to plunge through multiple walls of flames, my lungs didn't stand a chance of powering me through the townhouse to the front door. How soon before the fire invaded this level of the house, too? There were no windows down here, no doors to the outside. *Unless*—

I ran to the small metal door by the wine cellar. Worst-case scenario, I was looking at a dead-end crawl space. Best case? A subterranean tunnel that had once housed dead bodies under Savannah. A wild laugh bubbled up.

What other option did I have?

The metal door swung open to an unnerving mouth of darkness. I rummaged through the tools on Maura's workbench until I found a flashlight. Then, shaking, I lowered myself into the crawl space. The ground was packed earth, gritty on my palms and shins. It was, indeed, a passageway about two feet wide, with rough stone walls.

I sat back on my haunches. I couldn't do this. I might be heading to a cemetery, to Forsyth Park, but there was no guarantee I'd find an exit at the end of it all. What if, instead of escaping, I was only lodging myself further into Maura's trap? I thought of my dream-self, tangling tighter and tighter into the heart of the labyrinthine rose garden.

Lightheaded, I pressed my back against the wall. Took a deep inhale of the damp stone air. My body was starved of oxygen, and my windpipe still burned where Maura had squeezed. But she had already recovered once tonight; there was no telling how much time I had before Maura came for me again.

I started to crawl.

My breathing filled the space. I hated hearing myself like this—grunting, each breath edged with panic. The dirt tore at the skin of my bare knees and I ground my teeth against the pain. As I crawled, I thought of Maura rearing awake. I thought of the ghost of my brother. Were there more like him down here? If so, running away wasn't an option.

Movement flashed in the beam of my light. Reflexively, I drew into a ball, bracing for an attack. But when I eased my eyes open again, I was alone. Just me and my ragged breathing, rasping against stone.

Barely, I called up enough saliva to swallow. Then I placed my raw knees back against the dirt and shuffled forward. As I crawled, more images flooded in: Dad swallowed in that cream-colored couch, ticking up the volume on a golf game. The banister outside of Rachel's apartment, its paint chipped in all the right places. Time collapsed around me, nesting into the heaving of my too-loud breath. Sweat trickled down the hollow of my breastbone and I inhaled the stench of my own fear.

At last, my flashlight illuminated a rough stone wall.

I was trapped, just as I had feared. Would I even make it back to Maura's basement? Not likely; my body was already unraveling. Besides, what if the door had closed behind me? I didn't know which option was worse—starving to death in a haunted underground tunnel, burning alive in Maura's townhouse, or having Maura plunge inside the tunnel herself to rip me from the bowels of the earth. As I approached, trembling, I shone the flashlight up the stone wall.

A set of rungs was soldered into the rock.

My borrowed heels slid against the metal rungs, landing me back down in the dirt again and again. Finally, I ripped off the shoes and clambered barefoot up the crude ladder with the flashlight gripped between my teeth. My legs wobbled, knotted calf muscles aflame.

A splintered wooden surface greeted me. I pounded at it with my elbow, hearing hollowness on the other side. But it wasn't budging. With the final reserves of my strength, I cried out, ramming my shoulder against the wood. The flashlight dropped from my mouth and smashed to the stone below, shutting off.

A slit of night appeared between the slats, tinged with streetlights. The wooden door opened with another shove. I scrambled outside, falling to my knees in the grass of Forsyth Park, the night air like razor blades against my cheeks.

When I could stand, I ran through the park, feet slapping against the pavement until seams of pain laced my sides. At any moment, I expected to feel a tug at the back of my dress: Maura, coming to swallow me back up. But I kept surging forward, through the park and onto the dark streets. I could still taste soot and smoke on my tongue; a siren wailed somewhere in the distance. Was it possible someone had called about the fire? What would I see if I turned around to face the fleur-de-lis metalwork and gargoyles of Maura's townhouse?

I didn't dare.

A man walking a tiny, scruffy dog jumped to the opposite side of the sidewalk to let me pass. In that moment I saw, with exquisite clarity, what I must have looked like to him: a wild-haired, emaciated girl in a filthy silk dress, barreling barefoot down the streets of historic Savannah.

I kept running.

Seven weeks later

On my first Christmas without Dane, I wore a forest-green corduroy romper over black tights and ankle boots. Somehow, we'd made it through breakfast and presents. Dad's face flickered only once, while balling up the sparkly wrapping paper and shoving it into a trash bag. It was a task Dane had taken on in later years, hefting the trash bag over his shoulder. He'd called it "the spoils of Christmas."

I bit my lip now, watching Dad and wanting to say something. Since escaping from Maura's, all I'd wanted to do was provide some kind of closure. But what could I even tell him?

Dad sighed, casting the trash bag onto the floor. "It feels weird to be the one doing this again."

"Yeah." I focused on the miniature snow-dusted trees Mom had set up on the mantel.

"I'd worried a lot about today. I wasn't sure I'd be able to soldier through."

"Me neither." Here was my chance. I took a breath, feeling unsteady. "You know, Dad, Dane had something really terrible happen to him, even though he fought it tooth and nail."

Dad nodded mutely, staring at the ground.

"But he never forgot about us."

Now Dad was looking at a spot over my left shoulder. Was he holding back tears? "That's nice," he said, his voice gruff.

"Really. I'm not just saying that to make you feel better. It's true."

When Dad's eyes returned to mine, they were wet. "Okay, Holly," he said.

It was the best I could do.

Mom was in the kitchen preheating the oven. She saw me grab my coat by the door. "Where are you going?" she asked.

I patted the side of my jacket self-consciously. "Just going to step into the garden, get some fresh air."

She frowned. "Really?"

"I won't be long."

"Good grief." Mom caught one of my hands in her own. "Your nails are a mess. Maybe we should go for manicures tomorrow."

I tore out of her grip. "We'll see."

I'd been checking my nails and throat relentlessly since my escape. Within a day after the fire, the blackness had cleared and my nails returned to normal. But still I caught myself worrying the cuticles, the spots where the white crescents met my skin.

The winter air prickled in through my tights as I slipped outside. I crouched by the sundial in the center of the lawn and touched a fingertip to the cold stone—12:02 on the dot. With my eyes, I followed the line of the sun into the browning planting bed, to that gaudy birdhouse where my brother's clue had nestled. Sometimes I flashed back to riffling through Dane's canvases hidden in the basement, to sitting with my heart hammering in Lauren's fuchsia pouf. The entire debacle felt like a lifetime ago.

That fire I'd started had burned the entire townhouse to the ground. Police determined that Maura and Matias died of smoke inhalation, but they couldn't tell much from the state of the bodies after they'd been pulled from the rubble. Secretly, I'd devoured the articles that appeared in the news. They quoted the detective who'd been assigned to the case:

> Back in 2013, a similar explosion at a Texas fertilizer storage facility killed fifteen people. Ammonium nitrate is no joke. It's what the Germans used to make bombs during World War I. Moral of the story? Gardening— and fertilizer—is more dangerous than you might think.

Mom and Dad had stumbled across the news eventually. It didn't take them long to make the connection to Maura. Only Mom had cried.

I ran straight to Rachel's apartment after escaping the tunnel that night. She and Henry had taken me in, bug-eyed. I tried to explain myself, but thankfully my babbling was incoherent. The story I eventually crafted—for their benefit and my parents'—was that I'd been walking to meet my new roommate at a party when I'd gotten mugged. When I told them, tearfully, that I didn't want to relive the incident by suffering through a police report, they didn't push the issue. Since then, they'd all treated me with exaggerated gentleness, as if the wrong words might cause me to spontaneously shatter. I'd be living with my parents for now. Rachel had promised to come over tonight after she finished Christmas dinner with Henry's family. I was looking forward to leaning on her again in the coming weeks. Maybe, if I was lucky, I'd regain enough strength to return the favor.

I took Dane's roses from under my coat and placed them on the sundial. It was finally time to lay them to rest; my brother deserved that. After all, since his death, he'd been a prisoner of Maura's townhouse, too. Often I asked myself why I'd chosen to stay there for as long as I did. The enticement of solving the mystery of my brother's death, my building attraction to Maura . . . yes, okay, but those were only pieces of the story. Recently, it had dawned on me. Somehow, I'd sensed my brother was there and couldn't bear to walk away.

As I set the roses against the sundial, I thought of Dane. Of Eric. This small gesture wouldn't erase any of the pain and trauma they'd suffered—I knew that—but it felt meaningful anyway. It was a small step in beginning to chip away at my guilt. Some mornings I woke up and that bedrock of guilt felt so massive, so formidable, I couldn't raise myself off the pillows for hours. That's when I would remind myself: this was the price of living. It was the guilt I'd chosen to keep.

Wind shivered into the garden now, cold against my tears. I stroked the roses with a finger, thinking back to Dane's and my last night at summer camp, when all of us campers had taken our sleeping bags out under the stars. It was amazing how vividly I could call up the smell of dead campfire and the shriek of crickets alongside that snap of fear upon waking. The feral hunch of that knobbed coyote spine as it nosed through the line of sleeping bags.

Was it just you? Maura had asked me, at this point in the story.

That night in my sleeping bag, I really thought so. But then—slowly—my panic had guided me to Dane's eyes in the dark.

Was it just me? No, Maura. It wasn't.

And I'm convinced it won't ever be.

ACKNOWLEDGMENTS

An enormous thank-you goes to my agent, Chelsey Emmelhainz, who worked tirelessly on this book, offered her brilliant insight, and made me feel truly cared for every step of the way. Basically, I hit the querying jackpot! To my whip-smart editor, Jenny Chen: thank you for all you've done to elevate this book into a finished product that makes me proud. Thanks to the exceptional team at Random House, including Mae Martinez, Kim Hovey, Jennifer Hershey, Kara Cesare, Jennifer Backe, Jocelyn Kiker, Alice Dalrymple, Julia Henderson, Susan Turner, and Ella Laytham. It's a surreal feeling to be backed by such skill and dedication!

A shout-out goes to my early beta readers, Amy Hollingsworth and Megan Reiffenberger, who were the first to shape *Such Pretty Flowers*. Additionally, I used multiple sources to inform the botanical elements of this story—chief among them were *The Illustrated Herbiary: Guidance and Rituals from 36 Bewitching Botanicals* by Maia Toll and *Wicked Plants: The*

Weed That Killed Lincoln's Mother and Other Botanical Atrocities by Amy Stewart.

Thanks to my friends for your cheerleading and enthusiastic check-ins along the way. To my mom for cultivating my creativity from as early as I can remember and, of course, for your expert botanical opinion. And to my dad: I'll never forget your excitement when I told you I'd gotten a book deal. (Now you're finally allowed to read it!) To my sister, critique partner, and best friend, Sara, who was there to answer my every publishing question, ease my anxieties, and hype me up in turn. I love you guys.

Finally, to Andy, for your sundial contribution and your unwavering love and support. Waldo and I are the luckiest to have you.

ABOUT THE AUTHOR

K. L. CERRA uses her writing to explore the complexities—and the darker sides—of relationships. When not writing or seeing clients as a marriage and family therapist, Cerra is likely walking her Boston terrier or exploring the local botanical gardens. She lives with her husband in a small beach town outside of Los Angeles.

klcerra.com
Twitter: @kl_cerra

ABOUT THE TYPE

This book was set in Ehrhardt, a typeface based on the original design of Nicholas Kis, a seventeenth-century Hungarian type designer. Ehrhardt was first released in 1937 by the Monotype Corporation of London.